DRAGON MATED

CASSIE ALEXANDER
KARA LOCKHARTE

ABOUT DRAGON MATED

Andi knew taking a chance on love with a dragon might be a risk, but she never guessed that the greatest threat would come from *herself*.

As a human, falling in love with a dragon shifter was always going to end in tears. Damian Blackwood's dangerous world of magic and assassins was never going to be safe for a mere human night nurse like Andi. But she couldn't have predicted that the darkest secrets would come from her own family. Secrets so devastating that they change everything for Andi and the man she loves. Her dragon mate.

Andi will do whatever it takes to protect him, even if it means destroying their love.

Even if it destroys her, too.

CHAPTER
ONE

Andi fought not to play with her phone in her pocket, saying a silent prayer that its recording app was still running as she sat down. Could it hear her uncle clearly? Why hadn't she thought to check it at home? Why had none of her uncle's men searched her? Was the fact that she didn't smell like dragon enough now...and how sure was she that she didn't smell like dragon and wasn't putting Damian in danger? Her knee bounced and she stopped it, watching her uncle walk around to the far side of the table with narrowed eyes.

Uncle Lee had demanded that she come alone to talk to him, and she'd done so. She needed to know just how much of her past was a lie and why her mother had hidden a whole other life from her. And how come Danny, her brother, was a dragon now himself.

She hoped like hell she was finally close to getting answers.

"Are you ready to listen, niece?" her uncle asked, sitting himself down in a chair that looked more like a throne.

"Yes. Assuming you're ready to tell me the truth, *uncle*," she said primly.

CASSIE ALEXANDER & KARA LOCKHARTE

He gave her a pained smile. "I think the first thing I should tell you is, I really am your uncle, Andrea."

Andi frowned. She'd been surrounded by "aunties" and "uncles" since she was born, and she'd always known that none of them were actually related to her. If she could believe he was really telling the truth, then it made knowing he was a deliberate murderer—a hunter of sentient, unearthly creatures—even more painful.

"Your mother and I were siblings. We were orphaned after the Shaanxi earthquake in 1556." He paused to let the date sink in as Andi did the math.

"You mean to tell me you're over four hundred years old?"

"Four hundred sixty-four, to be precise. Your mother only made it to four hundred sixty-one, alas."

Andi opened her mouth to say, *I don't believe you*, but after seeing her mother's photo album, with all the photos of her mother in exotic locales wearing historically accurate clothing, from black and white film into color, she wasn't sure anymore. "Go on," she said, crossing her arms.

"The chaos after the earthquake...it was phenomenal. They say now that eight hundred thousand people died. All we knew was that our village was wiped out. For the few who survived, it wasn't that we didn't want to help one another, so much as that we couldn't. We were just two more small hungry mouths to feed. Everyone was just desperately trying to get by." He brought a pipe and a silver match holder out of his pocket, both highly engraved, and took his time lighting his pipe while Andi waited. He sucked in a breath through the pipe's stem, then released it in a cloud of familiar smoke before continuing.

"We were, quite frankly, about to die. I went into the wilds, fully expecting not to return. My arms were the diameter of this pipe bowl," he said, gesturing it at her. "I could see the cut of your mother's cheekbones below her eyes. There was nothing left for us—not in the world, and not for our stomachs." He took another long draw on his pipe.

Andi steeled herself. She knew just how persuasive her uncle could be to get his way. "And then?" she prompted.

"And then...I found it. At the bottom of a deep ravine I'd practically fallen into myself—one I didn't think I'd have been able to scramble back out of alone. The corpse of a dragon. Green, luscious, meaty...dead. I did what anyone would do—and what you would've done too, if you had been there, if you'd known what life was like. I carved a piece off of it with a sharp rock, ate it raw, and for a moment, I felt like an emperor."

They'd eaten a dragon. Andi bit her own lips in horror.

"I expected to be sick. I could almost feel the meat land in my stomach, same as dropping stones into a shallow pond. But what happened to me afterward...." She watched his face go beatific at the memory. "I felt better. Stronger. Whole. And I knew I had to do two things immediately. One—go find your mother and give her some, and two—never tell anyone what I had found." Her uncle's dark eyes unfocused to look through her, at a past only he could see. "That's maybe the only thing I've felt bad about this entire time. Should we have shared? Probably. But if we had, would I still be alive today? I don't know." He inhaled deeply. "I told your mother, though, of course. She came into the wilds with me and helped me flay the beast. It was forty feet long, and we were small, so it took a long time. We smoked pieces of it in small caves on windy days, so that no one else could find it, and we set other pieces out to dry. It never seemed to rot or catch flies, no matter how long we waited between times to be safe, or when we hid it when we had to.

"I won't recount each century for you, Andrea, but as we carefully rationed the meat, we realized we didn't age as others did, nor did we ever fall ill. And eventually, we met others like ourselves—people who'd been graced by luck the same as we had, who knew the truth of the world and the others, and, as the Christians say, the scales fell from our eyes."

Andi now hoped her recording app was working for her own sake, because she couldn't begin to process all of this right now.

"And so what, you worked your way up, from eating a dead dragon in the woods to killing innocent sentient creatures?"

Her uncle chuckled. "Well, the answer is that they were never so innocent, were they? What do you think caused the earthquake to begin with? My bet would be on the dragon that crashed down to earth. And to think that people thought it was a comet."

"But it was dead, uncle...if I even believe you! Why kill all the rest?"

"Because, my dear niece, the world back then was a rougher, crueler place. And every early civilization experienced them. Marauding centaurs and chimeras in ancient Greece, qalupalik waiting to drag Inuit children under the ice, nian attacking people in our China, the grootslang of the Afrikaans. All those stories—and so many more—came from somewhere, don't you think? And someone had to kill them, even eat them, so that humanity would survive. We may not have been as sophisticated as we are now, and we certainly didn't kill all of them, as their continued presence here attests. But if we hadn't tried, if those before us, like us, hadn't tried, neither you nor I would be sitting here today."

Andi let his words echo inside her, the sheer horror of them building. Over four hundred years of killing had led up to their meeting tonight, and she realized there was no way she could ever hope to make him change. Her uncle had eaten a dragon once, and he wouldn't think twice about eating one again. Her pulse picked up in fear. "And now that you know you're hunting down living, talking people? Neighbors? Friends?"

"And now we are into the ends justify the means phase. Which is something you find intolerable, I know." There was a knocking behind her, and Andi almost jumped out of her skin. "Come in," her uncle commanded someone else.

The man who entered was a gentlemen dressed in a well-tailored managerial suit. He had darker skin and appeared older, his brown hair shot through with gray, but Andi realized that she couldn't rely on her sense of that anymore, what with the magic they were ingesting. He didn't look decrepit, but he could be a thousand and three for all she knew.

"Lee," the man announced, moving to sit at one of the tables like his seat was pre-assigned.

"Joshan!" her uncle said, sounding pleased. "You've heard of my niece, yes? Mei Li's girl, Danny's sister?"

"So much of you, yes," the man told her, giving her a warm smile. Andi was about to tell him she'd heard fuck-all about him when he went on. "Your mother saved my life once."

The words hit her like a punch. It wasn't fair that this man had stories about her mother that she didn't even know. Nor that those stories may or may not have involved her mother killing someone— not some*thing*, but some*one*, a person—to save him.

More people began showing up: men, women, scattered in ages and races, greeting one another with quiet handshakes and nods. Completely outnumbered, she felt shy, especially realizing that her uncle had placed her in the U-shaped grouping of the table's center.

"All right," her uncle announced when all but one of the seats were taken. It was hard not to feel like all eyes were on her as the group settled down. "This," he began, while waving in her direction, "is my esteemed niece, Andrea."

Everyone present murmured and made sounds of acceptance. Andi had to put her hands between her knees to not instinctively respond.

"While she's reluctant to join us," her uncle granted while nodding at her, "I know what's best for you, Andrea, and you belong here at my side. As your mother was. As your brother is."

Andi risked looking around at all the people intent on her. "But... I'm human."

Her uncle laughed. "So was I, once upon a time! And your mother, too. But the powers that we have access to can change all that."

"If that's true, then why did my mother die?"

"Because she chose to have you."

He couldn't have hurt her more if he'd shot her with an arrow. "That's not true," she gasped.

"It is. We rationed that dragon meat for centuries, Andi—a bite here, a bite there. We even aged in the meantime; look at me. For all that I've lived, I am not a young man. But it wasn't until the end, when we knew we were running out, when she decided to stop eating her fair share and give her portion over to me. She met your father and the rest, as they say, is history."

"And her cancer?"

"Inevitable, really. I understand magic more than I do biology, but I suppose you can only betray your own cells for so long. Though you had good times before then with her, right?"

Andi didn't want to answer that right now because the answer was yes, even if everything had been built on lies. She'd loved her mother and known she was loved back. But...she stood so quickly, her chair teetered and whirled on the surrounding room. "Was my father one of you?"

Her uncle snorted. "Hardly. He was a commoner. An unfortunate decision, born of nothing but well-timed infatuation."

"Well...if your organization is so strong and powerful, why did you let him use her?"

"Oh, Andrea, let me make one thing clear. Your mother was using him. She got what she wanted. Your brother and you." Uncle Lee gave her a tight smile. "Monogamy's a fairly recent concept when you've lived as long as we had. She wasn't bothered by his other family in the least. Although I suppose she had no idea the effect discovering it would have on you two."

Andi reeled. "He left her to clean toilets, uncle!"

"And did that matter to her? No. No matter what your mother did, she always had pride in her work." Andi took another look around the room and found twenty pairs of eyes looking at her expectantly. "Andrea," her uncle went on, ever so reasonably. "I won't stop you from leaving. But you need to know that I want you here."

"Why?" she said harshly, the thought of it bitter on her tongue.

"Mei Li was quite the alchemist and herbalist. I feel sure you could be too. And you have modern medical training! We could use someone like you. There's been a hole in our little congregation since your mother's passing," he said, and pointed to the empty chair beside himself.

"And why isn't Danny in it?" she asked, crossing her arms.

"Because there's a chance Danny could change and take out the antique table, if not everyone else in the room," her brother answered from the shadows, stepping forward. He looked much worse than when she'd seen him last, at the cemetery beside their mother's grave. He was sallow, like a drunk with a bad liver, a shade not normally found in any "skin tone colors" of a crayon box, and his bright eyes were rimmed with red. The way he held himself said that he was tired, and he was hunched forward slightly like he might lose his balance at any moment.

She turned to face him. "Aren't you afraid they're going to eat you, too?"

"Nah. I'd fight back too hard," he said, giving her a lopsided grin, despite his apparent exhaustion.

Andi turned to her uncle while pointing at Danny. "How?"

Her uncle shrugged. "As I said, your mother was a master alchemist."

"While cleaning toilets."

"She was not without resources. She just chose not to access them, in her efforts to provide you with a normal life."

"A normal life?" Andi mocked.

"Andi-bear, just ask the question you really want to," Danny said wearily. "Why did Mom choose her degenerate son for her experiments and not you?"

Andi inhaled sharply and grit her teeth. It was too horrible to ask, knowing what those experiments were borne of and what they'd led to, and yet, he was right. She couldn't have admitted it to herself beforehand, but it was definitely why she'd lied to Damian and why she'd had to come here. She wanted to learn her uncle's plans, yes, but she needed to know why her mother had betrayed her more. "Okay, fine," she spat. "Why you?"

"The answer's in the question, Andi. You were going to get out." He looked at her and shook his head in the way that always infuriated her, like he knew something she didn't—some fact she was too stupid to understand. "You know, when she and I started the experiments, and she swore me to secrecy and said I could never tell you or anyone, I actually thought I was the special one. Me. You would be out playing with friends, and she'd be compounding oils to rub on me, making me eat strange things that didn't taste good, putting stinging drops in my eyes. Always trying to summon out the dragon that she hoped was in my blood." He chuckled ruefully. "And to think, I felt so lucky. Like I was the chosen one."

"Because you were," Andi whispered, and she couldn't hide the tinge of jealousy in her voice. She'd always known Danny and her mom were close, just like she'd always known Danny was the favorite one. Everyone had! It was obvious! He didn't even have to learn how to peel his own oranges until he was freaking twelve! Even their dad wanted him! The world had been handed to Danny on a silver plate, and he'd taken that plate and spit on it and thrown it out the nearest window.

"No, Andi," Danny said, and his voice had a serious timbre she was unaccustomed to hearing from him. "You were."

"Yeah. Right," Andi said, with maximal sarcasm.

Danny tossed his hands up in the air in frustration at her, a familiar gesture from him. "I don't care what you believe, Andi, but it's the truth. She chose to keep you ignorant and safe, to save you from this...and yet, here you fucking are."

"Now, now," her uncle chided, as Andi wavered.

Was Danny telling the truth? For once in his life? She couldn't ask her mom anymore.

Andi was struck by another fresh pang of grief, like a knife in the center of her chest. She used to get them all the time right after her mother had died, when she'd reach for her phone to call to tell her mom something and then realize that her mother wasn't there. The pain never went away or felt less sharp. The only thing time had dulled was that she didn't get stabbed as frequently.

Even if her mom had tried to save her from all of this, she knew she would've wanted Danny to be safe too. And she didn't have to be a nurse to look at him and know he wasn't well. Whatever was wrong with him—whatever had happened—she could undo it, somehow, if he gave her a chance, if he'd just give her time. "Danny, come with me," she began, reaching a hand out for him. "It's not too late."

"It is," her uncle answered for him, and made a dismissive sound. "And mind you, your mother was never ashamed of this, Andrea. She just knew how hard it would be for you to have a foot in both worlds. Apparently, being a woman in America is hard enough already? Who knew?" he said with a shrug.

She stared at Danny, willing him to ignore their uncle and respond to her. They'd used to be so close—before her own mother had apparently set them off on different courses. But it wasn't too late. It couldn't be.

Danny looked away from her...in defeat? Ashamed? Or just irritated that she was trying to meddle in his life again? "Tell her the rest, Uncle," Danny said.

"Indeed," Uncle Lee said. "A Joining is coming, Andi. I need you by my side more than I fear Mei Li's ghost haunting me. Other worlds are set to overlap with ours again, and fresh terrors *will* fold through."

Andi gave Danny another three seconds to do something—anything—to show her that he needed saving. Even a strong blink would do. When he didn't, she sank in on herself and attempted to switch gears. Her phone was still recording. Maybe this was her chance to get some information for Damian, right before asking him to help pay for her future therapy. "How do you know?" she asked, tearing her eyes away from Danny to face her uncle again.

9

"Because members among our group have dedicated their magical lives to determining when it will happen. It is not an if, but a when."

"Well...when?" Andi demanded, and some of the people surrounding her politely coughed in surprise.

"Soon," her uncle told her with a tender smile. "When you live as long as we do, time becomes quite relative."

"So, soon enough for you to rationalize killing people, but not so soon that you have to be held accountable for your actions?" She twisted as she spoke to include all of them. "You realize that's what you're doing, right? Killing people?"

"If we have to kill a handful of monsters so that true humans can live...." her uncle droned, and she realized he'd said the phrase before.

She whipped her head back to face him. "Are you a true human anymore?"

His eyes widened and his nostrils flared. "Probably not," he admitted. "But I remember what I once was," he said, tapping his chest firmly. "This was a burden placed upon me, Andrea. A gift...but also a curse. I am among the only people able to see the world for what it is, and act on what I see. And if you could just forget whatever lies the dragon you know has told you, you would see my truth, too, Andrea. Your dragon friend is secretly a beast hiding in human form. They pretend to be one of us, but when the Joining occurs, where will their loyalties lie? You think your dragon friend so noble now...have you ever seen the beast inside? You think it wouldn't rather take the side of another monster in the chaos of a fight? It has even fewer ties to this world than the descendants that we kill do! What cause can possibly bind it to the earth when it can fly?"

A man behind her banged his hand on the table for their attention. "You never said she knew a dragon, Lee." Andi turned in panic and saw it was the same man who said her mother'd saved him earlier.

"I didn't need to. Because we have our own dragon, now," her uncle said, gesturing toward Danny.

"No, you mean *you* have a dragon."

"And I have been generous with his skin, have I not?" her uncle asked archly. Andi flashed her brother a look of concern and saw his shoulders flinch. How were they trapping his dragon and keeping him still? Did they sedate him? Was his dragon some other entity trapped with him, like Damian's was, and if so, how the hell could Danny even begin to explain the tortures they were performing on him to the creature?

"I'd rather see Mei Li's notebooks, honestly," a man with an Australian accent said. He had a suit on as well, but unlike the rest of the men, he wore cowboy boots instead of dress shoes. He was gnawing on a toothpick that shone under the room's subtle lighting, and Andi had a feeling it was ivory. "Why settle for the egg when you could get the emu?"

Acid flashed across Andi's tongue as she felt like the conversation was sinking to a new and more frightening low.

"I have her notes, and I'm recreating her medicines as best I can," her brother interjected. "Without me, you have no connection to her. And Andi's our best chance at continuing her art."

"What, you think intelligence has some blood link?" a dour-sounding woman sniffed. Andi twisted to see her. She was Latina, with straight black hair longer than Andi's, and she had a glamorous golden rose brooch on the lapel of her black dress. Her tone and her gaze were disaffected and ancient, but her body was youthful, preternaturally so—she didn't look a day older than seventeen. "If so, you should meet *my* nephew."

"No. It's that she cares," Danny said, ignoring the rest of them to look only at his sister. "If you can make her care about something, she'll move heaven and earth to make it happen."

"I'm not helping you here, Danny." It didn't matter that her brother was right about her. She knew too many people on the opposite side, and on no planet would she ever hurt someone sheerly to gain from it. "I do care about you still, somehow. But I just can't."

"Not today and not tomorrow...but you will," Danny said, advancing on her with the same intent she'd seen in him a thousand times for others. There was something poisonously charismatic about Danny. Somehow, his entire life, he'd always known how to get his own way. "Now that I'm changing, Andi-bear, I can feel it, in my bones. Eventually, even despite your best efforts, we'll be fighting on the same side."

"He's right," her uncle told her, with a knowing nod.

Andi shook her head. "No. Absolutely not. You can take your destiny trash and shove it." She backed up, angling her way out of the tables, searching for the door. "I'm leaving now," she declared, daring anyone to say otherwise.

"Are we really letting her leave here when she knows the location of a dragon?" Joshan pressed. His suit was every bit as nice as Damian's. They spoke of money and personal tailoring, and if he caught Damian, the thought of what he would do to him—or what anyone else present would, given the chance—made her want to die. He stared at her, shamelessly trying to memorize her face and she threw up her hands to hide from him.

"We are," her uncle announced. "She will come to us willingly, or not at all." His eyes narrowed as he looked at her. "The time will come when you will be forced to choose. Us or them. I am confident you will make the right choice, Andrea, as befits your lineage and history."

"I won't join you. Not ever." She clenched her hands into impotent fists. "Stop pretending that it's destiny."

"I can't help it. It is. But run along now, back to your friends," he said, dismissing her like she was still a child. It made her so angry, him always thinking he knew what was best for her—it didn't matter how long he'd lived. But she took a step back and then another and then twisted to see the path she'd taken in so she could run back out it as she heard him go on. "As for the rest of us, I have other entertainments planned. We've recently caught a thorn in our side."

Andi couldn't help herself, mere feet from the door, she turned around to see two men dressed like janitors pulling in a cage. Inside the cage was a person.

Her stomach dropped. It was the small blonde woman from the coffee shop and again outside the hospital the night prior. And the woman had known who Damian was, after Andi said his name. Andi looked around for someone else to help her stop things and realized all the tables that edged the room were similar to Uncle Lee's tables at home that she'd seen all the time growing up. Dining room tables. She knew what they intended to do to the woman and knew she couldn't live with herself if she left.

"You can't!" she shouted from the back.

The blonde woman's head snapped in her direction, as did everyone else's. The woman glared at Andi with intent. "Save yourself, girl. Or call a fucking friend."

Andi only had a moment to decide. If she walked away, the strange woman would die, and if she called in Damian, he would. So she stalked around the edge of the room to play the only card she had, ignoring everyone else but her uncle to stand in front of him once again—only this time on his side of the table. "If you kill her, I will never come and work for you, no matter what my brother says."

"If we kill her, we could bathe you in her blood until you were forced to drink some. Then you'd know what it was like and gladly talk about your dragon," Joshan said lightly, smoothing a contemplative hand down his chest.

Her uncle moved almost faster than she could see, nimbly leaping over his own table and crossing to the next while flipping his pipe in his hand to hold the bowl. And then she watched in disbelief as he stabbed the pipe's stem through the other man's throat.

Her uncle—the man who'd given her her favorite stuffed unicorn when she was seven—had just killed someone. In front of her. And not in a pretty, dancing kung-fu movie pretend way, but in a way she was used to from the hospital. Real, brutal, and unforgiving.

The stranger slid out of his chair, sputtering, as blood sprayed wildly. Andi ran for him without thinking, although no one else present moved. By the time she reached his side, she could see he'd already lost too much blood, but it didn't stop her from clapping her hand to his throat, feeling the last of it, hot and sticky, seep out. There was nothing she could've done in time, and besides, if she saved him, wouldn't she only be endangering Damian?

Her uncle didn't even clean the man's blood off of his pipe stem before putting it back into his mouth to talk around it. "No one threatens my niece," he warned the rest of the people present, and then turned toward her, her kneeling near his feet. "Does it matter to you that this woman has killed many of my friends?" he asked her.

"No," she said, wiping her hand off roughly on the dead man's wool suit jacket. "Was he a friend?" she asked, pointing with her bloody hand at the man on the floor.

A smile fluttered across her uncle's face at realizing he'd been caught. "Not much of one, no."

CHAPTER

TWO

Damian sat stunned for the length of a breath listening to what sounded like Andi betraying him.

"That is your woman?" His sister turned toward him, green eyes wide and flashing with anger. She'd intuited things by the way he'd frozen the second he heard Andi speaking on their intercom. Everyone else in the SUV looked to him for instruction, one by one.

"She's a traitor!" Ryana went on—the only one not shocked into silence, her voice rising in volume. "You have to kill her, Damian, right away. This kind of insubordination cannot be allowed to stand!"

Out of his peripheral vision he saw Austin reach out and clamp a hand down over Ryana's mouth, stilling in her sheer surprise.

But his sister wasn't wrong. The Hunter they'd been tracking for a few days had led them here and now they were listening in to Andi—his *woman*, his *mate*—consorting with the enemy. It didn't matter that she was trying to refute the other Hunters. The mere fact that she was here and she hadn't told him she was coming— she'd lied to him. He should've known better. He'd been so blinded

15

by his feelings for her, but looking back, of course something had changed that night when they'd first used her as bait to lure her uncle, when he'd kidnapped her on his yacht. When Andi had pushed him away afterward and told him that she wouldn't see him again until midnight tonight, how could he not know? Because how precise that'd been of her. Precisely when this charade would be finished.

Andi had lied to him and put him through the worst two days of his life—all of him and his dragon longing for her, and for what? So that she could betray him here, with Hunters? He felt the gemstone he'd had Mills make for her—*from his own flesh!*—trapped in his pocket against his thigh and it felt like it burned him.

Mills's hand reached out for his shoulder and caught it, squeezing it tightly. "Damian," she said, her voice low and sensible.

"No," he disagreed. He didn't want to hear what wise things she would say in an attempt to talk him down. He just wanted to be pissed. They all listened in to the rest of the conversation as Ryana angrily shoved Austin away.

"You fell for a human whose mother was a servant?" She made a sound of extreme disgust.

Over the intercom, Andi's story continued. About her uncle, mother, and brother—just one big happy Hunter family.

Then the janitor they were tracing must've gotten closer because they could hear her uncle intone at full volume: *if you could just forget whatever lies the dragon you know has told you, you would see my truth too, Andrea. Your dragon friend is secretly a beast hiding in human form. They pretend to be one of us, but when the Joining occurs, where will their loyalties lie? You think your dragon friend so noble now...have you ever seen the beast inside? You think it wouldn't rather take the side of another monster in the chaos of a fight? It has even fewer ties to this world than the descendants that we kill do! What cause can possibly bind it to the earth when it can fly?*

And Damian felt the part of his chest that he hadn't gouged out with his teeth to make a living gemstone for Andi tighten, as though he were biting himself still. And worse yet, the janitor moved away, so he couldn't hear her response.

Did she defend him? Or did she think what her uncle said was true?

Had her opinion of him changed?

Did it matter now he knew she was capable of lying?

"I know she loves you Damian; I see it in her aura," Mills said.

"Love?" Ryana asked, her voice going high. "Oh no, no, no." She maneuvered around to face him in the SUV, crouching in the wheel well, tearing a higher slit in her ornately beaded evening dress, beads scattering across the floor as she attempted to get into his line of sight. "No. It doesn't matter how you feel—how strong you think you are—you do not *love* a simpleminded, weak skinned human. It would be like me saying I was in love with a puppy. Father would've already—"

"Ryana!" he shouted, and the SUV was quiet. "I am not my father."

"Clearly," Ryana sneered, then looked over at Austin. "Touch me again without permission and I'll have Lyka peck your eyes out."

A fire lit in Austin's eyes—what Damian knew was the thrill of making future bad decisions. The undaunted werewolf gave Ryana a challenging leer and readied to try his luck as Zach waved his hands trying to bat the tension out of the air and stop his brother's foolishness. "Damian, we need a plan."

"I've infiltrated the rest of the vehicles here that have Bluetooth," Jamison announced. "We'll know where they go. I suggest that we attempt taking them one by one."

"Why?" Ryana asked impatiently.

"Because they do have a dragon in there. We're significantly outnumbered, and—" Zach jerked his chin at Damian.

"I do not need your pity. And right now, I would very much enjoy fucking things up." He felt his dragon surge inside him, summoned by the thought of violence. If Andi's uncle wanted to see what kind of monster he was, that could be arranged.

"As confident as I am that you could kill Andi's brother, I'm not sure that'd be so good for your relationship, Damian," Mills said, trying to calm him.

The janitor's phone came into range again, a stranger's voice suddenly filled the car: *"Save yourself, girl. Or call a fucking friend."*

They each looked to one another again.

"Is that...Stella?" Zach guessed, and Damian watched the werewolf's knuckles go white as he clenched his hands into fists.

"Max, start the car," Austin quipped, as his brother looked back at him, stricken. "I'm kidding," he reassured him. "You need me, let's go," Austin said, putting one hand on his gun and the other on the SUV's door.

"I can't untangle centuries of cruelty here, uncle. I can only say what I know is right, right now. If you hurt her, you might as well be hurting me," they heard Andi proclaim. *"I have been hurt a lot lately...and I am growing tired of forgiveness."*

There was a pregnant pause wherein they all held their breath as one.

"Very well. Release the girl."

"You can't be serious," said someone else, unknown.

"Please don't make me kill you, too," said Andi's uncle. Not a threat, just a pleasant suggestion.

They all heard the sound of groans and then her uncle addressed Andi again. *"Andrea, the sooner you take your mother's place, the happier you'll be. You shouldn't fight it."*

Andi's voice came over, as clear as Damian's heart was dark. *"I don't care what you think you know. You don't know my destiny...or me."*

That makes two of us, Damian thought.

"DID THEY HURT YOU?" Andi asked the strange woman walking beside her for the twentieth time. Andi was still in the outfit she'd last worn at her mother's funeral years ago: black slacks, black flats, and a black silk shirt, with just enough makeup on to cover up her current level of exhaustion.

Whereas the woman lightly limping beside her was in street gear: a purple sweat shirt, short-shorts, and tennis shoes, with blonde hair pulled up into a messy bun. Her shorts were so short and her skin so pale it was easy for Andi to see the large bruise spreading on one leg, even underneath the tattoos she had sweeping down her thighs, a trail of spinning nebulas and stars.

"Are you sure you're okay?" Andi pressed.

The woman rolled her eyes and straightened herself to walk normally. "I'm fine. Like I already told you."

Andi didn't believe that for a second. She knew the woman wasn't human; otherwise, her uncle wouldn't have been interested in her, so she could only imagine how hard she'd been hit to make her limp. "Who are you? How did you know who I was? Why were you following me?"

The woman stopped and whirled on her. "My name is Stella…and you're fucking insane. People think I'm crazy? Compared to you, I'm Mr. Rogers."

Somehow, getting roughhoused hadn't done a thing to budge the woman's makeup—Andi could clearly see Stella's perfect cat-eye eyeliner by the streetlights. "Answer my other questions," Andi demanded.

Stella inhaled and exhaled deeply as they kept walking together just slower than a jog. "I've been tracking them—your uncle's group back there, including the asshole Australians who captured me—for revenge reasons, for a while now. I knew they were interested in you, but I didn't know why."

"Was he right?" Andi asked her. She couldn't fully claim why she wanted to know, but she needed to hear it from this woman's mouth. "Did you kill his friends?"

"Yes, but, he slaughtered most of my family. So I guess you could say he started it, but who the fuck knows. The ladder down into the cesspool is pretty fucking long."

"Are you going to turn around and try to kill him?"

"Your uncle?" Stella asked, her voice rising. "Yeah. Lady, thanks, but I don't owe you.... And if I meet your uncle in a dark alley, only one of us is coming out alive. If that makes you want to spit me back—"

Andi waved her hands. "No...just don't tell me anymore."

"I don't know what world you live in where everything's safe and shit, but that place is not here." Stella's eyes narrowed on hers. "But you do know Damian, don't you."

"If you tell them he's a dragon," Andi warned, feeling a wave of proprietary protectiveness. "Do you work for him?"

"No...but don't worry. I would never sell out one of my own. Especially not someone who could pick me up and throw me to the moon," Stella snorted.

Andi relaxed, fractionally. "All right, then. The less we know about each other, the better, I think."

"Agreed," Stella said, then paused. "You know it doesn't stop with tonight, right?"

Andi rocked up onto her toes and then back again. "What do you mean?" she asked, even though she was afraid she could guess.

"Those people back there...they'd do anything to get ahold of a dragon. There's only so much your uncle, no matter how 'esteemed'," she said, clearly mocking Uncle Lee's vocabulary, "can do."

"How do you know?" Andi asked, hugging herself, trapped between wanting to know everything and wanting to run away and hide.

"Uh, other than him or people like him killing my brother? And being willing to eat me tonight?" Stella snapped her fingers aggressively in front of Andi's face. "Get with the program."

"I am!" Andi said defensively. "It's just...hard."

Stella pretended to weigh things, an imaginary object in each hand. "Yeah, I can guess it would be. My dead family, versus your alive and wanting to kill me family. Tough decisions," she said, and then threw both her hands up to flip Andi off.

Andi took a step back. She knew Stella's anger was righteous, but getting hit with it still burned. "For what it's worth, I didn't know."

Stella looked her up and down and snorted. "I believe you."

"Good, because—" Andi began.

"Because no one else could've sold them that naive line of bullshit that got me free if they'd had even an inkling of what the fuck had been happening all this time," Stella cut in. "But I'm still not offering you absolution, lady. So, you did the right thing tonight, this one time. So fucking what? You want an award? You want me to clap for you? Where the fuck were you five years ago?"

Andi stood there and took the brunt of the other woman's anger. "I...I'm sorry." She felt foolish the second the words were out of her mouth.

Stella inhaled and it felt to Andi like she was going to yell a lot more, then she deflated. "Yeah. Me too." The street they were on ended at a streetlight where it intersected another and Stella jerked her chin over Andi's shoulder. "You go your way, and I'll go mine."

Andi nodded helplessly as the other woman turned around.

It was an extremely long way back to civilization and Andi didn't even know what kind of state she was going to be in by midnight tonight, when she knew Damian would be waiting to talk to her, just like she'd promised him. She walked down four more long blocks of the "walk in the center of the street because cars are less scary than shadows" variety until she got to a bus stop with a run that was still working this late. She sat down inside it, still not feeling very safe, remembering the last time something like this had happened to her —when she'd been at the bus stop waiting for David—and how Damian had been there for her, trying to protect her. She couldn't believe she'd tried to do something like this without him. But she also couldn't believe she'd just saved Stella from being an appetizer buffet, either.

Or that, given the choice, her uncle would gladly turn Damian into a main course.

Andi wanted to put her head in her hands and cry until it all went away, but one of her hands was still bloodstained. Tears wouldn't help, and it wouldn't be safe to not be situationally aware. So she curled into a ball instead, hugging her knees to her chest, praying that the schedule on the bus stop wasn't wrong.

It wasn't. It just took forever. And then the bus almost drove by her without stopping, probably because she looked like a small black shadow since that's the only color she was wearing. She felt infinitely relieved to be under the dim lights aboard, even if some of the other late-night passengers smelled of piss-on-their-shoes funk. She found a seat to herself and it stayed that way for three stops, her mind whirling fast enough to pull in two. Half of her was dying to see Damian. The other half knew that dying could be literal and she didn't know what to do about that. She stumbled off the bus, looking like any other drunk aboard, heading straight for her apartment, but before she could go inside, a car she didn't recognize drove up and stopped ahead of her. A stranger stepped out in driver's livery, and he held up a sign like he was meeting someone at the airport. It said *PRINCESS* on it in all capital letters.

She walked over to him slowly, remembering the first time she'd met Damian, when he'd been pretending to be his own driver so he could meet her before he could trust her to care for Zach. Back when things had been simple and good.

Back when a relationship between a dragon and an unfortunately-well-connected-to-hunters-human had been easy.

"Are you Princess?" the man inquired. He was a hundred pounds too light to be Damian, plus two-to-six inches too small in all directions.

She gave the stranger a half-hearted smile. "Depends. Does Princess have a last name?"

The man checked his notes. "Doesn't seem so."

"Then yeah. You're here for me," Andi said. She beat him to the back door of his car and opened it for herself before pausing. "Hey, do you have any towels?"

ANDI USED one of the complimentary bottles of water to wash off her bloodstained hand as best she could with one of the blue car paper towels he'd offered her, well aware she was making a mess and not caring. Damian could definitely compensate this poor man for his upholstery. She glanced up to see where they were going and for a horrible moment she thought he might be taking her to work. They were definitely headed the right direction, but then the car drove past her hospital's exit and headed to the center of the city, where Blackwood Industries' skyscraper jostled others for position, winning out by the five floors that made it taller than the rest.

"Are you sure this is the right way?" she asked, looking out.

"Absolutely," the man declared, weaving through streets as empty as the ones she'd just been walking on, until they reached the front of the glass-wrapped building that bore Damian's last name.

Andi made to get out, then stopped. "So what now?"

The driver twisted. "I was told to give you this." He handed her a gold key card.

Andi groaned. This was fifty shades of bullshit. She didn't want a magically romantic reconciliation—or whatever the hell else Damian had spent the last forty-eight hours planning.

She just wanted to see him. She needed to touch him again and have him touch her and have him tell her everything was going to be all right, even if it was a lie.

Andi took the card with a sigh, hopped out, and walked for the building's front door, which the card unsurprisingly opened.

"YOU FEEL confident that you can follow them all at once?" Damian asked Jamison, his hand already on the door handle.

"Totally," Jamison promised him. "It's just fifteen bogeys. And if anyone tries to fly out tonight, I'll hack the airport to stop them."

"Think about it...if we can get them checking into fancy hotels, security cameras will log them and their people's faces, and we can branch out from there," Mills said breathily, already lusting over the potential data.

"So when I want to do this, I'm an asshole, but when you all want to do it..." Damian began.

"We're at war, now. We get that," Zach said.

"And we weren't a few days ago?" Damian muttered.

"Go take your angst out on your girlfriend," Austin said, reaching over Damian to open his door for him.

Damian got out of the SUV and shot his werewolf friend a dark look. "Ryana's warned you. If you misbehave and she hurts you, I'll have no choice but to take her side. She's a lot more cunning than you're ready for."

"You truly know me, brother," Ryana said, grinning wildly at him. "Go kill the human quickly and then come back."

"Yeah, that's not gonna happen," Damian overheard Austin tell her as the door closed and Max pulled the SUV away with a wave.

DAMIAN FACED the empty street alone, prepared to run after Andi. She and Stella had turned the corner, and it would've been an easy enough thing to follow them. He was upwind, there was no way that Stella could scent him. And it would've been even easier to catch up to them like he wanted to, grab Andi, shake her and ask her, *what the fuck?* He made to do just that, then caught himself.

She told you herself the streets are not safe for her! His dragon's concern surged inside him, intimately worried about Andi's well-being. Andi had said as much to him the other night, and his dragon had been listening. How ironic that his cold-blooded half was apparently doing all the feeling for both of them right now.

But technically, nothing was safe—not the buses she used for transportation or the job that she had or actually, come to think of it, her personally. She'd chosen to do this alone, without him. Was it traitorous? Yes. Could she possibly be in danger right now? Also yes.

Go after her! his dragon pressed him, unwavering in its commitment, and everything in his being wanted to go with it.

But his mind knew better.

Whatever had happened tonight, this was what she'd wanted and how she'd wanted it, too. Solo, without him. Andi had known the risks. And somehow, she'd navigated a room full of Hunters so that both she and Stella had survived. She was nothing short of magnificent.

She'd also somehow lied to him easily, apparently without compunction, for days, and he was right to be hurt by that. It was a betrayal. But the reason it stung wasn't just that she'd been a liar. No, it hurt more than that because he knew she was his mate.

He knew they didn't have to face challenges alone anymore, so why would she do something like this without him?

Couldn't she feel it too?

He prepared to blow up about it again when he remembered an inconvenient fact...that he'd never, ever, told her. And as she was human, she didn't know.

Maybe Ryana was right. Maybe he was repeating his father's mistakes, by being mated with a human. But now that it had happened, what choice did he have? It was his destiny to be with her.

Even if she was a liar.

Even if he'd been lying to her, too, all along.

He stood there, incandescently angry, both at her and himself. His emotions ground inside of him like rough stones, chipping away at one another, as he hauled out his phone to summon an Uber, and came up with a plan.

DAMIAN WAS in the skyscraper named after him so infrequently that he forgot that he owned it sometimes. But there was a penthouse floor that well-paid maids kept up for him and Zach, despite neither of them hardly ever using it. He let himself in and took a cold, fast shower, trying to calm himself to think. After that, he discovered that the closet only had suits inside. He dressed himself in one, carefully removing the necklace he'd created for Andi from one pocket and putting it in the next, then took the elevator up to the helipad.

His mood was as dark as the clouds overhead when the elevator opened up. Andi had lied to him. Outright. If she could do that, what end to it was there? There'd been gaps in the conversation they'd overheard. Had she sold him out? Had she considered it, even briefly? Her uncle was offering her eternal life. Eternal beauty. He couldn't imagine those things mattering to Andi, but what human wouldn't be tempted?

Especially when it was him against her entire family. Her brother, her uncle, her mother, and a lineage that went back for centuries. Could he blame her if she ran to them instead? Even if it broke him?

What haunted him the most, though, was what her uncle'd said. He'd asked her what she knew of the beast inside of him. He hadn't heard her answer, but he knew the truth—not much. She'd asked questions of his dragon through him, but her uncle wasn't wrong. His dragon wasn't him. And with the Heart of the Dragon on earth now—thanks to his sister—and with his curse of eventually becoming his dragon clearly back in play, Damian stood at the edge of the roof looking out at the city below, his hands tight on the railing.

He knew they were meant to be together. It wasn't something he could verbally express, so much as it was something he felt, all the time, in his soul. Their destiny was an immutable, physical thing, as real for him as the sun in the daytime or the moon and stars at night.

But...she didn't really know him.

Not all of him.

And if he was going to tell her that they were mates, he had to be honest with her from here on out. Never any secrets again. No matter how much it scared him, and even if she'd cut him, first.

He kicked off his shoes quickly, unbuttoned his shirt to take it off, and stripped off his pants, folding them carefully on top, knowing the precious jewelry his pocket still held. Inside him, his dragon watched, bewildered.

What are you doing?

What I probably should've done a long time ago. He dropped the control internally, setting his dragon free, but it didn't rise to possess him. *What?* he demanded of it.

This makes no sense.

It doesn't have to, Damian thought at it, willing himself to relax. *I shouldn't have to hide you...not now that we want the same thing.*

But...each time we do, my time grows closer...and with the Heart near—

I would rather risk losing myself to you than her thinking she doesn't know all of me. That she can't trust all of me. And I include you. Whether I like it or not.

He stood naked on the tallest building in the city, and once more, he let go.

His dragon hesitated and then emerged, in a liquid-feeling rush, like Damian had jumped into a hot spring. Once again he was suspended in the nothingness inside the beast. Only this time, it didn't hurt.

He'd taken the pain of being trapped inside his dragon for granted for so long now, almost all of his life, that he never thought to mention it anymore. It was just part and parcel of losing control, of letting the dragon make his humanity disappear, the equal and opposite sensation to his dragon's "chains." But now.... Damian tried to push his hands out, searching for the walls his dragon so often built around him, he found nothing but a welcoming, enveloping warmth.

Was that a good thing? Or was this what it would be like when his time had come? He couldn't wonder for any longer. The elevator doors were opening.

"I AM NOT GOING ON A HELICOPTER," Andi began sternly, then at seeing the dragon, finished much more quietly, "ride."

Damian was his dragon now.

She hadn't seen it since it'd rescued her from the demon thing by his fountain weeks ago. Ever since then her brain had tried to trick her, whittling what she thought she'd seen down from a mind-breaking experience into a cheesy carnival freak show, convincing herself that instead of a shiny sixty-foot dragon she'd seen a sack full of boa constrictors all tied together and spray-painted gold.

But now, here it was, sitting on all fours like a sphinx, wings folded tight so as not to catch the cold night air—or more likely not to scare her.

Too late.

She gave it a low wave, before holding herself against the chill. "Hi."

The creature's massive head tilted in acknowledgement in return. All of its teeth were the length of her arm. She could've fit her entire head inside of one of its nostrils.

But the eyes...the eyes were still familiar. The same color as Damian's. Dark gold like the last flash of sun at sunset. She felt stricken by his presence, and it wasn't so much the dragon anymore, as it was being with *him* again. She put a hand over her mouth. Two days without him had been a long time.

She walked toward him and then she spotted a gouge on his chest, like a dent on a golden breastplate. She'd seen green blood in the photo he'd sent her. Was that why? It hadn't been there when she'd last seen his dragon, she was sure. She finished the distance between them at a jog. "What hurt you?"

The dragon ducked its head down to meet her, eyes nearly going crossed to look at her, as he gently nudged her away. She danced back, not letting it touch her, though she was close enough to feel the heat of its breath.

"Is there a reason for all this?" she guessed, gesturing at him. The dragon gently snaked its head down, until its chest was hidden and it was on a level with her, watching her, its pupils reptilian slits. "Damian," she began, and then switched gears. "Dragon." The beast's ears perked as she continued. "I had all these things to tell him. You... both of you, I guess. I don't know how it works." She pulled her phone out of her pocket and finally turned off her recording app. She thought about replaying her night for him, but at the thought of holding her phone up to one of his ears, she laughed. "Look, if I talk to you, can he hear me? I don't want to repeat myself. And, if I talk to him, do you care?" What was it be like to be trapped mute inside a fire-breathing reptile? She wished she'd asked Damian earlier. "Not like I'm talking through you, though. I guess, I mean, do you actually want to hear me?"

The dragon rearranged itself around her and she realized it was now blocking the wind as it faced her.

"I'll take that as a yes," she whispered. Its tail snaked alongside her and she sat down on the cold cement, putting her back against his scales to warm herself. "Okay...so," she started, and began.

DAMIAN LISTENED inside his dragon as Andi recounted everything. From the time on the boat with her uncle, up through that night's fight with him. The scent of her—apples, caramel, and the sea—was intoxicating. She smelled like home, and he knew his dragon was fighting the urge to lean closer to breathe her in.

"I really was mad at you, though, Damian. And I meant what I said about this," she said, her eyes widening as they took his dragon's form in. "You're a lot. And I'm just me."

She shrank into herself more, and he tightened his tail's wrap along her back and side.

"And I had to know what'd happened with my mother. I didn't lie about that." There was something about his inability to talk that seemed to let her speak more freely. "Which was why I went and saw my uncle tonight, without telling you. I knew you wouldn't have let me, or you'd have sent an army after me. But lying to you for the past few days hasn't felt right. I'm not a liar, Damian. That's not me." She stared up at him, as if willing him to believe, and then finished telling him everything else from her evening, most of which Damian had already heard secondhand. When she was done, she shook her head and spoke just above a whisper, like she was talking to herself, not him. "To think, he wants me to come help him...and my brother thinks I'm going to fight at his side."

She was quiet after that, and Damian would've paid any amount of money to know what she was thinking. "I've put you into danger, Damian." Her voice was low and she looked up at him with concern. "Stella told me as much, too," she said, moving to stand. "Now that they know you exist, I don't think they'll stop. And if they find me and I lead them to you, I could never live with myself if I hurt you."

His dragon did his best to give her a bemused look, at the thought of a slip of a girl hurting the hulking beast wrapped around her.

"I mean it," she protested, reading him easily. "I knew you wouldn't take it seriously. But you're not invulnerable. Look at what happened to you," she said, flinging her hands at the partially-hidden injury on his chest.

What happened to me was you, Damian wanted to say, but couldn't.

She walked over to stand in front of his nose, folding her hands behind her back. Where was the brave girl who'd walked right up to him and touched his cheek not long ago? But Damian remembered when he'd yelled at her to not touch Zach's wolf at the hospital and all the things her uncle had put into her head tonight.

She knows we're different now, he told his dragon. *She finally believes.*

Then does she not like me?

She doesn't know you. I've done too good a job of keeping you hidden.

His dragon considered this. *Is she...afraid of me?* it asked while watching her, poignantly wishing she'd lay hands on him, well aware of how still he needed to be to not scare her off.

Well, you are going to murder me eventually, Damian said dryly.

There are two sides to your family's curse, human. That you are murdered, yes, but also that I must do the murdering.

Damian grunted in response. *I suppose.*

His dragon pondered free of him in what way it could best make its affection for Andi known, without seeming monstrous. Damian knew the beast didn't long for her physically, that would've been ten different kinds of impossible, yet it did yearn for her love.

"You've been very quiet," Andi said softly, a silly attempt at a joke because otherwise the only sound up on the skyscraper was the whistling of wind...and now a phone alarm. Andi startled, then focused on what was beeping—his pile of folded clothing. She cast a glance back, then went over to dig through his pockets and find his phone. "It's midnight," she said, turning the alarm off. "Do you want to turn into a pumpkin, or shall I?" Another small object fell from her hand and started rolling away—the necklace he'd had Mills make for her, from his own flesh, bitten from his chest. He lunged for it with a paw and she shrieked and closed her eyes, going completely still, like if she couldn't see him he might forget about her too.

Like he could ever.

His dragon nudged her thigh softly, so softly, with the tip of its nose, and watched her eyes open back up. And then it gestured to the ground where it was carefully rolling its paw up to reveal the ember of a gem beneath. She gasped at seeing its strange light and knelt down to pick it up, finding it strung on a necklace. "Is this for me?" she asked him, showing it to him.

His dragon blinked slowly. She inspected the stone in her hand

and his dragon tried to content himself with the fact that even if she wouldn't touch him, she would be keeping a piece of him near, as she clasped it around her neck.

"It's lovely. Thank you," she said as she pressed it to her throat with a hand.

A brisk wind struck up and his dragon thwarted it by flicking out a wing to protect her. Damian watched her eyes travel the length of it with something like awe, and then his dragon acted before he knew what it was thinking.

It put its paw up for her. Clearly offering.

No! They are looking for us now! There is no way we can safely get away with this!

The night is clouded and I'll be careful, his dragon said, pushing his concerns and him aside.

CHAPTER

THREE

The dragon's paw was as big as she was and she knew without a doubt what it was for. She hesitated, but only for a moment—long enough to scoop Damian's clothes up for him.

Because who wouldn't want to fly?

"Don't drop me," she teased, crawling up into its scale covered palm. The dragon bowed its head to look at her. "What?" she grinned, as it placed its other paw over the top of her, its fingers and claws forming a loose cage as it readied to take off. She felt the power inside of it surge as it sent weight back into its haunches before leaping forward, wings grabbing hold of the sky.

Without thinking, she screamed. They'd been on the highest skyscraper in the city and now there was nothing beneath them anymore—just the cityscape, same as if she were on a plane. She clung to him, freezing and fearless, staring down at the rolling hills of lights below her, and then she bothered to look up.

He was holding her to his chest like she was something precious. His scales were gray now in the darkness, but she could see his wings stroking through the air, his tail like a whip behind her, and ahead of her his chin and throat straight as an arrow as he aimed them at their destination.

It didn't matter to her where they were going as long as they stayed aloft. It felt like she'd left all of her problems back on the ground—that this was what it felt like to be free.

"This is amazing!" she shouted loudly, hoping he could hear, squeezing the claws that protected her tight. "I love this!"

Then they banked and began to slow down, into a stomach clenching spiral like a roller coaster's highest turn. She shrieked and laughed, tempted to fling her arms up but too scared she'd drop Damian's clothing, until his wings flared out and she realized they were going to land someplace that she knew—the top of Damian's castle.

The beast made a nimble landing, considering two of its four paws were still holding her. After coming to a stop it slowly splayed its fingers out, releasing her to the castle's rooftop cobblestone. She stumbled forward, breathless. Her eyes were dry, she was freezing, and her body was shaking from the adrenaline. "I loved that!" she shouted, whirling, to see him and finding Damian standing naked there in all of his chiseled, brooding, perfection. It'd been two days since she'd seen him—two days too long—and her eyes soaked him in all at once. His broad shoulders, muscled chest, arms that could probably throw someone to the moon—Stella wasn't wrong about that—and below that the slight V of his flat stomach leading directly to his heavy cock. Andi rocked with ache from missing him, even as she blushed to see him so exposed. "I love," the words left her body again, her excitement priming her to repeat things, only this time there wasn't wind to rip them safely from her mouth. "Flying. I love flying."

Damian walked over to her, unashamed of his nakedness, and took his clothes out of her arms to put back on. He started with his slacks. "Yes. My dragon also loves flying," he told her, although there was something faintly accusatory in his tone. "You should see your hair."

She quickly pulled her wind-whipped hair into a bun. She could make out the same injury on him as his dragon had. "You should see your skin," she frowned, trying to lay a hand on his chest but he moved back, quickly buttoning his shirt back up.

It was very unlike Damian to be dressing in front of her unless he had someplace to be. "Where are you going?"

"Why do you care?"

Andi blinked. "Are you...mad at me?"

"Yes," he said flatly, pulling his suit jacket on. "But I'm also mad at myself."

For what? Andi's head tilted, imagining bad things instantly. "You heard what I told your dragon, right?"

"I did," he said, straightening his cuffs. It was a reflexive maneuver, she could tell—like he was nervous—and anything that made him nervous made her doubly so. His brow creased in disappointment, and he made a thoughtful noise before speaking again. "I told you once you were a pretty knife, princess. Well, congratulations, tonight you cut me."

"Damian—" she began, as he squared off in front of her.

"You called me your boyfriend and then pushed me away for days so you could do what you liked. You hurt me. On purpose."

"I had to lie to you, you know that—"

"No, actually, I don't."

Andi crossed her arms. "You know, I could get used to your whole dragon's not-talking thing."

He snorted. Wind struck up and brushed his straight black hair into his eyes. "You don't actually have a defense, do you," he said, pushing it back with one hand.

"I was doing what I thought was right. I deserved answers, Damian, and I wasn't going to get them with you at my side." Andi hugged herself, angry at him and herself in turn. *At least we have that in common tonight?* "I didn't want to do it, you know. Do you think I enjoyed lying to you? Being scared, knowing that I had to go see my crazy family alone?"

His eyes searched hers, stepping forward as she retreated. The sky had been dark and cloudy when they'd flown through it, but that was nothing compared to the storm Damian brought with him now. "But you did it anyway."

"And I came straight to you to tell you everything!" She threw her hands up in exasperation. "Even knowing it would piss you off!" The stone of a castle parapet was at her back.

The corners of his lips cruelly lifted, taunting her, as she realized she was trapped. "Why?"

"Why what?"

"Why me, Andi?" He moved to stand so close to her that they were almost touching.

Andi blinked and blurted out, "Because you're the person I tell things to." She was surprised by how wrung out she felt after fear with her uncle, the elation of flight, and the stomach-churning queasiness of fighting now. It left her with few defenses.

"Why?" he pressed again. "Why am I that person?"

She bit her lips and shook her head. "I don't know!"

They were toe-to-toe and he was breathing hard and she didn't know what he wanted from her as he bowed his head toward hers. "Lie to me again, why don't you, princess."

"I love you," she said. She didn't think she meant it at the time. She was just pissed off at the way he was treating her and had thought of the worst possible thing for her to say. She watched the words hit him like a slap.

But then...oh, but then, it was like she'd uncorked a secret reservoir, the place where she'd been shoving her emotions with him all along, trying to dole them out into societally acceptable pieces, not letting herself get too hopeful or appear too wanton. But now that the lid was off and the words were spoken, she could feel it all jumbling together inside her like a science project volcano. His eyes searched hers, his expression more wounded than anything any monster could've done to his chest.

"I don't believe that's a lie for a moment," he whispered, leaning down.

"Too bad," she told him, looking up, because she didn't want to believe it herself, and then his lips were on hers.

She could've pushed him back, but she didn't. He was still mad at her—she could tell from the way his lips bruised hers, his tongue invading her mouth like it needed a new home, his hands rough and demanding all over her body. But that was okay; she was mad at herself too. Not because she'd lied to him—she was her own person, goddammit—but because she'd gone and cracked the edges of the box around her soul and let actual feelings in. She did care about him, and the more she let herself think about it, she realized she more than cared for him. She wanted to be with him, now and forever, and she didn't care how ridiculous that sounded because everything about being with him now felt right and.... *What the hell was she thinking?*

Her uncle wanted to murder Damian and her brother swore he knew she was going to fight by his side.

If both those things were true, what the fuck was she doing right now?

"Damian..." She said his name hoarsely, pulling back. His mouth was on her neck now. He'd pulled her to him bodily, one hand on her ass, the other in her hair, and she could feel his raging hard-on pressed between them.

"Andi..." he said much the same, and she could feel the flutter of his smile on her skin. "I missed you," he said, before another kiss. "Never leave again," he commanded, and then nipped her. It made her bounce on her toes and her nipples perk up. Her hips swayed against him, her foolish body asking him for more just as she was trying to disengage.

Because it didn't matter anymore what she wanted with Damian —what he was ready to give her, what her body wanted to take—as he aligned himself with her, his hands pulling her against him.

She couldn't risk it.

She couldn't risk him.

It was too late.

If she was with him now, she'd never let him go. He was already in her soul. If she let him back into her body, she'd never find the strength. If she acted for even a moment like he was hers, like she was his.... She couldn't. She had to go back to who she was, her old life, without him, where no one could disappoint her or be disappointed in her, ever again.

A safer world, where she couldn't accidentally lead the man she loved to her uncle to be slaughtered.

His mouth met hers again, drinking her in, and she allowed herself one last sweet taste of him, giving as good as she got, and then somehow found the strength to twist her head to the side, breaking the contact between them. Her chest was already tightening, knowing what she was about to do, and tears started hiding in her eyes.

Damian left his forehead pressed against her temple. She heard him swallow and felt his rough breath hot against her cheek. His desire was a physical thing. She felt it in all the places that he touched her and also everywhere he didn't—a shared current of electricity.

She'd never felt so wanted before in her life.

God...I know I don't believe in you...but help me, now, please.

"I need to go home," she whispered.

He didn't move a millimeter and his straining erection was still pressed against her belly. "You once made me promise not to leave you." His voice was like gravel in her ear.

She concentrated on everything she'd seen that night. Danny, her uncle, and Stella. That was reality. Not the way he made her feel. *This wasn't real. It never had been.* "Yeah, well, I lied, all right? You already know I'm a liar. You told me so yourself."

Damian pushed himself off the wall he'd boxed her against with a groan. "Andi," he began.

"I need to go home, Damian. Now. Through a mirror, so no one sees." She couldn't believe she was saying the words. It felt like she was two separate people—the one speaking and living in this moment, and the other silently screaming inside—looking on in horror. She brought her hands up to unclasp the necklace he'd given her from around her neck. "You need to take this back, too."

And everything else you've ever given me, so that nothing reminds me of you.

"Absolutely not!" he snapped. "Andi—"

She whirled on him. "Please don't make this harder than it is for me, all right?" Tears started streaking down her cheeks, and she saw his eyes widen, his muscles bunching beneath his suit jacket in all the ways that wanted to hold her tight and kiss her tears away.

"Did I...scare you?" he asked her slowly.

"No, Damian." She shook her head, trying to memorize him—same as that Hunter had her, earlier in the night. The memory made her even more resolved. "You don't scare me. You never have. Even when you are scary...if that makes sense." She ran her hands into her tangled hair and wished that she could pull it out. "This is the world's biggest case ever of 'it's not you, it's me.'"

"Andi," he said softly, catching her hands in his own, pulling them down. "What's going on?"

"My uncle wants to kill you," she said simply, letting herself feel solace in his touch for one-one-thousand before twisting her wrists away. "And if I lead him to you—if I were the reason you died—that would break me."

He looked bemused, and then he had the gall to laugh. "Princess, your protectiveness is charming. But people have been trying to kill me since I was ten. I can handle it. Your uncle doesn't frighten me."

That was when she knew she'd made the right choice, that as painful as this was, it was worthwhile. "He should, Damian," she whispered, sinking in on herself. "But...you're never going to take him seriously with me around. Or...worse yet...you'll freeze up at some important moment, wondering about how I'll feel when you have to fight him...or my brother...and then, where will I be?"

"You'll be mine," he growled, grabbing her shoulders to straighten them.

"Not if you're dead. And if you're dead because of me...." she swallowed, unable to finish the sentence.

He advanced on her half a step, his golden eyes serious. "And if I'm not? If I win?"

"By murdering them?" she asked, her voice rising, watching the realization hit him as her words did. "I don't know, Damian. I can't promise how I'll feel." Her throat felt like it was closing up at the thought of it—in panic. She'd already lost her mother. Did she really have to lose Danny, too? By Damian's hand? She choked back another sob at the sheer awfulness of it. "It can be the right thing to do and still hurt me. Maybe that makes me weak, and maybe I'm running away too, but that's why this has to end."

"End?" he repeated, and she wasn't sure if he was arguing with her or just hypnotized by the word. "What do you mean, *end*?"

She stepped back, leaving his hands empty and tried to catch her breath. "I mean, we need to stop seeing each other. From this moment on." She watched each word land on him like a physical blow.

"Impossible," he said. He shook his head quickly, as if he could disbelieve this entire moment out of existence.

"Not really," she said softly. "Because it takes two people to be in a relationship, Damian. And I don't want to be in this one anymore. It's too hard. Too...terrible." She forced herself to watch the effect her words had on him—she owed him that much—and he might not believe her if she let herself look away. A beautiful blaze of anger and confusion streaked across him like a comet, and then... Andi had seen a lot of people die at the hospital but she'd never seen anyone die outside of it until tonight. First the Hunter by her uncle's hand, and now, Damian, by hers.

She hadn't even had to stab him.

"Until when?" he demanded, his voice hoarse.

"I don't know." She bit her lips. There'd been a lot of Hunters in the room along with her uncle. And all of them knew she knew a dragon now, and the fight between Damian and Danny was clearly coming. "Maybe never." She closed her eyes so she wouldn't cry more, but it didn't work. The tears wouldn't stop, and it felt like there was something small and rabid clawing her heart out of her chest. "This was never going to work, Damian. We're from two different worlds...literally." She pressed the heels of her hands to her eyes and tried not to sob, and when she opened them again her image of him was shattered by the teardrops in her eyelashes, like watching him through a broken mirror.

"Andi...we're meant to be together," he panted in front of her, eyes wild, hands clenching in and out of helpless fists. "It's destiny—"

"No!" she shouted, startling him to silence. "I'm so sick of that word, Damian! You're not the boss of me, and neither is my uncle!" She sidestepped him so that the sky was at her back. "I make my own decisions! And right now? I want to go home."

He stepped toward her again, his golden eyes searching hers for any hint of kindness. "Princess, why don't you have faith in us? In me?" He sounded so wounded and everything inside her wanted to break and run to his side. She wanted to let him hold her, let him play his hands against her body, feel him move inside of her again, and above all else, to tell her everything was going to be fine.

But it would be a lie, wouldn't it? Because there was no way he could make her any promises right now. Nothing he could say would be true.

"Damian, I do. But I'm not so naive as to not have faith in my uncle also. I've known him too long for that." She took a step back from him and it felt like the first step of the rest of her life. "Please, don't make me repeat myself again."

He waited for a long moment, and then snapped his fingers twice. The magic cat appeared and took their current situation in with a curious yowl.

"I need a mirror, Grim," Damian told it.

41

The cat fell back on its haunches, looked at her, then started complaining to Damian.

"Grim, now!" Damian demanded.

The small cat made a frustrated sound, but a mirror arrived from nowhere to hover in the air between them. Andi walked around it to be on Damian's side so they both showed in its reflection. He waved his hand in front of it and the image of her bathroom showed on the glass.

"This isn't what I want, Andi," he said, offering his hand out. She knew she'd have to take it to make the journey. She carefully put her hand in his and felt his strong fingers wrap around hers.

"It's a good thing I'm not asking you then," she said, raising her chin high. She felt his pain radiating off of him in waves.

"Andi—"

"Take me home."

His hand squeezed hers tightly as he stared at her, swallowing again. "Don't let go," he warned, and she heard all the ways he meant it as he stepped into the reflection.

Andi stepped in after him. This time, she wasn't protected by the heat from his body—not like she'd been when they'd stepped into the pond at the cemetery. The freezing unhappiness of the horrible between-place assaulted her everywhere and she bit her lips not to scream because she didn't want Damian to overreact—and she didn't want to let any of the tiny cold hands touching her to reach inside her mouth. It was bad enough she had to breathe still, and she didn't want to open her eyes. There was a crashing sound as both she and Damian arrived on her bathroom counter. He'd managed to make a much more graceful landing, lightly hopping down to stand on the tile, whereas when she opened her eyes she found herself sitting amongst the hair products and makeup she'd used earlier and left out.

He was still holding her hand. She let him help her dismount the counter, to stand closer to the door, and it was clear he wasn't going to let go first.

"Andi," he tried her name again, his voice a symphony of tones imploring her to reconsider.

"Don't," she told him, letting go of his hand. His hand fell from hers much more slowly. Andi took one last long look at him, before opening her bedroom door and pausing. "Why were you mad at yourself earlier?" She knew she was going to regret asking, but she couldn't help it.

He closed his eyes before responding. "It doesn't matter anymore, princess, does it?"

She shook her head. "No, I guess not. Good-bye, dragon."

The second the door was closed behind her she leaned on it, slid to the ground, and cried.

ANDI STAYED in a ball inside her bedroom quietly sobbing. She didn't want to wake Sammy up. It was late, and there was nothing Sammy could do about it besides. No one else in the world would understand what this was like, being torn between the man she loved and her family. She'd never condone anything her uncle or her brother did, but Danny had sounded so sure about her destiny, and she'd be damned if she was somehow Damian's Achilles heel.

She loved him too much for that.

She loved him enough to hurt this badly.

She put her hands over her mouth and sobbed on the floor until she couldn't breathe, and then fished inside her nightstand for her bottle of Ambien. Just one ten milligram pill, nothing crazy, but she wanted to go straight to sleep. She prayed she wouldn't dream; she just needed to *not be here* for a little bit. She swallowed it dry, its bitter taste suiting her mood, and then looked around her room and found herself surrounded by too many memories. Everything in it reminded her of him—or her family.

She got up and started walking through her room—like if she weren't touching something she'd collapse because it was true—taking inventory. Anything that reminded her of her heritage? She didn't want to see it anymore. She threw the photo of her, Danny, and her mom from their trip to the zoo as kids into a desk drawer, facedown. All sorts of knickknacks and memories followed it: the teddy bear Danny'd given her—his Andi-bear—for Christmas when she was ten that they both knew her mom had picked out; the stuffed unicorn her uncle had given her—that she still had!—and when she was done, her desk and walls, and half her shelves were empty. The photo album that proved her mom was a Hunter? She spun it underneath her bed, where she'd never look at it again.

And then anything that reminded her of Damian? She didn't want to get rid of any of it, but seeing it now would only burn. She dumped one of her pillows out onto her bed and used the pillowcase, putting anything that reminded her of him into it: the empty French press she'd kept on her desk, the pajamas he'd given her, the sheets she'd washed and thrown into the back of her closet, and while she was there, she regretfully pulled the black silk dress she'd worn with him off its hanger, pouring the slippery fabric into the pillowcase before strangling it with a knot.

The Ambien was hitting now; things were slowing down. She lunged for her full-length mirror and turned it around while she still had the sense to. It would be cheating if Damian got to peek, and she took down the Fast and Furious poster for good measure, because if Damian couldn't see her then her Ambien addled brain said then no one could, not even Vin or The Rock. She held onto furniture now like it was a path, first the wall, then the nightstand, then crawled onto her bed, kicking off her shoes, curling back into a ball around a pillow, and that's when it hit her.

She'd really left him.

She held her naked pillow to her mouth to muffle the sound of her screaming and felt her emotions wrack her body. Her heart clenched inside her chest, making her gasp for air, and she knew that that's what people meant when they said they had a broken heart—it was all the adrenaline in your body flowing into your bloodstream, all your veins and arteries constricting, feeling like a heart attack. She wished that that were true. If there was something merely physically wrong with her, she could just call 911 and have someone else fix it, as opposed to the mess that'd happened just now.

It was the right thing to do, but that didn't mean it didn't feel like dying.

DAMIAN WAITED inside Andi's bathroom for as long as he could stand.

Go to her, his dragon growled. They were listening to her sob on the door's far side, and the air was thick with Andi's scent, especially the ocean.

We can't. Not now.

He put his hand on his side of her bathroom door and traced the path she'd taken down it, as he fell to kneel on her bathroom floor.

His mate had pushed him away. Andi had had her reasons—good ones—but her absence left him reeling.

She was the one, *the only one,* and now—he heard her manage to stand, moving around her room with little grace—she had abandoned him.

No.

It only felt like that.

That's not what she'd done.

She wasn't fighting him. She was fighting fate. And he remembered what that was like, when his father had died and he'd opted to not take his crown.

Which had led to his own fate, brought low here, inside Andi's bathroom. He wanted to tear down her apartment's thin walls to get to her and claim her again while knowing that the best thing he could do for her was to leave here immediately.

She was scared *of* her uncle and scared *for* him, and he was going to have to kill members of her family. On what obscene world could he expect to put their relationship through that and come out intact?

She is ours, his dragon growled. He felt the beast's claws flex inside him, looking to take his frustrations out on someone.

Damian both knew she was...and wasn't.

She is hers, he corrected the beast.

His dragon made an anguished sound. It didn't care for semantics, and it started tearing into him as he stood quietly, letting it run amok inside of him, hurting them both in a way that Damian himself, always in control, was never allowed. He moved himself onto the bathroom counter and opened the mirror up before his resolve could break and he sent himself back to his castle, in a swirl of air scented like caramel, apples, and the saltwater of her tears.

His dragon attacked him again, wordlessly, the moment he was free of the mirror, worse than it had ever been. *You need to stop,* he warned it.

You need to let me win, the beast growled back.

Damian clutched onto the side of the mirror he'd just exited, and Grimalkin appeared. "Well?" the cat demanded, tail straight as an exclamation point. "What happened? Where is she? And why was she crying?"

"Not you, too," Damian muttered. He put a hand to his chest and started staggering toward his bedroom door. It felt like his dragon was searching for his heart to shred.

If I found it, I'd eat it, his dragon told him. *But you have none,* it snarled.

He concentrated on making it to his hallway, keeping his hand along one wall. He ignored Grim's ongoing questions for his dragon's accusations. *You think I am not in pain?*

We didn't have to leave her! He felt the beast lurch inside him, trying to gain control and go back to his mirrors. He never should've let it out earlier this evening; he'd given it freedom it wouldn't easily forget—like the feel of her soft weight, safe inside its paws.... *You want it, too,* his dragon hissed at him.

It would be a lie to deny it. The thrill of her absolute trust in him, listening to her shriek with delight as his dragon flew her, the satis-

46

faction of her finally knowing him in his entirety. Damian closed his eyes at the memory, taking his path by heart, one foot after another, in internal agony as his dragon attempted to rend him in two.

The doors to the training room opened in front of him, and he felt safer the second they closed behind him again. Was his dragon stronger or was he just too tormented to control it? Did he even want control? His dragon wasn't wrong; they did want the same thing. Andi, in their hands, paws, at their side, to be inside her—it was just that he knew it wasn't possible.

When would it be?

"Damian?" Grimalkin appeared inside the room with him, prancing in concern. "Are you even listening?"

"No," Damian said, his voice low. "Hardest setting," he announced, bracing for a barrage. The walls of the training room were mounted with weapons created from Grim's magic and Jamison's technological imagination, and he would welcome whatever attacked him with open arms.

Grim waved away his command with a tail-stroke. "Damian, I asked you a question," the cat snapped.

Damian glared at his guardian. "Hardest setting! NOW!"

Grimalkin glared back at him and disappeared, as fifty of the lasers Jamison had mounted into the walls dropped down from panels and began charging.

You always try to drown me out with acts of physical performance, his dragon snarled.

"That's not why we're here," he answered the beast aloud.

The first shot out and he dodged it without thinking, the red light clipping his suit's shoulder, the scent of ozone mixed with vaporized wool smoking in the air. He twisted in time to miss another near his cheek, feeling its heat like a painful kiss.

No? his dragon asked archly, sure it was catching him in a lie.

"No," he told it.

The other forty-eight came online, aimed at him and he didn't bother to try. Fifty pinpricks of pain, burning him on the outside, same as his dragon was ripping him apart in his mind. The air was full of the stench of his suit being burned off of him, and then past that, his own skin. He watched the spots where they hit him, as they coalesced on his chest, where it looked like he was exploding into light. He was magically enhanced, and he healed almost as fast as they harmed, but they *were* hurting him. They were smaller versions of the big gun that Jamison had made to kill him, if his dragon ever got free. It felt good to hurt. It felt good to feel—something, anything —that was not the sheer anguish in his heart. His dragon quieted inside of him as it realized what was going on, that he was just standing there, taking the blows.

"I wanted to prove to you that I can bleed."

He felt the beast coil and writhe inside himself. *So?* it hissed. *You think if you punish yourself, I will stop hurting you?* It redoubled its efforts, raking him with its claws. *I will never rest until I am with her again!*

Damian suffered unimaginable pain both inside and out. "And do you think that I will?" he shouted.

It considered this, sensing the truth in him, then continued regardless. *But you let her go!*

Damian brought his hands to his hair to tear at it, lasers following glittering paths up his arms. *I had to! It was what she wanted! She's scared—*

But she is our mate! his dragon howled, as if that alone could fix everything. *She loved flying! Why is she scared? I don't understand!*

Damian fell to his knees and felt the lasers dance a path down his back. He wanted to yell at the beast, but the torment it felt was only an echo of his own. He couldn't blame it for not knowing what to do with its emotions when he could barely handle his. He ached indescribably inside and out and the scent of burning wool and cotton had shifted into the cooking scent of flesh. *She feels trapped, dragon. Something that you should know all about.*

His dragon recoiled and Damian felt it thinking hard. *Then I want to break her free.*

It sounded so mournful, so pained, and in that moment, they were almost the same creature again, because Damian wanted nothing more than that as well. To somehow untangle Andi from all her entrapments with her brother and her uncle—and to free himself from his life of being hunted and being haunted by his curse. Would that he could come to her as a man, just a man, and love her freely. *Oh, dragon. As do I.* He sobbed into his hands.

It was the crying that did it. His dragon didn't care if he stood there and obliterated himself one atom at a time with angry light, but the second tears sprang to his eyes, he felt it reconsider. *All I know,* Damian thought as he swallowed, grabbing hold of his emotions again to hide them, swallowing down his pain and fear, putting all of the armor back on that he'd let Andi crack, *is that we cannot crush her. She doesn't have our scales.*

His dragon went still and slowly sank in on itself until it disappeared, leaving him on the ground, scorched.

CHAPTER

FOUR

At some point the lasers must have turned off, and his body had gone to sleep to heal because the next time he woke it was to the delicate pinpricks of Grim's teeth, nipping at his fingers. "Damian," Grim said, letting go as he roused. "The others are waiting for you."

"Why?" he asked, sliding a hand over his face and rolling flat. He was a mess, but it didn't matter, because things weren't going to get better any time soon.

"I believe they've got *actual* enemies for you. So you can stop fighting yourself," Grim said, sounding peeved.

Yes. Fighting, his dragon said agreeably, unfurling in his mind, before gently continuing. *You like fighting, don't you, human?*

In general, yes, Damian said, then snorted. *Is this your way of trying to be nice to me?* His dragon didn't respond as they walked down the hall.

THEY REACHED the conference room quickly, where the rest of his team was waiting, and Mills sucked in air at the sight of him. "Oh, Dami-

51

an." She was dressed in business casual, black pencil skirt and a flowy cream-colored blouse, for their presumable business meeting, her long hair tidily up in braids, quite a contrast to what little was left of his suit on him, and all of his body smeared with green. He knew he reeked of sweat, blood, and ozone. "Grim, you should've made him shower."

The cat hopped up onto the table and yowled an apology Mills couldn't understand.

"He says he did the best he could," Damian translated, his voice a rumble. "And he told me there was a fight coming up."

"Yeah, about that, Damian...." Jamison began, sounding hesitant.

"Are you cosplaying the *Incredible Hulk* intentionally? Because if so, good job," said an unaccustomed voice with a slow ironic clap. Damian turned his head, scanning across his crew's faces until he found someone new in their midst. Stella, the small and likely insane werewolf girl Andi had saved last night, now wearing black motorcycle leathers.

What was it Andi had said? That Stella had warned her?

"You," he said, rounding the table, angling for the woman.

"Whoa, D," Zach said, putting himself in Damian's way, his crisp black suit making him look every bit like an unsuspecting bystander.

Damian shoved the werewolf aside without thinking, knocking him back into the wall so hard he bounced. Jamison ran out the door as Austin ran to his brother's side, and Damian continued on for Stella. "What did you tell her?" he demanded.

"Tell who?" Stella asked, instantly jumping up and pulling out her handgun as she backed away. "I know you're a fucking dragon, but this is a Ruger Super Redhawk loaded with 454 Casull. It can take down a buffalo."

"Damian, I know things are rough right now," Mills began, appearing at Stella's side. "But we invited Stella here, to help us with the hunters. Remember them?"

Damian cleared the distance between them until the muzzle of

Stella's gun was resting against his sternum, rising and falling in the rhythm of his breath. "What. Did. You. Tell. Her."

Ryana appeared on Stella's other side. "Really, brother? Did murdering one little human do this to you? You're very out of practice."

Max ran forward to sweep Ryana back to safety as Damian heard Austin say, "Oh, shit, are we really doing this?" and then a mottled gray and black wolf the size of a picnic table leapt out of nowhere and careened into him. Zach. Damian swatted it back and then felt its fangs clamp on his hand and wrist—yanking him to one side as it fell. The pain traveled up his arm slowly, like it was coming from a great distance, and it was absolutely nothing compared to the pain in his soul since he'd left Andi behind.

"Zachariah!" Mills snapped, and then another werewolf ran at him from the side, a shaggy auburn blur, buffeting him with its shoulder, knocking him down. "Austin! Cut that out!"

Damian knew they were his friends, that he shouldn't fight with them, that there'd be more appropriate fights to come, and yet, he moved his hand inside Zach's wolf's mouth to grab hold of the inside of his lower jaw and squeeze. The wolf whined, but it didn't let go, and his brother's jaw found the meat of Damian's thigh to viciously bite and pull.

"Boys! Stop it! All of you!" Mills demanded. She strode forward to put a foot on his chest. Her hair was down now and it seethed like a living thing, winding itself around each of his limbs.

"You murdered her?" Stella accused him. She hadn't used the wolves' distraction as an excuse to run away; instead, she'd moved her half-cocked gun up for a headshot.

"Of course not," Mills answered on his behalf, as a strand of her hair came up and wrapped the barrel of Stella's gun, too, whipping it away from the woman. "Explain yourself!" she demanded. "Starting with you, Damian!"

Damian lay there, gnawed on by werewolves, strangled by

magical hair, and it was all he could do to keep breathing. Not because of anything they were doing to him, but because she was gone. The day his entire crew had prepared for, for when he'd finally go wild, was here—only, instead of it being his dragon's fault, this was all *him*.

"Andi left me," he confessed. "To protect me from her uncle and her brother." He let go of Zach's jaw and the wolf began to release his arm in turn.

Stella took a step back, retrieving her weapon as Mills's hair proffered it back to her. "Well, she's not wrong. He's a fucking scary dude."

Jamison ran back into the room with his dragon-shooting armature on, the weapon making a high-pitched whining as it charged. "Back it up, buttercups," he announced, focusing the aiming light on Damian.

Mills waved him down. "We're all right," she said, then stared down at Damian. "Aren't we?"

Damian was fairly sure he'd never be 'all right' again but he forced himself to answer, "For now."

"Hell of an operation you've got here," Stella told Mills, as Ryana wrested herself free of Max's arms to come back to the fray, peeking her head over his so that she was upside down in his field of vision.

"So, you didn't murder her?" she tsked. "For shame."

AFTER THAT, Mills tasked the two wolves with making sure Damian showered, shouting, "The three of you...go cool off!" They herded him down the hall like oversized border collies with a reluctant sheep, if that same sheep could also become a fire-breathing dragon. Grimalkin brought up the rear, hissing any time a wolf so much as looked his way and they went into the communal showers outside the training gym together.

Damian stepped under the nearest shower, with the remnants of his suit still on him, and let the hottest water hit him, listening to the sickening sounds of his friends changing back to human nearby. The first time he'd ever seen his friends change on a no-moon night, and it was to stop him. He really was fucking cracking up. But he had unfinished business with Andi—no matter what she thought. He had to pull himself together.

"Take off what's left of your shirt and pants, Damian," Grim counseled, hopping between the water jets. "You need to get clean."

Damian did as he was told and saw the river of blood pouring out of the wounds on his arm where Zach's fangs had pierced him, and again, on his thigh where Austin had. The blood swirled, a watered-down emerald green against the shower's bright white tile. The amount of blood leaking out of him lessened as his wounds healed from the inside out.

"Dude, I cannot believe I bit you," Austin said, coming up beside him to clap his shoulder hard, staring at the green splashes on the floor. The tattoos Austin had rippled over his muscled chest and down his arms. "So let me just say, Zach started it."

Zach snorted, coming up beside them both. "Thanks."

"It's true!" Austin protested, with a lopsided grin, before shaking himself like a dog. "What the hell were you thinking, shifting?"

Zach groaned. "I wasn't. I'm sorry, Damian...you were coming in hot—"

"I was," Damian agreed, waving his friend's apology away as the last of the green washed off of him. "I...don't usually let my emotions get the better of me. I should be the one apologizing. I'm sorry." No matter what Andi believed, he *was* scary.

It was just a mystery to him that somehow her uncle was scar*ier*.

The werewolf brothers shared a pointed look. "Are you...okay?" Zach asked.

"If you're asking if I'm going to dragon-out on you, the answer's no."

"What about the rest of it?" Austin pressed, one eyebrow high.

Damian inhaled, considering the honest answer: *No. I am fucked up. And I am going to remain fucked up for quite some time. Possibly forever.* But he couldn't let on. He didn't want to worry them anymore than he already had.

Zach put a serious hand on Damian's shoulder before he could speak again. "Do you want to talk about it? Before my brother offers to take you to a strip club, I mean."

"That's not my only go-to, Zach," Austin snarked before rebounding. "Although now that you mention it...pussy does solve a lot of problems."

Damian took a deep inhale. "Not when the only pussy in the world I want is worried her brother is going to kill me. Or me, him." Austin hissed and Zach winced as he turned the water faucet off. "You see my conundrum," he went on. Grimalkin materialized a set of towels nearby, and each of the men took one.

Austin cinched his, appeared thoughtful, and then held his hands up like he was selling products on a TV infomercial. "Have you thought about alternate sources of pussy?" he asked.

Zach rolled his eyes to the heavens, and not for the first time, Damian thought it was interesting that their tattoos matched, because nothing else about them did. He stared at his brother flatly. "Not helping," he said, then faced Damian. "Did you tell her? The mates thing?"

"Of course not." Damian sighed. "I wanted to, but she'd already gone through so much tonight. Besides, it's not like it's a magic wand. We'd still have the same problems." Damian raked a hand through his wet hair.

"But if she's your mate, then this is temporary," Zach said, trying to logic things out. "She can't escape fate, right?"

"Purportedly. Only I forgot the part where she's also fated to fight by her brother's side."

Austin groaned. "I mean, really, Damian. There's so much no-fate-pussy out there." Zach went to punch his brother's shoulder as

Austin danced aside. "Wait, I know a guy. Two doors down from me, third hallway. Wears goggles, shifts into a bear? Named Max?"

"I'm not using the Forgetting Fire on Andi to erase her memory of her family. That's fucking dark." Damian glared at the shaggier wolf.

Zach moved so that he occupied Damian's field of vision instead. "Okay. I agree that my brother's an idiot, and that things are hard. But let's acknowledge that this is not a problem we're going to solve tonight."

Damian stared into Zach's eminently reasonable ice blue eyes for a long moment, reminded of all the reasons why he let Zach run Blackwood Industries without him. "Agreed."

"Good. So let's focus on the now. Mills and Jamison have some targets for us to take out. You like beating things up. These Hunters sure as shit deserve to be beaten. It'll be an easy win. Let's go take it."

Damian slowly nodded.

"Thanks, coach," Austin said ironically, bobbing up in front of his brother, his rust colored hair just beginning to dry. "And when we're done?" he said with a dangerous grin. "I know this place by the interstate. Pussy as far as the eye can see."

DAMIAN WENT UP to his room to get dressed and brought his orrery down with him from his office. It chimed musically as he took the stairs. By the time he returned to the conference room, Mills's hair was rebraided. "So, Andi's gone?" the witch asked, her brow furrowed with concern.

Damian sat down again beside her, putting the orrery down between them. "She's trying to protect me from herself. Her brother told her she's going to fight by his side, so she's trying to take herself out of the equation."

"Destiny doesn't work like that." Ryana crossed her arms, frowning at the thing Damian had brought.

"That's what I told her, but she's human." Damian spread his hands out on the table. "She doesn't want to betray me. But she doesn't want to look at me and know that I'll have to kill Danny. So, although it pains me, I cannot blame her."

Max grunted, putting both his elbows on the table. "No one said it has to be you who kills him, Damian. We've got plenty of weaponry."

"And don't forget the big gun," Jamison said, gesturing at the armature he'd set down in the room's corner.

"I'm fairly sure any one of us vaporizing him will feel the same to her." Damian shook his head.

Zach cleared his throat. "So, is there a solution to the Hunter problem that doesn't include killing him?"

"For as long as he's a traitor to dragonkind...." Ryana said, letting her voice drift meaningfully.

"Yes, sister, your opinions on traitors are well-known." Damian snorted.

"She's right, D," Austin said, and Ryana gave the shifter a begrudging nod. "I know you care for Andi, but he's on the other side. This is no time to get soft. I mean, would he hesitate if he had the chance to kill you?"

"I don't know. I haven't met the man before," Damian muttered, but then realized that wasn't true. "Wait, we did see him fight in Rax's casino that one time." Danny had come in, wild and half-draconic, to save Andi from the other Hunter—back before Andi'd realized all of her family's Hunter ties.

"I remember that fight," Mills said, tapping a finger on her lips.

"Yeah, we saw him stick his claws through that guy's eyes into his brain. Who could forget?" Jamison's lip curled in disgust.

Damian would've...because of everything that night that'd come afterward. Him in Andi's bedroom, satisfying her thoroughly before holding her as she drifted to sleep in his arms. He realized all he had of her now were memories. His hands moved to the edge of the table and grabbed hold, like he was trying to pull his happier past closer.

"Just how strong is he?" Ryana asked in concern.

"Damian was born a dragon. He would win," Max said, sounding certain. "If he wanted to," he amended. "Which he'd better." Max's tone changed to the stern whipcrack of Damian's youth, when the bear-shifter had put him through his paces in the Realms.

"I would," Damian agreed. "But what then?" His jaw clenched and he stared at the grain of the wooden table, thinking hard. Why wasn't there an easy solution? How could he thread this needle, survive, and still keep Andi's gentle heart?

Zach cleared his throat. "Okay, so, what's with the crazy desk toy?" he asked, gesturing at the thing Damian had brought with his chin.

Damian took a deep inhale and tried to focus. "You heard Lee's talk of the Joining in the car, yes?"

Austin grunted. "It sounded pretty made up, like he just wanted an excuse to kill people."

Damian looked over at his sister. "Do you think a Joining and a Conjunction could be the same thing?"

Max's head snapped toward her too. "Why is he asking?"

"Because that's why I'm here. The prognosticators said one was coming. It instigated the war in the Realms that I escaped," Ryana told him.

"What the fuck's a prognosticator?" Stella asked.

"Good question," Austin said, looking to Damian for translation.

"This is my orrery," he said as answer, pushing the thing forward and flicking one of the hovering crystal globes. It made a melodious sound as it flew out of orbit on its chain, and then swung back into its original path. "I brought it with me from the Realms, and each of these represents a different Realm," he said, pointing at them in turn. "I can't claim to understand all their interactions with one another, largely because they're practically random. But there are people of the Realms who stare at these all day long—crazy people, called prognosticators—who claim to make predictions of future movement based on prior movement."

"That's not an incalculable amount of objects and motion, Damian," Jamison mused, rapping his metal fingers on the table thought-fully. "I wish you'd shared it sooner. We could've—"

"Been charting it all this time? Why? It has no bearing on earth. Or it didn't until now, perhaps," Damian said with a shake of his head. "But with Lee's talk of a Joining, I'm worried it's the same as what we call a Conjunction." He used his hands and forearms to press the line of hovering globes into a chiming line. "It's an align-ment of the Realms creating a rift on each one, allowing anything that wants entrance through, up, or down to whichever Realm it seeks."

"That seems bad," Stella murmured.

"The strong will survive and the weak will perish," Max intoned.

"Kind of like the Book of Revelation? Where all those old guys had wild end-of-the-world visions?" Jamison asked.

"If believable people had actually experienced it once before and then written books about it afterward, then yes," Ryana stated.

"Fuck," Austin cursed.

"Pretty much," Max agreed.

"And this happens in the Realms every few centuries?" Stella asked.

Damian nodded.

Zach frowned. "But we're not part of the Realms, right?"

"Earth is more like here," Damian said, making a fist beside his orrery, releasing the globes to float back to their paths. "It has more periodicity than the Realms do, but there's no reason it couldn't be part of a Conjunction. And you all already know there's bleed through when Realms touch Earth, via rifts. Plus, a Conjunction-level event doesn't always have to come out in monsters. It can be releases of raw energy—volcanos, tidal waves, that sort of thing."

"Earthquakes?" Austin guessed, remembering Lee's story.

"Quite likely."

"What can we do about a Conjunction though?" Jamison asked. "If it happening is just a mathematical probability?"

Damian leaned back to consider and met Ryana and Max's eyes

in turn before speaking again. "Harden Earth's defenses. We'll let the other wardens know—prime them, prepare them—and give them as much access to tech and magic as we can in the interim. We'll have to buy new warehouses to create, store, and ship warded weapons and ammunitions."

"Your shareholders won't like that much," Zach said with an ironic snort.

"My shareholders can go fuck themselves," Damian said. "But, no, really, that's why you're in charge of them, not me. You're better at making things palatable."

"Or hiding them from the books entirely," Zach said.

"That, too," Damian agreed. Zach gave Damian a mock salute.

"Back to the Hunters, then," Austin prompted, looking to Mills.

"Damian," Mills said, laying a soft hand on his arm, "I've made a decision. And it's not going to make me popular."

One of his eyebrows rose as he sighed. "Why should anything tonight get any easier for me?"

She patted his arm twice before addressing the group. "Austin, Zach, Stella, you're all going out. Max will run the fire brigade, just in case. Jamison and I will observe and run assistance from here, and Damian, you and Ryana will stay home."

It took him a moment to parse what she'd said. "Me? Home? That's unthinkable. Why?"

Mills pointed at the handprints he'd clutched into the hardwood in front of him earlier, with each of his fingers clearly visible. "That's why. You've had a bad day, Damian. You said so yourself. And your dragon right now...his aura reads a little untrustworthy." She waved a hand at his body, indicating the magical energies he had that only she could see. "We need to keep you inside."

Damian would've fought her, only he knew she could only tell the truth.

"Stand down, brother. Stay home with me," Ryana said from his other side, pressing her hand atop his.

If he hadn't already been bitten by two werewolves tonight he might've fought harder, but as it was…. "All right," he reluctantly agreed.

THERE WAS a soft knock on Andi's door around six p.m. She blinked to life inside her darkened room. She'd had a long night—or day, really —of nightmares, running from the stupid angry rotting dog-thing again, and waking to reality brought no relief. Her memories caught up to her in an instant, everything from the night before: Danny, her uncle, Stella…and Damian.

"Andi?" Sammy asked quietly from the hall. "You okay?"

"Yeah," Andi lied. "Come in." She pushed herself up in bed and yanked on the chain for her reading light.

Sammy entered and looked around. "Oh, wow."

"What's up?" Andi asked, her voice thick with sleep.

"You didn't answer when I knocked. Why are you wearing all your clothes? And…those clothes?" Sammy had actually driven her to her mom's funeral; she recognized the outfit Andi had fallen asleep in last night. Then she saw Sammy looking at all the walls, where all her family photos were gone and her shelves missing mementos, like her very own personalized tornado had ripped through. "What happened?"

Andi blew air through pursed lips. "Ambien side effects."

Sammy's eyes widened. "Maybe it's a good thing you don't know how to drive then." She walked over to the reversed Fast and the Furious poster on the floor. "What'd Vin and The Rock do now?"

"Wrong room, wrong night," Andi said, hauling up sheets to cover her dressed oddness as Sammy rehung the poster. She prayed Sammy wouldn't ask about Damian. If she did, there'd be no way for her to lie. "Not the mirror," she said, as Sammy reached for it next.

Sammy gestured at her vaguely. "Yeah, you kinda don't want to see this right now, trust me." Andi snorted, as Sammy snickered. "Do you want some help? Or some dinner?"

"Nah, I'm not hungry. I'll grab something from the cafeteria on my way in."

"Your loss...I ordered ramen. I'll put some in the fridge for you, though...just in case." Sammy gave her a sweet smile. "Anything you want to talk about?"

Andi shook her head quickly. "No. I just really need a shower."

"I wasn't going to say anything, but...." Sammy said, and Andi laughed.

"Get out already," she said, waving her roommate off.

Her phone buzzed. Andi sat down on her penguin-sheeted bed and reached for her phone, knowing that hope was foolish and disappointment was inevitable.

Wanna hang? Danny asked.

Like that was a feasible thing. Ditching Damian only to spend time with her brother—especially when all this was at least his fault. *New number, who's this?* she texted back.

Very funny. But he knew her well enough to know that her sarcastic joke was still a "no" and didn't reply.

Andi stripped out of her funeral attire and stuck it in the back of her closet to be forgotten too. She was never wearing that outfit again if she could help it—right down to the flats—so the only thing she wore into her bathroom was the necklace Damian had given her.

She took it off for inspection, cupping the stone in her palm. It wasn't anything she could identify. It looked like smoky quartz or a blurry diamond, but with a tiny spark of light inside. Like the hot head of a pin—or a very small trapped genie. She gave her imagination a wistful smile. Technically, she probably should've given it back because what if some hunter-person saw it on her and then traced it back to a jewelry shop and found out he'd bought it for her? But she wasn't willing to give everything up just yet. Ninety-nine-point nine-nine percent of their relationship had been swept away last night. Couldn't she keep just one thing? Some proof of their having been a *them*, to survive the next however long she had to last without him? She put the necklace back on, stepped into the shower, and let cold water hit her like a slap.

Just like when he'd thrown her into the pool beneath his castle, when he'd been worried about her being scarred by unearthly blood. How safe she'd felt in his strong arms—even as she'd yelled at him—and how she'd known then, standing in the chest high water, feeling his gaze on her: intense, angry, and interested—that she'd wanted something more. She knew if she looked at herself in the mirror again she'd see the small scar the acidic blood had left beneath her breast.

It was nothing compared to the scar she now had inside her heart. She set her forehead against the cool tile and cried.

"It won't be so bad, brother." Ryana had joined him in his bedroom and redecorated the place as she liked. She had Lyka disappear his bed and replaced where it'd been with bench-like couches and a low side table full of all sorts of food he barely remembered from their childhood.

"I do live here, you know," Damian said, sitting down, noting that all the couches faced his wall of mirrors.

"Grimalkin can change it back when we're through," she said, sweeping her wings out behind her as she sat down, with Lyka taking a perch on her shoulder. Ryana waved a hand at the wall of mirrors and assorted images of the rest of his team started showing, via whatever was reflective of them nearby. They saw Zach and Austin from the SUV's side-views, while what was clearly a rearview mirror showed both the men up front and Stella in the SUV's back seat.

"Ryana, no." He paced over to the mirrors, waving a hand to turn them off.

"Why?"

He shook his head quickly. "Mills and Jamison are monitoring them. They don't need us watching too."

"But why can't we?"

Largely because Damian had never considered doing it, he'd never been sidelined before. "Because it's rude."

"You mean you don't have a mirror making sure your woman is safe at all times?" Ryana asked, her head tilting sideways. Lyka, sitting on her shoulder, mimicked the motion, twisting her beak.

"No. Andi doesn't want that, and neither do I."

Speak for yourself, human, his dragon muttered. He pushed it back.

"But we're royalty," Ryana said, completely sincere. "How do you monitor your servants, without spying?"

He laughed. "That's easy. I don't have any."

Ryana's eyes went wide as she clutched a hand to her chest. "No. Say you're kidding. You're a prince, Damian—"

"And I manage just fine, with Grim's help. And the others." He sat back beside her. "They can deliver a lot of things these days, not everything's bespoke. The castle cleans itself, and we make do."

She shuddered, sending ripples down her wings and disturbing Lyka, who went to fly in lazy circles near the ceiling. "How...odd." He watched her stare into space, considering her servant-less future, and he realized he'd been unkind.

"I'm sorry, Ryana. I know you just got here, and I've hardly taken any time to teach you."

Her green eyes focused on him again, as she got a sly smile. "Yes, well, I hear being mated to a traitor takes up a lot of time."

"Ryana," he warned, but he knew from his childhood it was already too late.

"You do realize you could've stayed home, killed my mother, and already had two or three cursed children of your own by now? And then *I* would be at home, surrounded by a fleet of servants, *and* I'd have access to all my old books, with the opportunity to be an amazing aunt?"

He snorted. "You don't like children, I haven't forgotten."

"I don't have to like things to make a point," she said, grinning.

"And just who would've suited me better, in your imaginary future?" He could hardly remember any of the women he'd been with before Andi.

"Ceraliea," Ryana said, without hesitation. "She was heartbroken when you left, you know. Cried for weeks, or so I was told."

"Our nanny's daughter?" Damian struggled to put the name to a face, and then frowned, remembering. "Ryana, she was half-horse."

"So?" Ryana sank near him and pretended to swoon. "Where your love was concerned, she was all woman!" She broke into peals of laughter, as he groaned. "Oh, it's just as easy to rile you as it's ever been, so there's that," she said, dabbing the corners of her eyes daintily.

He inhaled and exhaled deeply. "Give me time regarding Andi. The wound's still fresh."

Ryana snorted. "What kind of sister would I be to you if I waited long enough to be kind? Truly, have you been away so long?" She rolled her eyes, and then coquettishly turned her head, focusing her attention on him again. "Be honest brother, did you miss me?"

"Up until about five minutes ago, yes," he said, and she chortled. "But really, you were the only thing about the Realms I missed. Not the servants or the spying or the one woman who magically chose to have a horse's head for some reason."

"Half-horse makes more sense than entirely-human," Ryana said, still snide, then sighed. "I am glad to rank slightly higher than Ceraliea on that list." Her hands played with her skirt, a nervous habit he remembered from their youth, and Damian realized the gulf of differences now between them. While the fire their childhood had forged them in had made them close, they'd still been apart for two decades. "I always understood why you had to go," she said, smoothing her skirt back down. "I just didn't like it."

"It was your mother or me, Ryana. She was interested in ruling; I was not. If I'd taken you then, your mother would've skinned me...or I'd have been trapped on a throne after I strangled her."

"I know," she said, subtly nodding. "It's just that it was hard without you."

He could only imagine. "I am sorry for that."

"Me too." She straightened herself again, taking back some of the regal bearing she'd lost to taunt him. "In any case, if you don't spy on people, what do you do to pass the time?"

"Train." Damian shrugged.

One of her eyebrows arched high. "Let me rephrase: what do people who aren't you do to pass the time? Normal people of this planet?"

Damian thought quickly. "Grim, a TV, please."

Several of the mirrors on his wall disappeared, replaced by a large flat screen TV that showed both of them in reflection.

"Oooh! Is that a different kind of mirror?" Ryana got up and walked over to it, placing a hand upon the screen.

"Of a sort." The only television he'd seen recently were the murder reenactments that Andi found so fascinating. He didn't want to show those to Ryana though. "Hang on, I'll be right back," he told her, escaping to the bathroom so that she couldn't see him 'spying.' Once there, he waved at the mirror over the sinks and Austin's face, still in the SUV's rearview mirror, showed. "Austin!" he hissed quietly.

Austin jumped sideways in the car, as the car veered. "Fuck, Damian, I nearly pissed myself." Stella cackled in the back seat as Zach, driving, cursed.

"Sorry, what's that film you like? The holidays one?" Austin made them watch it every Christmas.

"*Die Hard*. Why?"

"No reason," he said, cutting the connection and returning to his sister. "I have a treat for you. A traditional earthly holiday film."

. . .

IN THE BEGINNING, it took twice as long to watch as it normally did, because Damian kept having to stop it to explain what things were to Ryana, although she got the underlying story immediately.

"This is a romance, Damian!" she squealed. "You're so soft now!"

"No, it isn't," he growled. "There's explosions. And deaths. And a holiday celebration."

Ryana reached over to pull a bucket of something crunchy onto her lap to eat, sharing it with Lyka, feeding the bird by hand every other bite. "Most good romances include death, or hadn't you noticed?" she said and he snorted. It seemed like his would, so he couldn't deny it. "They don't have to, though," she went on quickly, as if reading his mind.

Shortly thereafter she gave into the story and stopped asking questions, completely absorbed. Damian watched along with half his attention, while the other half was still on his phone's empty screen in his hand, trying to decide what to do. He wanted Andi to know that he thought of her—continually—but he also wanted to give her space to decide. It was a horrible position to be in, and he found himself envying the certainty of John McClane on screen. He was thinking he would've paid all of Blackwoods Industry's fortunes to just have a problem he could fight his way through rather than one that required patience of him, when three things happened at once:

Grim appeared, hackles raised, tail like a fat white pinecone, shouting his name; Mills and Jamison burst through the door behind them; and Jamison's dragon fighting apparatus dropped from the ceiling to land on the ground. Jamison ran over to it and started pulling it on.

"What's going on?" Damian shoved up and off the couch, putting himself in front of his sister protectively.

"They're fighting a dragon! You need to send Jamison there!" Mills exclaimed. "Grim! Show him!"

One of Damian's remaining mirrors showed Zach, Stella, and Austin looking harried in some kind of office complex via a window's reflection. They were fighting on short brown carpeting, surrounded by desks, with even more windows at their back.

"It's just like the film!" Ryana shouted with glee.

"I need to get over there," Jamison told him, having strapped on the weapon.

Damian took everything in in a second. "Nothing personal, but fuck that," he said, transporting only himself through the glass.

CHAPTER
FIVE

S omehow, even with the spheres of magic that Jamison had developed to hide them, bursts of machine gun fire had the werewolves pinned down. The Hunters didn't have to see who they were shooting, because as long as they kept up a barrage at the door, they knew they'd get the fighters inside eventually. Damian was lucky that they hadn't broken all the windows yet—there was an intact pane in the room he was able to step through. The second he landed, he knew why they'd called. The scent of warm dragon blood hung in the air. There was only one dragon it could be from.

Danny.

His own dragon answered, aligning itself beneath his skin, readying to fight. *Finish this,* it whispered, its monstrous urges echoing inside him. His dragon showed himself a vision of him tearing the other dragon limb from limb, and then flying free.

But he flashed back to Andi, crying on his castle's roof. *What if this destroys everything we have?*

She is our mate, it hummed, its surety charging him like electricity. *She is our destiny.*

"Where is your sphere, Damian?" Zach hissed.

The magically imbued metal marbles protected anyone inside their radius, hiding them from view, but Damian was already inches from the door, bullets landing at his feet. He turned back toward Zach. "Why?"

"Because you don't even have a mask on!" Zach snapped, pulling his own off to throw it at him.

Damian caught it as the pull of battle rolled through him like a tide. "I won't leave any survivors," he said, tossing the mask back. "Wait here," he commanded the werewolves, pointing at the ground like they were puppies, flipping a heavy conference table over for their protection.

Damian stepped out of the room they were in and advanced on the nearest cubicles, kicking over the next wall. Three men running submachine guns advanced and Damian ignored them, feeling the bullets hit the scales just beneath his skin. He walked for the nearest one, who couldn't believe what he was seeing, until he could grab the hot metal of the gun's barrel and twisted it off with a snap. The fool kept pulling the trigger and the gun exploded in his hands, shrapnel shooting everywhere. Damian relieved him of the weapon, clocking him with it and cracking his skull, before hurling the gun at the next Hunter, nearly taking off his head.

"It's him, it's really him!" he heard the third tell someone else, excitedly, and whoever smelled like dragon finally advanced.

The man wore a mask just like Zach's, and he was as broad in the shoulders as Damian was. Damian remembered the fight at Rax's casino. Danny—Andi's brother—was a slight man. Wiry and fast, but not bulky. But he knew they'd been doing experiments on him....

His dragon lunged inside him. Killing Danny was the answer to all of its problems, whereas Damian hesitated. "Who are you?" he demanded. Before he murdered the man, he needed to know his name.

"The man who kills you," the man taunted, and then he leapt for Damian.

Damian dodged the blow and let him take down another wall of cubicles like dominos, as the remaining man with the submachine kept firing. Damian scooped up a desk chair and threw it at the man with the gun, who yelped and ducked, as the draconic man found his footing again, and whirled, launching himself at Damian's knees.

He was definitely faster than a normal human—but not as fast as Damian. Damian sidestepped him and stomped on his back, catching him flat on the floor. He flipped himself onto his back as Damian dropped down, bringing his elbow down to crash into the man's sternum. Damian heard it crack—not a very dragon-like sound.

"Who are you?" he hissed, reaching for the man's mask. Austin flew out of nowhere, catching the man's hand as it came up with a knife for Damian's neck. It fell to the drab carpeting and bounced.

Damian ignored it and ripped the man's balaclava off, and the man underneath was Caucasian, definitely not Andi's twin brother. Stella lunged beneath him and snapped the man's neck before he could.

Zach caught up with them after dispatching the last gunman. "What the fuck, Damian!"

Damian eyed him. "Are you going to bite me again?"

"I should," Zach growled. "You endangered all of us, acting on your own without a plan. Without even a mask!"

"We would've had it covered with Jamison," Austin agreed.

"You didn't need Jamison when you had me." Damian looked down at the Hunter's dead body. He was relieved it wasn't Danny, but that meant that that problem had merely been kicked down the road—not solved.

"The fuck we did, D, I saved your goddamned life!" Austin said, picking up the knife the man had dropped to show Damian. Its blade was bone. It was a talisman harvested from another unearthly creature, and Damian recognized the carving on the hilt, as did Zach.

"That's dragon bone," the dark-haired werewolf rumbled. "And *you* hesitated."

"I'd have lived." Damian stood up, glowering. What were they thinking, shouting at him? He was nigh invulnerable, the night was young, and Andi wasn't far. His dragon's energy suffused him, and he didn't want to fight it as it urged him to mount the stairs to the top of the building where it could take flight, because she was close —so close. *Go to her,* his dragon wheedled.

Stella took two quick steps up to Damian and punched him in the stomach. "This is exactly what she was afraid of, you idiot!" Then the three men gawked at her as she started dancing, cursing, holding her wrist, and Damian was so surprised he became himself in an instant.

"Did you just punch me?" Damian asked her, blinking.

Go to her! Now! his dragon insisted, but its spell over him was gone.

No, he growled, shoving it back. *We have to wait until she wants us.*

Zach reached for Stella's injured hand. She offered it to him reluctantly. "There's a reason we just shout at him," he said.

"Or turn into wolves first," Austin added.

"Oh, fuck all three of you," Stella said, yanking her hand back from Zach. "But especially you," she said, focusing in on Damian. "Because Andi told you that this would happen and you didn't believe her."

Damian took in his unmasked self, the dragon-bone knife that would've actually pierced his skin, and the man wielding it who he'd waited to kill. Stella was right...as was Andi.

"This is your second strike, Damian," Zach informed him. "I don't know what we do at three strikes, but you'd better cut this shit out."

Damian fought back a growl at being chastised, but the wolf was right. "I know."

Zach gave him a begrudging nod and touched his earpiece after that. "We'll debrief later. Jamison, are we clear?"

Damian didn't need to wait for Jamison's okay. He could use his dragon's ability to feel-see heat, and the only thing he sensed were cooling bodies.

But the scent of blood had come from somewhere, and the knife alone wasn't enough to make someone change. He knelt down and ripped the Hunter's shirt off, revealing an eight-by-eight panel of scaled skin bound against his chest with slippery green edges.

Stella gagged. "God. That's fucking fresh."

That was the dragon he'd scented. And he'd been right—in a fashion. The man on the ground wasn't Danny, but the portion of dragon skin he wore was. Peeled right off of Andi's brother, to help the Hunters' cause.

"Disgusting," Austin said, lip curled.

Damian grunted in agreement, pulling it off the Hunter. It was a piece of hide from a dragon's stomach, with overlapping scales in mottled army green, in sharp contrast to the bright green blood still fresh on the rawer side.

His dragon resurfaced inside him at feeling the rough skin of another dragon's hide against his palm. *In this instance, your sister is correct,* it told him. *Traitors should be killed on sight.*

DAMIAN RODE back in the SUV with them, their mood far more muted than it should've been after a successful night. They'd taken all the Hunters' talismans with them so it was just as impossible to ignore the scent of Danny's blood stinking up the cabin as it was to ignore the knowledge that the dragon that *was* on their side wasn't guaranteed to play nice.

For his part, Damian stared out the window or played with his phone. Still nothing from Andi. And what would he send her if he could? *I hope your brother stops skinning himself for the Hunters soon,* or, *You were right, I hesitated,* or, *Currently, my friends think I'm an asshole.*

But he knew that even if she wanted to be apart from him, she would be worried. It wasn't in his princess not to worry, because she cared. It was part of what drew him to her—her profound depth of empathy. She needed things to work out, her friends and patients to be healthy, her relationships to be good. She was like some benign

75

force of nature, radiating a wholesome kindness that his own scarred and scaled-self found impossibly alluring, wanting nothing more than to bask beneath her benevolent sun.

So he decided he could risk one word, and he could pretend it was more for her sake than for his.

Alive.

He sent it before he could talk himself out of it as Zach put the tour bus in park in their garage, and he willed himself to expect nothing in return.

"You're going to dispose of these, right, Wind Racer?" Stella asked, handing the bag of talismans she'd collected over to Zach.

"With dragon fire," Zach said. "The next time we can trust him, that is." He gave Damian a meaningful look.

"Which is now," Damian grumbled.

Stella snorted. "I'll believe it when I see it, big guy."

"Which means you'll come out with us again?" Zach pressed. He was half a head taller than Stella, and he didn't need his suit on to look like he still meant business; you could hear it in his voice. She ducked away, heading for her motorcycle, nearer the front stair.

"Sure, I guess," she said, shrugging one shoulder as she pulled her jacket on.

"Hold up," Damian called to her, walking to her side.

"I don't give rides to strangers," she said, standing beside her Suzuki GSX-R. She had real gear on, stiff black leather, and was pulling her light blonde hair into a low ponytail for her ride.

"Are you all right?" he asked her, entirely conscious of the way that Zach was now staring at his back.

"No thanks to you and your washboard abs." She frowned, reaching for her helmet.

"About that...I owe you an apology."

She squinted at him and finished pulling her helmet on, before tapping the side of it where her ear would be. "I don't think I heard you," she shouted, like she was deafened inside.

Damian knew very well she wasn't, but also understood this was a burden that he'd earned. "I'm sorry," he said, much louder.

"What?" she shouted back at him.

"I am sorry!" he said, at high volume. "For threatening you this evening...and endangering you tonight."

She glanced past him, at where Zach was, and her lips curled into a grin. "Apology accepted," she shouted back. "Call me if you want to go out again." She made an imaginary phone with her gloved hand and waved it by her ear before straddling her bike and taking off.

Zach came up behind him and clapped his shoulder. "Just because you apologized doesn't mean you get to skip debriefing."

"I didn't think it would." Damian was resigned, and Stella wasn't the only one he needed to make amends to. He headed back inside with Zach, and found Austin waiting on the stair, looking peeved.

"I know. I'm sorry," Damian began, but the werewolf waved his apology away with a hand and cut to the chase.

"Did you *really* watch *Die Hard* without me?"

ANDI WAS on her last break on her longest shift at work ever. Both of her patients were despicably healthy, one of them even had transfer orders, so there was nothing for her to do. They were sleeping, for crying out loud, no neuro checks or vascular checks. They were just normal people.

Plain, boring people.

Like her.

She tried not to huff as she turned over on the breakroom couch. There were other people in the room who legitimately needed sleep, so she shouldn't be rude, but what was there to do? She still had three hours of work left after this. How was she going to make it? She didn't want to read books on her phone, because all of known fiction was a fucking lie, and she didn't want to look at Instagram and see happy people with daytime lives, her old nursing school friends with their real tans acquired from actual sun, holding babies and smiling by pretty food.

No, she needed legitimate distractions from all her internal agony. She wanted to do things and save people and not have a goddamned moment to herself to think about the consequences of her decisions, or how awful her family was and how she'd had to leave Damian. She was still in a bad mood when her break was finished, quietly closing the breakroom door behind herself to find her charge nurse waiting in the hall.

"We transferred your room four out and got in a crainy."

"While I was gone?"

"Yeah. Zenaida was going to take it, but one of her kids called, they threw up, so she's going home. It's yours now; we put them in three."

An actually sick patient meant stuff to do. "Halle-fucking-lujah," Andi breathed.

"Excuse me?"

"Sorry. It's just, tonight's been—"

"Don't say it." Sheila glared. Everyone in the hospital knew you never said that it was slow or quiet. There was no surer way to curse your shift.

"Yeah, no," Andi said, shaking her head quickly with a grin. She went to her rooms and got a fast report from Zen, and then hopped into her new patient's room to do an assessment. But much to her horror, they, too, were relatively stable, past the craniotomy.

Andi closed the doors and checked over her shoulders for witnesses before announcing, "Tonight's been slow," to her very-well-sedated and missing-a-portion-of-their-brain-now patient, welcoming any chaos that that might bring.

Her phone buzzed. She pulled it out and found a simple one-word text from Damian: *Alive.*

A sense of profound calm washed over her—one she couldn't

deny. She'd wanted to protect him from herself, yes, but everything he did was dangerous, so she was happy just knowing he was all right, even if she didn't feel comfortable responding to him. She didn't want to lead him on, but she sure as shit didn't want to block him. She sighed and rocked back on her heels, feeling like a ten-ton weight had been lifted from her shoulders.

"Hey," she told her patient, pulling one of their eyelids open, their wide pupil focusing only on the ceiling. "It's not slow here anymore. I take it back."

DAMIAN'S DAYS fell into a rhythm after that. Mills announced targets —despite the fact that they didn't know where Danny and Lee were, there was a never-ending stream of Hunters coming into their city, it seemed—and he and the others carefully took them out. They even closed a rift which Jamison's gear had predicted. In the beforetimes, that would've been a cause worth celebrating, but everything felt dead without Andi.

Each day was a struggle to contain his dragon's anger and his growing apathy toward all else in his life. The only thing he had to look forward to was the moment between two to four a.m. each night when he broke and texted her.

Alive. Alive. Alive. Over and over again. Even though it wasn't true, because was this living, really? He was killing things, yes. Protecting his friends and family—also true—but he might as well have been a robot. He'd trained so hard, he could do the things he did in his sleep, and slowly it felt like waking and dreaming made no difference to him; everything was just painfully the same. His life, if it could be called such, was wrapped in drab gray fog.

Alive.

He never got any response.

Was he bothering her?

Alive.

Had she blocked him?

Had she changed her number?

Alive.

He did his best not to scroll up through the texts and torment himself with the photos of her body that she'd sent him or her half-hidden face in the photographs the paparazzi had taken. But sometimes his resolve broke; he couldn't help himself, and it hurt far worse than any of Jamison's lasers.

Because he was still himself, he had urges—strong, monstrous, and dark. And dreams of being with Andi haunted him at night, and came at inopportune moments throughout the day, but the idea of touching himself and imagining her stopped him cold. Coming for her while knowing she wasn't there to answer when he called out her name felt like exactly the kind of thing that might break him.

More, if he were being honest with himself. *Break him more... because he was already pretty damn broken.*

"Damian," Grimalkin greeted him, batting at his face one morning till he woke.

"What," he grumbled. He'd been having a perfectly nice dream. He and Andi had been in a deep forest, walking side by side, and it'd felt so real he'd been able to forget actual reality—until Grimalkin had started in. "We're not under attack, there are no klaxons. Come back later," he said without opening his eyes. If he could fall back asleep, there was a chance he could go back to his walk and her smile.

"I brought this for you, Damian," Grimalkin said into his ear, his whiskers tickling against Damian's neck.

Damian shivered and growled, sitting up. He was too awake to chase his dream now that Grimalkin had ruined it. "Explain yourself," he told the cat. Grimalkin stepped sideways, revealing a small crumbly pile of white cheese on a wooden cutting board, looking for all the world like a miniature avalanche. "I should've known this conversation would be cheese related," he said flatly.

Grimalkin pranced to stand behind the platter. "This is the pule cheese I made you get me. I hid it from Austin, obviously."

Damian wiped a hand over his face, like the last of his dream was a cobweb he needed to knock off, and he scratched at his stubble. He remembered the hassle of getting this particular cheese for Grimalkin. More than the expense—although it was quite expensive—the stuff came from donkeys milked in Serbia. "I got you five pounds of it," he recalled.

Grimalkin looked affronted. "I've. Been. Rationing," the cat informed him, before batting the cutting board closer to Damian's thigh. Damian sighed and reached for one of the crumbles and Grimalkin swatted at his hand with his paw, claws out. "What do you think you're doing?"

"Trying five hundred dollar a pound cheese?" Damian guessed, setting the crumble down and looking at his hand, where Grimalkin's tiny wrath had left four small red streaks. He was bemused by the injury; not many things were able to hurt him.

Except for Andi.

"It's not for *you*," Grimalkin said, as if he were insane. "It's for her. Take it back through the mirror and make things better."

Damian realized what a sacrifice this was for his guardian and how dire his situation must seem for Grim to offer it. "Cheese doesn't fix everything, Grim," he said, knuckling the cat's tiny head.

"But it almost always helps," his guardian informed him sagely, while leaning into his hand. "Unless...she doesn't like cheese? No. You couldn't be mated to someone who didn't like cheese. Impossible."

Damian chuckled. "I'll ask her next time I talk to her."

"But when will that be?" Grim pressed. Damian didn't know how to respond, and the cat panicked, sensing that. "She's your mate and you don't even know?" The cheese disappeared, and Grimalkin hopped into his lap with a discomfited sound, to start kneading nervously against his chest. "She was supposed to be the one to lick you forever, Damian."

Damian took a shuddering inhale, feeling a fresh pang of loss as he stroked a hand down the cat's soft back. "I know."

"Hey, so," Sammy began, from her spot beside Andi on the couch, with the Investigation Discovery channel playing in their background. "Is your man avoiding me?"

Andi looked at her roommate over the Ben and Jerry's she'd been sincerely eating for dinner. "No. Why do you ask?" Andi knew she'd been lucky. She and Sammy had been on opposite schedules for a while now—Sammy out on dates or Andi asleep—but she should've known this moment was coming and prepared.

"Because. I want to know when I get those drives." Sammy grinned at her. "I bet he's scared of me crashing his fancy-ass car."

Andi gave her a tight smile. "Probably!" she agreed.

"Although, I bet he's insured out the wazoo," Sammy went on, considering. Then she stared at Andi, and realized Andi wasn't frozen on the couch just because of her ice cream. "Wait a minute," Sammy started.

"I can explain everything," Andi tried, even though she couldn't.

"Did you guys *break up*?" Sammy asked, each word rising in volume.

"Yes," Andi answered slowly.

"And you didn't tell me?"

Andi took the longest inhale of her life. What was there to tell? Girl meets dragon, girl's family hates dragons, girl breaks dragon's heart? "Also, yes."

"Wait. What?" Sammy blew air through pursed lips at her, clearly stunned by her betrayal. "I'm torn between being really pissed about you not telling me and wanting to know what happened, and I'm not sure what to yell about first."

"Well, at least you're honest," Andi said. "Unlike me," she added, before Sammy could for her. Sammy held out her hand, and Andi passed the ice cream over with the spoon, taking a savage scoop of it before twirling the spoon in midair to indicate Andi should go on.

"We, uh, had some differences. I guess."

"Uh-uh. Not good enough. Phone," Sammy said. Andi reluctantly pulled out her phone and queued up Damian's number, handing it over. Sammy held the spoon in her mouth while she scrolled back.

"Don't go too far or you'll see things you don't wanna see," Andi warned.

"If you're broken up, why's he still texting you?" Sammy asked, talking around the spoon like it was a cigar. "What's this 'alive' shit? Is he suicidal or something?"

"It's hard to explain. Really. But...he's not in my life anymore, Sammy. And neither is his car," Andi explained while Sammy scrolled. She watched her roommate's eyes widen. She'd gone too far, for sure, and seen the photo of Damian's hand and then she turned off Andi's phone.

"Are you all right?" Sammy asked, handing the phone back with a frown.

She wanted to lie again to Sammy, but the thought was more than she could bear. "Not really, no," she admitted.

Sammy set the ice cream down and wrapped Andi against her side, and they watched the rest of their TV show while the ice cream melted—Andi content to be held in the safety of her best friend's arms. She'd done so much quiet crying in the shower over the past few weeks she didn't have any tears left in her, just a seemingly bottomless pit of sorrow that followed her like her shadow. She felt on the verge of falling in all the time despite her best efforts to avoid it.

But it was what it was, and as long as Damian was still alive, she knew she'd be okay.

"We're going out tomorrow," Sammy announced, her chin placed on Andi's head protectively.

"You and Mister PhD?" Andi guessed forlornly.

"No, you, me, and Eumie."

Andi'd been avoiding Eumie as well. "They might have plans."

"They'll break them for you. I can't believe you've been suffering a breakup alone."

"We weren't together very long." It just felt like they had. It felt like *everything*.

"Shut up and let me be nice to you, you stupid, stubborn girl," Sammy said. "I swear, sometimes you're just like Danny."

Andi sighed into Sammy's arms. "Not really."

ANDI MADE it through work that night on autopilot, then went straight to bed when she got home, because she knew Sammy was a woman of her word, and sure enough, the soft knocking at her door started at 5:05.

"Coffee, dinner, movies," Sammy announced, when she heard Andi rustling.

"Gimme twenty," Andi asked, hiding her face with a pillow. "Although, I don't need babysitting, Sammy." Despite the fact that she still hadn't yet put a fresh pillowcase back on the pillow she was using....

"Don't make me fight you," Sammy threatened, and because Andi knew she meant it, she got up.

Sammy drove them to Jones and Shah for coffee—which was good and bad. Andi still got free coffee, but she remembered the time Damian had accosted her there, back when she'd been trying to pump David for information about her brother, before she learned that everything about Danny was bad.

"And you're sure he wasn't mean to you?" Eumie asked, having closed the bakery early to join them, and all too ready to join Sammy's 'cause Damian physical harm' brigade. They were looking masc today with heavy denim jeans and a 'Team Building 1999!' T-shirt on underneath a flannel jacket.

"Yes." *Except for the times I wanted him to be mean because it was hot.* Andi knew she was going to have to be Wonder Woman to deflect all the questions they were going to pepper her with tonight if she didn't manage to head them off at the pass. "It was just a doomed thing. From the start. Which, yes, both of you tried to warn me, and I swear next time I'll try to listen." She gave her chest a decent Catholic cross.

"I don't think I told you it was doomed. In fact, I clearly remember telling you to get some," Eumie said, with an evil chuckle.

Sammy glared at the baker. "I might have said the doomed thing? But then I was swayed by the car. I should've known though that any man who could afford a Pagani would also be an asshole. The connection between cash and dickery is clear."

Eumie offered their coffee up in a silent toast to Sammy, who obliged with hers back. "In any case," Eumie continued, "let's figure out what movie we're going to see." They grabbed one of the omnipresent local papers and flipped over to the showtimes page, putting it on the table between the three of them.

"No rom-coms," Andi begged. "And no action movies, either. Or fantasy. Or sci-fi."

Eumie gave her a look. "Is there a genre of movie he didn't ruin for you?"

"Foreign films?" Andi guessed. "Wait...no."

Sammy closed her eyes, zigged her finger through the air, and planted it on the page. "This is what we're seeing," she said, lifting up her finger. "Diary of a Middle-aged Man. The Art Deco House. Seven."

Eumie grit their teeth and inhaled sharply. "I can already tell that's going to suck."

"I'm not the one who wants to go," Andi said, looking pointedly at Sammy.

"Adventure is misery fondly remembered," Sammy said, staring the both of them down.

"What fortune cookie did you get that off of?" Andi asked.

"None, because you never let us order Chinese," Sammy said, sticking her tongue out.

It was true, because nothing that got delivered could begin to compare to the memory of Andi's mother's cooking.

Two and a half hours later, during which Andi had only thought of Damian forty times, so a probable win for Sammy, they were in the back of the theater watching credits roll.

"Oh, God. That was so bad," Eumie groaned.

"Fuck yes, it was," Andi agreed.

"I mean," Eumie went on, "that was like an, 'Are You There, God, It's Me, Margaret' only written, directed, and acted by a forty-year old white man going through a midlife crisis."

"That dude was pushing fifty. I don't know who he thought he was kidding," Sammy said, moving to stand behind Eumie. "Honestly, when I went to the bathroom, I thought about not coming back."

"If you had ditched us after forcing us to watch a movie bad enough to be covered by the Geneva Convention...." Andi threatened, standing too.

"I would've had to help her murder you, Sammy," Eumie promised.

"And no jury would convict. We'd just show them that movie as evidence, and get off scot free."

Sammy snickered as Eumie pressed an affronted palm to their chest, the three of them navigating down the aisle. "Where's my diary? Who's going to write my story? Any three days in my life have been more interesting than that asshat's life in its entirety."

"I don't know, Eumie," Sammy said, matter-of-factually, "have *you* ever committed adultery with a sexually wise beyond her years student? Did *you* ever cut the brakes to your wife's car because you couldn't be bothered to get a divorce?"

Eumie pretended to think in the hallway's brighter light, illuminated by a series of old-timey chandeliers that helped the Art Deco theater live up to its name. "I did sleep around with some wandering heroes. Does that count?"

Sammy laughed delightedly. "Wandering heroes, eh? I like the sound of that. I'm not having a one-night stand, I'm just a *wandering hero*."

"More like wandering ho," Andi said, and then danced out of hitting range.

"You!" Sammy shouted at her, laughing. "I don't want to hear it from you right now, missy." She tossed her empty box of Red Vines in the trash. "Go back to being depressed or something."

Andi stuck her tongue out at her friend, then rejoined their line. "Don't worry. I still am." She heaved a sigh. "It's gonna take a while for me to get back to 'wandering ho' status." *If ever.* Damian's memory was going to eclipse any other man she met...possibly for life. In fact, right now it felt like there was no point in even trying.

"Wandering ho is a state of mind," Eumie said with a grin. "And I have faith in you. Because the walls in our building are very thin." Andi felt herself turning beet red, as Eumie wrapped an arm around her, laughing. "But not tonight."

"No. No boys now. Tonight is just hanging out with friends," Sammy said, wrapping Andi up on the other side. Andi took a moment to relax into their collective safekeeping, even if it involved being teased mercilessly. "Also," Sammy went on, "I feel like if we're wandering heroes, we should have a theme song."

"Sammy, you know I love you, but you cannot sing," Andi said. Sammy was fond of early morning shower karaoke, and sometimes there was not enough Ambien in Andi's bloodstream to sleep through it.

"Since when has that ever stopped me?" Sammy said, and inhaled to start.

They turned the corner as one, heading for the small theater's lobby where they were greeted by another group of ten or so guests, of differing heights and ethnicities, all dressed in black. The only commonality they had were embroidered gold roses on their lapels, and then odd, organically strange pieces of armor or jewelry everywhere else. At seeing her, they snapped to attention and so did Andi.

Because she realized she knew exactly who they were, especially when the youthful looking Latina woman who'd been seated near her uncle appeared in their midst.

Hunters.

CHAPTER
SIX

Sammy's bad singing stopped in confusion, and Eumie moved to stand in front of both of them, both arms out. "Sammy, go get the car," they demanded.

Andi's stomach fell into the Earth's core. The Hunters knew who she was, but they didn't know who the dragon was. Of course, they'd assume it was one of her friends. Andi'd been so busy trying to protect Damian, she'd never thought she was putting anyone else in danger.

Whatever happened right now was going to be her fault.

"And Andi...go with her," Eumie said, putting a strong hand on Andi's shoulder and shoving her Sammy's way. Andi knew Eumie'd been to every protest their city had ever had. Of course they could sense trouble brewing.

Andi rocked with the shove but didn't go, instead taking point. "Sammy, do what Eumie says, okay?"

"What the hell?" Sammy protested.

"Rambunctious!" Andi snapped, using the safe word she and Sammy'd used to indicate that they needed help on dates before she and Damian had perverted it.

Sammy looked between them, and then ran for the theater doors.

The Latina woman Andi remembered from her uncle's meeting strode up, surveying her coolly. The Huntress was wearing much the same outfit as she had on their prior encounter, only with the addition of jarring jewelry, white bone earrings that bobbed as she shook her head. Her forearms were covered in vambraces of some kind of reptilian scale, and at her hip was a sword. "What interesting company you keep, Andrea."

"My uncle said I was off limits," she said. She now hated the man, but she wasn't above using his protection now.

"Lamentably, your uncle's out of town," the woman told her with a slight accent. "But you're right. You are off limits. For now. But that doesn't mean we can't have other entertainments in the meantime."

"My friends are not dragons, okay?" Andi had no idea how she was going to explain all this to Eumie later, and...was Sammy really safe outside? A bolt of bitter fear ran over Andi's tongue. "So whatever the fuck your plan was for this evening, move along."

"Gladly," the woman said, putting her hand meaningfully on her sword's hilt. "After we talk with this one," she said, jerking her chin at Eumie.

"No." Andi reached for her pocket. She would fucking call Uncle Lee or Danny and get him to straighten this out if she had to.

"It's okay, Andi," Eumie said, taking a deliberate step forward. "Get in Sammy's car and go home."

"You don't know these people, and I'm not abandoning you." Andi scanned past the sea of black shoulders. The kids who'd been manning the concession stand had taken off—probably bribed.

"That's where you're wrong. Everyone knows the Mother of Monsters," the Latina woman said. "Except, perhaps, you."

"Mother of...what?" Andi said, putting herself in the woman's way while wildly scanning for something she could use as a shield or a weapon.

"Andi, go." Eumie said behind her, resting a hand on Andi's shoulder. Their hand briefly took on greater weight and as Andi looked over at it, she saw Eumie's strong blunt fingers with short baker's nails grow lean and elegant...and tipped with claws.

"What the—" Andi said, and looked back in time to see Eumie unfurling themself upwards, almost like a growing vine. Andi gasped as her friend, whom she'd known for years, became something else entirely. Eumie's torso slid into a thick snake's tail with a bold green and gold scale pattern right below their breasts, stretching back for half the length of the lobby, as it held Eumie's human portion up high.

"Xochitl," Eumie said, acknowledging the woman.

"You will regret not having killed me the last time, Echidna," the woman said, drawing her sword. It was made of what looked like a curved rib bone and her unlined face was possessed by an expression of unholy glee. "I've found the last of Orthrus's lineage. Did you think you could hide them from me forever?"

Eumie surged ahead on their strong snake tail. "If you knew where I'd hid them, would you be here?"

Andi stumbled backward as the woman named Xochitl brought down her sword, and Andi heard the sound of it scraping against Eumie's scales, as Eumie launched up at a chandelier, whipping their tail in the opposite direction from Andi to catch a brace of Hunters in the chest, knocking them back into a wall.

"Andi! Go!" Eumie shouted from above, before dropping down and winding back bodily the way they'd come, diving into a theater with all the Hunters hot on their tail.

Andi's instinct was to run after them in case there was any way she could help, but thinking quickly, she knew the theater itself would be empty except for the chairs, and there wouldn't be anything she could use as a weapon there. She looked around and ran through the saloon doors to the concession stand's far side and looked around.

And found...not much. She could throw water bottles at people? Which sounded stupid, listening to the sounds of an intense fight happening down the hall. *Fuck.* Then she spotted the industrial sized bag of popcorn kernels they refilled the popcorn machine with. She grabbed the corners of the bag and lugged it out the way she'd come, through the saloon doors, to pour it over the lobby's tile in a golden wave.

The sounds of fighting became louder as Eumie returned to the lobby, using their snake's tail to propel themselves at speed, with just Xochitl plus another three Hunters hot behind them. Xochitl was deft enough to stay in the space Eumie's tail had swept clean, but the others weren't. Two Hunters went down with head-hitting thunks on the ground, just like cartoon characters, and the third paused, stymied. Andi cheered and then took in Eumie. The baker was bleeding from several gashes on their tail, and an ominous one spreading on their chest just under the "1999!" of their shirt. One of Eumie's hands was clasped against it, and they were breathing hard as Xochitl advanced.

"You don't have to do this!" Andi screamed at Xochitl and started throwing water bottles, which the woman dodged, seemingly without even looking at Andi.

Eumie spared Andi a wild grin, and Xochitl hacked into the meat of their tail, like her sword was an axe. Eumie bellowed as Andi shouted, sweeping her arms full of every projectile the concession stand had and running back through the saloon doors to pelt them at the other woman, who was in the process of pulling her sword up for another strike. The Hunter at the back of the lobby started mincing forward on the tile, and other Hunters came out of the theater where they'd been fighting, leaning on each other, holding broken arms, helping ones with broken legs limp along, and Andi started throwing water bottles at all of them.

"Fuck all of you!" Andi said, putting herself into their paths. Eumie lashed their tail safely away as Xochitl raised her sword, leaving a broad stripe of blood on the tile. Andi didn't know what she was going to do next, but if they were going for Eumie, they were going to have to get through her, and if her brother or uncle thought that she would *ever* help them after this, much less speak to them again, they were *so fucking wrong.*

Then all of the Hunters paused as one, like a squad of adults playing red-light green-light, and several of them reached for their ears.

Xochitl was the first to recover, and then clearly curse in a language that Andi had never heard before.

"We can finish here first," said the man nearest her.

Xochitl's eyes narrowed. "No. If we don't participate in taking the beast down, we can't lay claim to the spoils." The woman stared up at Eumie, who was weaving gently back and forth, staying in motion, ready to evade any attack. "Until next time, *Mother.*" She saluted Eumie sarcastically with her sword, and then licked the blood off the blade before sheathing it and running for the theater's exit.

As the doors opened, Andi heard the honk of a car approaching outside. It kept honking—*Sammy!*—as the Hunters rushed out and Eumie sagged to the tile, holding themselves off of it with their braced hands.

"Are you all right?" Andi asked, crouching at their side.

Eumie looked over at her. They'd lost an earring in the battle. "Are you?"

"Yeah...may I?" She already had her hands hovering over Eumie.

"Please," Eumie said, flipping over onto their back and then clutching their chest with one hand tightly as they groaned. Sammy was still honking the horn of her car outside for them, as Andi pulled up Eumie's shirt and saw small pulses of blood. Something arterial was cut inside. She ran to the napkin dispenser, popped it open, and grabbed all the napkins inside.

"Are you going to heal?" she asked, returning to apply pressure with a fistful of them.

"I'm not entirely sure. It slows down the older you get, and I am very old. No hospitals, though, promise me."

CASSIE ALEXANDER & KARA LOCKHARTE

What could a hospital possibly do for Eumie anyhow? Andi bit her lips before answering, "Okay." Eumie's close cropped gray hair and easy smile were so familiar, and yet, everything else.... "Who are you, Eumie?" she asked. They only had moments before Sammy would come in with too many questions, surely.

"Eumie, your neighbor, the owner of the Greek bakery below your apartment." They put their hand over Andi's and squeezed. "Because I am now who I choose to be. I am no longer constrained by my past—periodic attempts by my past to murder me aside." A faint smile traced their lips.

They both heard footsteps running up outside. It would only be moments until Sammy could look through the glass. Eumie groaned and writhed and Andi realized why Damian hadn't wanted her to see the wolves change at the hospital that night long ago. It was a disturbing sight to see. Like a Transformer transforming...only with flesh. Their tail parted violently, like Eumie was being torn, and then the scales inverted as it lost mass, becoming the legs Andi was familiar with seeing in summertime—still showing every one of the wounds the hunters had given them. They looked even worse on a human-sized scale. Sammy barged in and stopped three steps inside the door.

"Whoa," Sammy said, eyes wide, taking in the sweeping blood-stains on the floor, the chandelier hanging by a wire above, and Eumie's half-naked form. "What the fuck happened to Eumie's jeans?"

"Nevermind that," Andi said. "How close can you get the car?"

SAMMY BROUGHT her car right up to the doors outside, jumping the curb, as Andi found an apron in the back to wrap Eumie in, and then it took both the girls efforts to get the baker out the door and into the back seat of Sammy's car safely. By the end of it, they were smeared with so much blood, how was there any left inside of Eumie?

DRAGON MATED

At least their blood is red, Andi thought. One less thing to have to explain.

Sammy started driving like she was racing again, and for the first time as a passenger, Andi didn't complain. She sat with Eumie's head in her lap in the back seat, leaning over Eumie, still applying pressure, hoping that whatever healing processes Eumie had were working inside.

"What the hell happened?" Sammy asked, eyeing them in the rearview as she yanked her Subaru WRX onto the freeway.

Andi looked down at Eumie, whose eyes were closed. It would be impossible to explain, and it wasn't her story to tell.

"If someone doesn't start talking by the time I get to the hospital...." Sammy threatened, wringing the steering wheel anxiously.

"No!" Andi exclaimed.

"No?" Sammy twisted her head back—which was worrisome at their current rate of speed—to gawk at Andi.

"Just home," she said, and tried to fight down flashbacks of telling Damian the same thing at his castle.

"Eumie's bleeding in my back seat with no jeans on and you want to go *home*?" Sammy said, her Irish accent rolling each word.

"Yes. It's what they wanted."

"Did they have more blood in them at that time?" Sammy pressed.

"Sammy, I'm sorry, you just need to trust me. Shit's weird, all right?"

There was a harrowing moment as Sammy shifted gears and blew past other cars on the road, before downshifting and taking the appropriate exit. "This is such a bad idea," she muttered, still driving at speed.

"I know," Andi said. "Believe me, I know."

SAMMY'S CAR squealed to a stop in their parking lot, and Andi helped navigate Eumie back out of the car, doing the best she could to apply

95

continuous pressure to the wound on Eumie's chest. The baker woke up enough to hiss in pain, and it didn't look to Andi like anything about them had improved.

"Are you getting better?" Andi asked, feeling frantic. It wasn't too late to call 911—and what were they going to tell the authorities if Eumie did die?

"Not really, no," Eumie admitted, grunting as they tried to help the girls get them up the stairs.

"How can I fix you?"

Eumie inhaled and gave a harsh laugh. "That boat sailed long ago."

"Cut the crap, Eumie," Sammy said, using her keys to open up their apartment. Andi saw her hands were shaking, and knew it wasn't from the land-speed record she'd set getting them home. Her roommate and best friend was scared because their other best friend was dying. "I know you hate authority and all, but now is not the time to become a conscientious objector to modern medicine."

They dragged Eumie to the couch and lay them down, and Andi realized all of her couches were destined to be biohazards, only if Eumie died tonight it wouldn't be something that flipping a pillow could solve.

"There has to be something. Some way," Andi pleaded, stroking Eumie's short cropped hair back.

Eumie's eyes closed again and Andi's free hand searched for a pulse. "Can you get some cao wu?" the baker murmured.

Andi blinked. If she'd just heard Eumie right, she'd asked for a Chinese herb. In really excellent Chinese. Jesus Christ, did everyone secretly speak Chinese better than she did? "Eumie...what the hell—"

"You know," Eumie said, opening their eyes to pierce Andi with a look.

"Cao wu?" said Andi hesitatingly, achingly aware of how terrible her accent was. She'd had no one to practice with ever since her mother'd died. She and Danny never spoke Chinese with one another.

Eumie nodded subtly. "It looks like pieces of burnt tree bark."

"Almost all Chinese medicinal herbs look like burned tree bark!"

One of Eumie's eyebrows rose. "You know that I know that you know."

"Well I don't fucking know!" Sammy said, throwing her hands up in the air, pulling out her phone. "That's it, I'm calling 911."

Andi caught her wrist. "No."

"Why?" Sammy said, beginning to fight with her.

Andi let go and got in Eumie's face again. "You're like one hundred percent this is going to work if I get some?"

"As sure as I can be, considering," Eumie said, gesturing at their current state with one hand.

Andi rocked back on her heels. "Fuck my life." She grabbed Sammy's hand and put it where hers was. "Hold here."

ANDI RAN out onto the small stoop outside with her phone. She knew she was wasting time—*time Eumie might not have!*—but she needed to think things through. Because what she was thinking about doing was a huge-ass risk.

Her first instinct was to call Damian and tell him to get Austin over here right-the-hell now, but if the sinking feeling in her gut was right, the only thing that would've detoured the Hunters trying to kill Eumie was bigger prey, and the only thing she knew about "worth" killing more was Damian. If she called and distracted him... no. This was why they were broken up. Even if she was holding his necklace through her shirt as she paced.

So with her free hand she found Danny's number. He was dangerous, too, but a known danger.

Danny? she texted him.

His response was instantaneous. *I'm dealing with some things right now, Andi.*

Andi bit her lips. What if he was also on his way to fight Damian? If he was, then wasn't distracting him a good thing?

Then why did everything about the situation make her queasy?

I need your help, she texted quickly.

A slightly longer pause, then an onslaught of questions. *Where? Why? Are you all right?*

At my apartment. Because a friend is hurt. And I'm pleased you care.

What kind of friend? Danny asked.

She frowned at her screen. *The kind of friend that needs you to bring me some cao wu. It looks like burned tree bark.*

Andi watched the dots at the bottom of the screen whirl for an uncomfortably long period of time before the next message resolved: *Almost all Chinese medicine looks like burned tree bark.*

I know! Andi blinked at her phone, her fingers typing faster than she could stop herself. *Did Mom feed it to you?*

A second later, Danny replied. *Yes.*

She had another irrational pang of jealousy, feeling left out all over again, even now that she knew the truth of things, as Danny sent another text: *On my way.*

Andi went back into the apartment and found Eumie and Sammy the same as she'd left them. She went to their small kitchen and grabbed some fresh dish towels. "Okay," she announced, retaking her spot beside Sammy. "The thing you asked for is on its way." She saw Eumie's eyelids flutter in response.

Sammy glared between the two of them. "Don't code-word me. What's going on?"

Andi shook her head, suddenly realizing why Damian had found using the Forgetting Fire on her so tempting after she'd first seen his dragon. "I want to, Sammy, but...." Andi let her voice drift.

"You think I'm so innocent, Andi? Remember when you met me!" Sammy said.

Andi did. She'd first met Sammy when she'd been dating Danny, and about thirty seconds afterward she realized Sammy was too good for him. That didn't stop them from dating for the next eight months though, during which Danny'd been stealing cars semi-professionally, and taking them to the roving chop-shop Sammy worked at. She'd gotten straight after she'd dumped Danny, but Andi would be a fool to think Sammy hadn't seen the underside of life.

"So, those people in black were clearly trouble, and...?" Sammy prompted.

"They were after Eumie," Andi began. "But that's not my story to tell, and besides, they could've just as easily been after me."

Sammy's head tilted practically sideways, like a dog that'd just watched a magic trick. "What?"

Andi calculated the value of their friendship, divided by the cost of lying to Sammy now, and decided it was too steep. Plus, if Sammy was going to be put into danger by virtue of just knowing Andi, didn't Andi owe her the truth? "If I tell you a secret, do you promise to take it to your grave?" Andi asked.

"Of course," Sammy said, crossing her legs, settling in to listen.

"Okay, so not everyone's what they seem, Sammy. I know you know that."

Sammy rolled her eyes. "Yeah, Danny told me about you and him going off to hustle frat boys at pool halls back in the day. If that's your dark secret, I'm not impressed."

"No. I mean more different than that. Like a lot more. My most recent ex-boyfriend wasn't just like a normal rich dude, Sammy. He was also a dragon."

Sammy's eyes narrowed, then she rapid-fired questions. "Why was he dating you then? Were you like, what, his Asian side-piece? And why the fuck would you let anyone from the KKK touch you?"

"No! Not that kind of dragon." Andi went to press her hand to her forehead, but caught herself in time; it was covered in blood. "Like a mythical being, big wings, claws, teeth, scales. A Lord-of-the-Rings kind of dragon. Like a werewolf but a dragon version. He could change back and forth at will."

"What...the fuck?" Sammy's ginger eyebrows went high in disbelief, and then she guffawed. "You're like the world's worst liar, Andi. Jesus."

"That's why I'm not lying!" Andi groaned, watching her roommate utterly disbelieve her, as she wanted to melt into the ground. "I just never thought I'd be saying anything like that out loud."

"Oh, I can't imagine why," Sammy said, shaking her head before she scoffed. "I'd be pissed at you if it weren't so ludicrous."

"Just because it sounds bad doesn't mean it's not true," Andi said, wincing. "But whatever. The thing is, he's got enemies, and so does Eumie, and that's why those people attacked us tonight. And that's also why I dumped him."

Sammy pursed her lips tightly. "So that random groups of ninjas wouldn't stalk you?"

"Pretty much. I was worried for him. He has to fight a lot of people. And I didn't want to get in the way."

"Which is why he keeps texting you that he's alive?"

"Yeah."

Sammy sighed deeply, as if from the bottom of her soul. "Were you high when he told you all this? No judgment, honestly."

"No, I wasn't *high*. I was," Andi began, inhaling, feeling the words and emotions choke her throat. "I was in love, okay?" She looked between Sammy and Eumie—she'd finally gone and said it out loud for real, in front of witnesses. Only one didn't believe her, and the other was possibly dying.

But that didn't make it any less real for her, and it wasn't past tense. The intervening weeks since she'd seen Damian hadn't changed a thing about her feelings. She'd loved him then and she loved him now, and she was probably cursed to love him forever just like he was cursed to become a dragon for how hollow she felt when she stopped to let herself think about it—like there was a hole inside her that not even the thrill of saving lives or pints of high-end ice cream could fill.

The tears she'd kept at bay outside of her bathroom rushed up and threatened to jump out of her eyes. "I loved him, and people

were going to try to kill him, and I got scared that protecting me
from them or something was going to get him hurt, and—"

"Whoa, whoa, whoa," Sammy said. "For reals?"

"Yeah. Even if you don't believe the dragon part, you saw what
those assholes did to Eumie." Andi sniffled to control herself.

"Not that part, Andi. You mean, you fell for him? That hard?" she
asked, her eyebrows high, as Andi nodded. "And...you weren't just
dick-ma-tized?" Sammy went on lightly.

Andi blinked and stared blankly at her.

"It's a medical condition! I read about it on the internet. As a
nurse, I'm surprised you don't know more about it," Sammy said
with a snicker and a leer.

Andi rolled her eyes to their popcorn ceiling and snickered, too,
tears banished. It felt so good to talk about him finally. And to tell
someone else she loved him. It made her feel a thousand times less
alone. "Yeah. Okay? Maybe I was. But I was everything else-ma-tized
too. He was a good man, Sammy, and I had to leave him behind.
Because if this happened to him because of me," she went on,
looking forlornly at Eumie, "I just don't know." She laced her hand
through the baker's and squeezed. Eumie gave her a fluttering
squeeze back. "Hold on. Please."

"Wait," Sammy announced. "That photo...I saw...does he dye his
spunk green?"

"Oh my God, no, it's not green, but his blood is, and fuck you for
asking, Sammy." She waited for Sammy to laugh again, but this time
her roommate just swallowed instead, and then the doorbell rang.
"Stay here," Andi told her and ran to get it quickly.

Andi darted outside and hauled the door shut behind her, pulling
it closed and keeping her hand on the knob as her brother came near.
He looked a little better than he had the other night...tired, but
significantly less jaundiced. Still angry, though, and tense. "Did you
bring it?"

"Yeah," he said, handing a small paper bag over.

"It's not for my dragon friend, if that's what you're thinking."

"Friend?" Danny asked archly, like they were sixteen again and he was the man-of-the-house, interrogating her dates, and then laughed. "Nah, I know."

Andi's heart lurched. She wanted to ask him how he knew, what he knew, but instead she said, "Thanks. I owe you."

He broke into a sly grin like she remembered from their childhood, while also rolling his eyes. "I've heard that before."

She rolled her eyes right back. "Yeah, you're still ten thousand bucks in the hole with me, technically. So what's the street rate on this," Andi asked, shaking the bag, "and I'll take it off your tab."

The door knob in her free hand twisted hard. As Andi's hand was still slippery with Eumie's blood, it was nothing for Sammy to shoulder bump the door open. "I heard someone that...Danny?" she said, stepping out and crowding the already small space further. Andi reached behind her to reclose the door, keeping Eumie hidden. "You're...alive?" Sammy asked him, then looked to Andi. "And you knew?" she asked accusingly.

Danny cut off anything Andi could've said to save herself. "Hey, Samantha," he said, giving her a nod and an appreciative glance. "You look good. Still working at the shop?"

Sammy's eyes narrowed, and Andi remembered they hadn't parted on good terms. "I liked you better when you were dead," she said, frowning deeply at Danny before grabbing the bag from Andi's hands and wheeling back inside.

"It's been a busy night here," Andi said once the door was closed again.

"Sounds like," Danny said with a chuckle. "She knows that's poisonous right?"

"Somebody in there does," Andi said. She knew she needed to go back inside and help Eumie, but she also felt like she might never see her brother again.

Which would be a good thing...wouldn't it?

"Take care, Andi-bear," Danny said with a nod. He turned to trot down the stairs, and then paused to turn back. "And tell your so-called friend to lay low. There's practically a Hunter convention in town right now."

"I'd noticed," she said, catching herself before crossing her arms and getting Eumie's blood on even more of herself. Danny gave her a mock salute and took the remaining stairs two by two, before hopping into his car, a vintage dark-green souped up El Camino, and driving off with a thunderous roar.

After he'd gone, and before she went back inside, Andi wondered which friend he'd meant...Eumie or Damian.

CHAPTER
SEVEN

D amian was waiting in the foyer for Austin to come down. Mills had announced another set of targets for them and it was a large enough group she'd invited Stella to come, especially since Zach was indisposed.

Damian had spent most of the afternoon in his office trying, and failing, to write a letter to Andi. All he wanted to do was tell her how he felt. To somehow promise her a future. He didn't trust himself to text her—especially when there'd been no sign she was getting his texts anyhow.

But he couldn't make the words flow either. He'd waited too long and didn't know where to begin anymore. Anytime he opened up the door to thoughts of her inside his heart, his emotions poured out and drowned him, and then his dragon started in. It was through talking to him, disgusted with what it viewed as his inaction and spent its days inside him committing violence. The only thing that quieted it was training to the point of exhaustion, and that only bought him a slim window for sleep.

He'd wound up throwing the pieces of paper into the brazier of

Forgetting Fire on his desk, wishing that he could forget his own futility as well.

"You ready?" Austin asked at the top of the stair. He was kitted out in the military things he enjoyed, dressed in black, with a mask pulled down around his neck like a scarf for later.

"As ever."

Austin came down and clapped his shoulders, giving him a wicked grin. "The interstate offer still stands, you know."

Damian snorted. "No, thank you. And I don't think Stella would appreciate the detour."

Austin laughed. "We could always leave her in the trunk."

"I don't think so," Zach said, coming up to see them off. Mills had already done her magicks on him, making him look like an older version of Damian for an international business call. There was no way for Mills to do it and not make Zach look like Damian's father, because they'd shared so many traits.

"Oh, come on, brother, I was joking. I would never put a member of Starry Sky in a trunk—unless I was sure that trunk had air holes," Austin went on.

"Don't make me aerate you," Zach jokingly threatened.

It was always strange for Damian to see Zach's performance, but no more so than when he smiled. It wasn't an expression he could remember his father making from his childhood, no matter how hard he tried.

"Wait for me!" Ryana announced, from the top of the stair. She had her wings tucked away, and was also wearing black. It gave her a curvy silhouette against the white wall behind her and made the red bird sitting on her shoulder all the more striking.

"Ryana?" Damian asked. There'd been no mention of his sister when they'd been planning this raid. "Mills didn't tell you to come, did she?" If she had, he was going to have some words with the witch.

"She didn't have to," Ryana told him simply, descending the stairs with a look of triumph. "I'm coming."

"You're not," he growled. He could barely keep himself together outside his castle's walls. He couldn't kill Hunters, manage his dragon, and be worrying about her, too. "You're staying here."

Ryana rolled her eyes. "Damian, I am my own person. Not to mention that I've been trained in fighting and statescraft since I was five."

"Statescraft? I'll take you," Zach said, turning toward her for the first time.

Ryana saw him and gasped. "F-father?" she asked, her voice going high, as Lyka shot up, to caw and fling herself at Zach's eyes.

"Whoa!" Damian said, swatting the bird aside gently as Zach ducked.

"It's Zach, it's Zach!" The werewolf waved his hands. "Sorry!"

Ryana regained her footing and snarled. "What is the meaning of this?"

Damian put himself in her path. "Zach pretends to be a person who doesn't exist to run my company. I'm too ageless to do it myself and also too busy. Not all fights require him, but most require me."

"But it looks *exactly* like him," Ryana said, her voice a whisper, peeking around Damian's shoulders to see again.

"I know. It's because I've been on Earth for twenty years. It has to be believable."

Her eyes narrowed on Damian. "So he has two jobs, and I can't even have one?"

Damian blew out air roughly. "Ryana, perhaps we should have this conversation in private."

"No, because I know what your answer will be." Her green-leather wings snapped out of her back to arch in defiance and Damian heard Austin gasp beside him. "You want to keep me in a box, like the Heart."

"It's different, Ry," he tried.

"You're not the only person Max taught how to fight!"

"Yes, but...the outside world is dangerous, wings," Austin said, taking Damian's side.

"So?" Ryana told him. "I have watched all of your suggested movies and then some. And what I have learned is that if I don't like my current situation here, I should probably beat someone up to get my way. Which means that the Earth and the Realms are not all that different."

Damian looked over to Austin. He was vaguely aware that after finding out they'd watched *Die Hard*, Austin had given her a list of other movies to catch up on. "And just what movies did he tell you to watch, Ryana?" he asked his sister while watching the werewolf tense.

"I have seen many *Alien, Terminator, Rambo,* and *Rocky* films. Highly variable in quality, but the message seemed to be the same."

Damian put a hand to his head. This was all his fault for not keeping a closer eye on her, yes, but....

Austin grimaced. "I should go check out the SUV, make sure it's all geared up," he said, angling for the door.

"Yes, you should," Damian said flatly.

"Nice knowing you, brother," Zach said, low.

Austin made to leave, and then stopped on the threshold and looked back, as they all heard Stella's motorcycle pulling up behind him. "The wings are why you can't come."

Ryana gave a dancing shiver and both wings disappeared. "There. They're gone now. Happy?" She crossed her arms.

"No. I wish you could be you all the time," the werewolf told her. "But we've already got enough Hunters on this fool's ass," he said, jerking his chin at Damian. "I don't think we could handle any more heat right now, honestly. And if they found out about you, they'd be twice as relentless."

"Why?" she asked warily, through half-lidded eyes.

"Because you're a lot better looking than he is," Austin said. He leaned against the doorjamb and surveyed Ryana appreciatively. "Also, if you go into business with my brother, you should watch *Working Girl* tonight."

"You should *not* do that," Zach said, shoving Austin out and closing the door behind him. "But the offer still stands, otherwise," he said, turning to find Ryana giving him a horrified glare. "Yes... well...I'll remind you tomorrow. Good luck, in any case," he said, waving to Damian, before making his own escape.

Ryana sat down on the stairs with a huff. "You're not going to let me go, are you?"

"I'm sorry, Ry," Damian said, sitting down beside her. He could hear the SUV idling right outside and scent a wisp of its exhaust.

His sister held up her hand to tick off fingers. "So far on Earth I've learned that we're hunted by cannibals, that your purported mate is a traitor, and that someone else has to pretend to be our dead father. I'm not sure that I like it here."

He pulled her in for a hug. "Andi's not a traitor," he reminded her.

"No...now she's not a traitor for the hunters...she's a traitor to you," Ryana said, pushing him away. "She's hurting you. I see it, even if they do not." She rolled her eyes in the direction of outdoors.

"They probably do. There's just nothing for it right now. What is there to say?" he asked her.

One of her eyebrows rose. "I *am* a fighter. You know it."

He snorted. "Yes. I remember our childhood. Vividly."

"I'd apologize, but as I recall, most the time you deserved it." She smirked for a moment, then became serious. "So remember I'm part-dragon, too. Even if there's not a beast inside of me, our father's blood runs through my veins, same as it does yours. We are creatures of action, Damian. I'm happy to be living, yes, but just breathing's not enough."

"I feel that. Deeper than you know."

"Good," she told him, then shoved him lightly. "Now go."

"We'll make a place for you tomorrow," he promised her, standing.

"Or else I'll make a place," she threatened, with a dangerous smile that showed all her teeth. He knew she meant it as he went out the door, getting into the SUV.

"What were you thinking?" he asked Austin, the second his seat belt was buckled.

"That it might be a good idea for your sister to be familiar with some of the best films from the twentieth century?"

"Nothing useful? Or kind?"

"Hey, now, *Rocky*'s plenty useful," Austin started, as they drove off.

"Wait!" Stella shouted. "Where's Zach?" She twisted in the back seat to see the castle dwindling behind them, showing her blonde hair in two low ponytails.

"He's got a business meeting," Damian said.

"He passed up a fight...for business?" Stella asked, like Zach might have grown a second head.

"Business is much like fighting when you do it at his level," Austin said, defending his brother's honor, looking back in the rearview. "You in or you out, Starry Sky?"

"I'm in," she said, crossing her arms. Her well-lined eyes narrowed. "Someone has to keep an eye on you two."

"You're not wrong," Austin said. He looped an arm around Damian's headrest and looked back at her after the next turn. "And when we're finished, how do you feel about detours?"

Jamison's coordinates were taking them to the mansion he'd shown them photos of earlier. According to Mills, this was tonight's best bet —Hunters in an isolated cluster outside of town—and if they worked cleanly enough, no one would know they'd been wiped off the board till morning.

Damian opened the glove box in front of him and pulled out earpieces for all of them, offering one to Austin and then one to Stella.

"You shouldn't have!" she breathily exclaimed like he was giving her a gift. "No, really, you shouldn't have," she said more normally, and didn't touch it. "I don't like being tracked."

"There's only three of us. We might get separated, we need to know if you get into trouble."

"Mmm, I'm more worried about what happens if *you* get into trouble," she said. "Does this have magic dragon-turning-offing powers?"

"No." His crew had been keeping a short leash on him after his first night. It'd been frustrating, although he supposed he couldn't blame them. "You'll just have to trust me for that."

She squinted up at him. "I don't know if you noticed, but I have trust issues."

"Oh, we'd noticed," Austin told her, putting his own earpiece in.

"You're wearing the earpiece or we're dropping you off," Damian said, tossing it up in midair.

"*Fine*," she said dramatically and caught it, plugging it into her ear same as Damian did with his. He watched her find gum from somewhere on her person and put it in her mouth, before looking out the window.

"You never did tell me what you told her," he said. Stella was one of the last people he knew who'd seen Andi in person, and in hindsight, maybe he'd missed an opportunity that night to just run after Andi, chase her down, take her home, and keep her hog-tied in his closet.

She shrugged a shoulder. "Just the truth. That her uncle would do anything to get hold of a dragon." Stella's head swiveled toward him. "Why do you care so much anyhow? I mean, she's a nice girl, but that shit's a dime a dozen."

"She is not," he said, with a low growl.

"Okay, okay, maybe not that common," Stella said, waving him down. "Especially being that she managed to rescue my ass by the power of being bratty. But really, dragon-man, why on earth would you choose to associate with a human that has so much baggage?"

Damian paused, trying to formulate an answer that would explain how much Andi meant to him and was met with the same problems that blocked his earlier letter. It was all too much, too strong. What metaphors were there to use? True north and magnets, the moon and tides? The way that thinking of her made him feel like he was beneath warm rain on a cool night?

"They're mates," Austin answered for him when he took too long, and Damian had to stop himself from punching the werewolf's arm.

Stella winced. "Ooof. That's...quaint. I mean, I would rather shoot myself with my Ruger here than be mated to anyone. Fucking's fun and all, but...."

"This isn't a topic we need to discuss," Damian said, turning back around.

Stella waited five seconds before saying, "Shoulda thought of that before you gave me this fancy earpiece," in a whisper, as his own earpiece echoed her words into his ear.

THEY DECIDED to take the first "targets" after a brief stakeout just after nightfall. The Hunters had attempted to turn the mansion into a safe house, but while there were guards on all the entrances, no one was watching the skylight on the roof. Jamison cut off all external communications as they started and blipped the security cameras sequentially, as the three of them climbed up. After that, it was nothing for Damian to wrench off the skylight and them to all drop inside. Between the element of surprise, the wolves' ability to scent and hear and Damian's skill at sensing traces of heat, they cleared the house of all its occupants and guards in under ten minutes.

"Nice work," Jamison said in all their ears.

"Training does pay off," Austin said, pleased.

"Which is why I do so much of it," Damian muttered. His dragon had been happy to help while they'd been fighting, but had now gone back to writhing inside of him, expressing its displeasure. He'd have to train for hours more tonight to get it to quiet unless Mills had other plans for them.

"And we didn't even *need* earpieces," Stella said on their line, before disappearing to shake down corpses for talismans like she always did.

"Grab some gear while you're at it," Jamison suggested. "I want to crack it later, see what exactly they know."

"Sure," Austin said, chucking a tablet with a bloody palm print on it into his rucksack, before moving into Damian's path. "I've been meaning to say something, Damian. I've seen the gym logs. Maybe it wouldn't be so bad for you to slow down for a night and watch a movie, too."

"And I'm sure you could suggest something," Damian said. "Rocky twelve?"

"Hey, no friendly fire." Austin held his hands up in surrender. "I just don't know how long you can keep this up." He gave Damian a concerned look. "Do you?"

"As long as it takes," Damian said without hesitation, as they all heard Stella gasp in their ears as one. They looked at one another, then ran for the hallway they'd last seen her go down.

Damian let his dragon's senses flare. They were alone in the building now—he was sure of it—but as he raced into the room where Stella was, he realized that wasn't why she'd inhaled.

"That guy seemed like he was going somewhere," Stella said, pointing at a corpse back out in the hall. "So, I thought, let's find out what he was running for, and...." she said, then stopped speaking to gesture helplessly at the room and the crates she'd already broken into.

The room they were in wouldn't have been out of place on a modern whaling vessel. Stella had used a crowbar to pry her way into several boxes, some of which had nets made of metal rope as thick as Damian's wrists. The last box she'd gotten into had what Damian knew was an explosive harpoon. He was sure its launcher was in another box nearby.

"What?" Jamison asked, sounding panicked as they all went silent. "What're you seeing?"

"My phone's live," Austin announced, pulling it out to swing around so Jamison could get a view.

"Fuck me," Jamison muttered.

"No, actually, I think they're aiming for me," Damian corrected with a snort. Box after box, and it was a massive room.

"D," Austin began. "This gear represents some serious intent."

"When money's no object," Stella said, kicking a box's wooden edge.

"Serial numbers. I need serial numbers," Jamison demanded. Austin stepped up with his phone and waved it around each of the parcels like a magic wand.

Stella looked to Damian. "And here I thought *I* was wanted."

"Sorry to disappoint," Damian told her, then glanced around. "We need to take all these out of commission."

"There's incendiaries in the bus," Jamison said.

Damian saw Stella's eyes go wide with delight. "Get on it," he allowed, and she ran for the SUV, with Austin hot on her heels. He walked up to the contraption the Hunters had purchased to use on him. Dragons and whales weren't interchangeable, given that magic was involved, but healing wasn't instantaneous. All they needed was one lucky shot through a wing to bring him down to where they could use the net.

"I'll call in the arson once I'm done fucking their bank accounts sideways," Jamison said.

"How does that work?" Damian mused, touching the harpoon's point gently, before picking it up, and spooling the rope for it around one of his shoulders.

"Easy. Take out all their liquid assets, run them through a few fairly transparent cycles of the wash, and notify the authorities right after you invest it all in a bulk purchase of South Miami condos. You don't need brute force when you can implicate them in an international money laundering scheme," Jamison said.

Damian chuckled darkly.

"You're taking this rather well, considering," Jamison went on.

"I'm surprisingly used to people wanting to kill me." But if he and Andi were still together, and she'd seen all these....

"This is crazy," Stella said, returning, her arms full of explosives. Her face was lit up like a kid's on Christmas morning. "I like it!"

"Don't get too excited," Austin told her, as he started putting timed bombs on piles of munitions. "When this is through, we're still taking you back to the pound."

THE EXPLOSIONS behind them started as they got into the car. The fact that the house was full of weapons was helping, Damian knew, listening to the firework-like sound of casings full of gunpowder go off.

"Souvenir?" Stella asked, as Damian carefully put the harpoon into the back seat of the SUV beside her. He tossed the nylon cord down, too, and pulled himself into the car's front passenger seat.

"No."

"Toothpick for your dragon?"

"No."

"Sex toy? Piercing needle? Both?" Stella pressed, with extreme sarcasm. Damian didn't deign to answer her.

"Don't be dense. It's for Andi's brother," Austin said. Stella looked pissed, and then horrified. "I mean, I assume and all," he amended, giving Damian a glance.

Damian hadn't wanted to say as much out loud. Some part of him worried that saying the words might somehow make it so. They hadn't seen another dragon-soldier since that first night, and none of them knew if that was a good or bad thing. "He *is* a dragon. And if for some reason I'm not around...."

An uncomfortable silence descended over all of them.

"And here I was worried you wanted us to call you Ishmael," Jamison muttered in all of their ears, breaking it. Damian would've glared at him if he was nearby—and the man must've known it. "Come on, Damian. I've been trying to figure out a way to make that joke for the past twenty minutes."

Damian groaned as Austin laughed. "Why'd you have to do it the smart way, Jamison? You've seen him naked at least forty times. The obvious Moby Dick joke is already *right there.*"

Stella snickered and hid from the rearview mirror in the back seat.

ANDI LET Eumie talk her through preparing the poisonous cao wu, wearing gloves the entire time. Eumie'd told them to turn it into a soup, so she'd added it to a can of chicken noodle that'd probably been in their apartment since they'd moved in. Her mother had made her plenty of medicinal soups from scratch when she was sick as a kid—it's what Chinese moms did—so she knew if she concentrated hard enough, she'd be able to feel the earthquake from her mother rolling over in her grave over her using Campbells.

Together, the girls helped hold Eumie's head up enough for them to take small sips of the woody scented broth, and right afterward Eumie'd passed out.

"Is that it? Is it going to work?" Sammy asked her. Eumie had stopped bleeding but Andi didn't know if that was because the baker was healing or because they'd simply run out of blood.

"I don't know," Andi said, squatting down on her heels at Eumie's side. She peeked under the sheet they'd put on top of them. Their wounds did seem...better? Maybe.

Eumie took a big inhale and then sighed contentedly, fluttering one eye open to look at Sammy. "Have we reached the adventure portion of the evening yet?"

"What?" Sammy asked.

"Earlier on in the evening. You said adventure was misery fondly remembered. Have we been miserable enough yet for that?"

Sammy went to shove Eumie but then stopped herself in time. "I know you're feeling better, if you're getting mouthy."

Eumie grinned. "I am. But if it's all the same to you two, I think I'm going to spend the night on your couch."

"I think that's wise," Andi said, squeezing Eumie's hand hard, as Sammy gasped loudly. "What?" Andi asked, looking at her room-mate. What horrible new thing could *possibly* happen tonight?

"You're going to be late for work!" Sammy said.

"Oh, fuck," Andi groaned. She looked down at herself. She needed a shower. She was covered in Eumie's blood. "Fuck, fuck, fuck!" Andi said, dancing down the hall, tearing off her clothes. "Grab my phone! Call into my floor for me! Tell them I'll be there as soon as I can!"

"What excuse should I give?" Sammy called after her.

"Think of something!" Andi shouted back, running for her bathroom.

ANDI BLITZED through scrubbing Eumie's blood off and washing her hair and got out, hauled on scrubs, and ran back into the living room in record time. "What'd you tell them?" she asked Sammy, shoving her feet into her work shoes, praying she could catch the next bus.

Sammy winced. "That you'd just gotten broken up with."

"What?" Andi asked, frozen and blinking, as she pulled on her coat.

"I panicked, okay? This night...it's been a lot!"

Andi closed her eyes and shook her head. It had been a lot, and she still needed to go to work for the next eight hours. "I'm sorry, I know. And we'll talk about Danny when I get back, swear," she said, holding her hand out for her phone.

"We'd better," Sammy said, tossing it over as she rocked to standing. "Want a ride?"

Andi glanced past Sammy for Eumie, who was breathing unla-boredly and whose color had much improved. "No, stay here with them just in case. If I'm fast, I can catch the bus. Love you both!" she said, and darted for the door.

. . .

Andi ran down the stairs for the bus stop at full speed where the bus was idling, but in the dark the bus driver didn't even see her coming. It did a California stop and kept rolling.

"Hey!" Andi shouted after it, waving both her hands. "Come back!" She ran clumsily in her Danskos, feeling Damian's necklace thump against her neck. She reached for it to keep it still beneath her coat. She hadn't thought about him in, what, twenty minutes? A new record.

A loud engine started up beside her, startling her, as she heard a wolf whistle in her direction. She turned, ready to give whoever a piece of her mind, when she saw Danny lolling halfway out of the driver side window of his El Camino. "Need a ride, pretty lady?"

Andi stomped over to him with her arms crossed, the thick soles of her shoes clonking on the asphalt. "Have you just been waiting outside for me this whole time?"

Danny grinned up at her. "So what if I have?"

"Or were you waiting for my 'friend'?" she asked with air quotes.

"Nah. Scouts honor."

Andi eyed him. "As your twin, I know you were never in scouts."

He laughed. "Why're you always so paranoid, Andi-bear?"

"Maybe because I recently found out my entire childhood was a lie?"

"Fair point," he allowed. "But I just wanted to talk to you alone. And I knew you'd come out eventually. So, you want a ride to work or what?"

Andi knew she was never going to make it to work on time if she caught the next bus. "Fine," she sighed, and circled the car to get in. She looked around as she buckled her seat belt. The car was twice as old as they were—and was clearly in the middle of a restoration. Certain parts were shiny and chrome, but the seats had fluff sticking out and she was pretty sure she was sitting on a sprung spring.

"How'd you like my Elky?" Danny asked, patting the dashboard.

"Depends. Is it stolen?"

"Oh my *God*, Andi," Danny groaned. "I'm sitting on my balls, so stop trying to kick them."

"Sorry. Habit." She watched her apartment complex fade in the rearview. "Does everyone know where I live? By which I mean all of your murderer friends."

"Nah. And Uncle Lee meant it, he wouldn't let anything happen to you. And neither would I."

"Wow, I'm so glad that the two people in my family who kill other people are on my side." Andi pinched the bridge of her nose. "What about the other people in my life? Do I have to worry about weirdos coming after Sammy because she's my roommate, thinking she's a dragon?"

"What?" Danny asked, following her train of thought. "Oh, fuck no," he exclaimed. "I'll make sure she's on the safe list too. She doesn't need that nonsense. I already put that girl through the wringer."

"How nice of you to admit it."

He snorted. "I'm a jerk, not an idiot."

Andi pulled her phone out quickly. "Say that again, so I can record it for her?"

Danny laughed, swatted her phone away, and pulled them onto the highway.

"BASED on the current movement patterns of the Hunters we're tracking, I think you all should come in," Jamison told everyone at the same time. They were driving back to town on an open stretch of road.

Damian frowned. "We don't need to stop for my sake." He'd done his best to behave after that first rough night—not because he didn't still hurt, but because his friends depended on him. But given the option, he'd much, much, rather fight Hunters than his dragon.

"We were just getting started. Do we have to?" Stella asked.

"Yeah, Dad, do we?" Austin asked Jamison, clearly making fun of Stella.

"Don't make me turn this car around," Jamison teased back in all of their ears.

Stella laughed, as did Austin, and even Damian snorted. Going out tonight had been good for him. It'd distracted him, if only for a time. He listened to Austin and Stella bicker in the background about who'd killed the most Hunters, trying to get Jamison to break their tie, as Damian attempted to ignore the defeated sensation beginning to ripple through him.

He didn't want to go home and sleep in an empty bed again without her. If he couldn't wake up beside her, what was the point of waking up at all?

"Guys," Jamison said sharply.

"I'm a better shot," Stella protested, patting the speed loaders she had holstered on her belt.

"The Judge begs to differ," Austin said, patting the Taurus Judge revolver at his hip with affection.

"That's Zach's gun, not yours," Stella sniffed.

"Incoming!" Jamison said, even louder.

Damian tensed. "Which direction?"

"Two in a bus behind you, just pulled on. Could be coincidence but—"

The bus barreled by out of nowhere, passing them at a high rate of speed only to arc to a stop in front of them, blocking all three lanes, and then another bus blocked behind them just the same, back half a block. Austin threw the SUV into reverse, then paused.

"They've made the SUV," Damian announced.

"Shit," Jamison cursed. "I've been wiping cameras right and left—"

"They probably got an eyewitness report," Stella said, crouching down.

Austin looked to him for answers. "Any ideas, D?"

Damian put his hand on the door, but didn't open it. The obvious action would be to change into a dragon, pick up the SUV, and fly it safely home. But there weren't men running out of the buses that'd stopped to circle them....

"They're here for me." He pulled his balaclava back on, even though he knew they couldn't see him through the SUV's deeply tinted windows. "They want to lure my dragon out."

"And shoot it with what, diesel fumes?" Austin mocked. Then they heard it. The distant sound of a Sikorsky helicopter dropping in, as they felt the beat of its blades start to rock the SUV. "Fuuuuuck," Austin drawled.

Damian's dragon was instantly thrilled. *I want to fight a mechanical bird!*

So now you speak? Damian told it, before looking at Austin and Stella. "When you get free, go and don't look back. I'll meet you back at home." His dragon seethed inside him in excitement.

"Wait!" Stella shouted as she reached forward to ineffectually try to pull him back. "Why are you doing exactly what they want?"

"Because as a dragon, I can burn that thing out of the sky—or pick up a bus to bat it down—to save you," Damian growled.

"Yes, but they don't know who the dragon is! Not with the masks we've been wearing! So send him out instead! Without any magic!" Stella said, pointing at Austin.

"What?" Austin asked, wheeling on her.

"They want you as a dragon, right? You don't do any good to them as man-meat! Why would they want a single serving when they could have a whole buffet?" She looked between the two of them. "They don't want you until you're a dragon, and they won't kill you until you're a dragon, so whoever the hell goes out now gets to live for sure—especially if they can't actually turn into a dragon!"

Damian's hand fractionally released the door. *We cannot fight in the sky?* his dragon complained.

No. The girl has a point.

"She's right," Jamison chimed in. "He'll draw fire, while you two can move the bus with spheres on."

"Double fuck," Austin groaned, and put his hand on the door handle. "Don't make me regret this, Starry Sky," he said, using Stella's werewolf pack's name.

"You're a Wind Racer, you should be great at running!" Stella said with snark.

Austin growled, and Damian told Jamison, "Get ready to take the wheel."

The werewolf revved the SUV's engine, drove it in a tight circle, and then bailed out of it after aiming it at the bus in front of them. They heard gunfire behind them but ignored it as the SUV lurched to a stop right in front of the bus's doors. Stella and Damian ran out of it with the protective magic of the spheres around them, making them essentially invisible except to one another. Stella ran up to the bus with an empty bag slapping across her back. "You clear it, I'll move it," Damian shouted at her, and she nodded, running up the bus's stairs to wrench the doors open with both hands.

Damian ran to the front of the vehicle, crouching down and putting his back to the bus's grill. He grabbed hold of the metal and then lifted, listening to the bus's structure groan, as gunshots went off from inside the bus, and the helicopter aimed at Austin more distantly, while the werewolf ran back and forth. He was faster than they could track as humans, even with their talismans on, but he couldn't run forever. The SUV whirled around, still under Jamison's control, providing him with a piece of cover, as the helicopter circled to find him again. Behind them, men started pouring out of the other bus and began advancing.

"We're gonna need this to work real soon, D," Austin panted over the earpiece, as Jamison wound the SUV around him like a protective cat, shielding him with it as best it could.

"I. Know," Damian said. His dragon was as near to breaching as he could let it be. He felt the creature tensing just underneath every piece of flesh he had—wrapped around every muscle, straining bone, so close to changing that it burned. He let loose a roar that was not his own and felt the vehicle behind him shift.

"I put it in neutral!" Stella shouted, returning to his side, kneeling down to take potshots at the advancing men as Jamison ran the SUV straight for the line of Hunters, sending them running like ants.

Now, dragon! Damian let loose the beast inside him, and he felt himself flare with unimaginable power. For the briefest of moments he and his beast were one, in a way that they had never been before. It was nothing to pick the bus up and send it spinning out of the way —even in his human form. Stella whooped and the SUV came racing their direction, with Austin already aboard, the helicopter racing close behind, gunshots ringing out.

"Get in!" Austin shouted at them from the passenger side, kicking the other door open. Damian picked Stella up and threw her into the driver's seat before diving for the back door, yanking it open to leap inside.

"Go, go, go!" he shouted and they all felt the SUV lunge forward as Jamison hit the gas. The whole SUV rocked with the force of the blows it was taking, but that wasn't the problem. It was all reinforced with military grade armor, and the tires could run flat if they had to.

The problem was that it was going to be practically impossible to lose the helicopter now that it was on top of them. There was nothing between them and the city to use for cover.

"Damian," Jamison warned, likely thinking the same thing.

"On it," Damian announced, leaning forward into the wheel well. "Open up the sunroof."

"Excuse me?" Austin asked, looking back, his eyes widening as he saw what Damian was doing. "Oh, shit," he said, then his hands lunged for the console to make the sunroof open. "Duck, girl," he snapped at Stella, as she squirmed over the front seats to be in the safer back seat by Damian.

She figured out what Damian was doing too, just as he finished tying the nylon rope he'd taken from their first target that night to the harpoon. "Wait!" she pleaded, and rummaged around in her bag, pulling out some bones on leather tethers. She wound and tied them to the shaft of the harpoon. "From us to them and back again," she prayed quickly, before letting them go and nodding at Damian. "They deserve a chance at vengeance too."

Damian grunted. "Jamison, get their hopes up."

"Everyone hold on," the man warned, before veering the SUV across all the lanes, like it was fighting a blown tire. Damian heard the helicopter getting closer, could feel the gusts from its blades, and the shots from above became less frantic and more precise—straight through to where a driver would be if the car currently had one, leather splitting open and upholstery stuffing popping out.

"Speed up, and then stop!" Damian demanded.

Jamison did as he was told, and as he stopped, the helicopter kept flying low overhead, unable to maneuver as quickly as the car. Damian quickly took the harpoon up on one shoulder and stood, bracing himself between the seats of the car, half his body outside of it. He threw the spooled rope out behind himself on the SUV's back hood, took careful aim, and threw the harpoon like a javelin.

It sailed over the helicopter, the nylon rope streaking behind it like a comet's tail.

"You missed it!" Stella exclaimed, having dared to look.

"Not at all," Damian said, as the rope fell from the sky to land atop the helicopter's blades. Their rotation wrapped it up instantly, the helicopter began to drift and then fall, as the weight of the harpoon at the rope's far end swung nearer and nearer like the end of a flail, until it reached the falling body of the helicopter itself and an explosion lit overhead as the harpoon made heavy contact with the helicopter's side.

"Kaboom!" Austin whooped. Damian sat back down inside the SUV as Stella cheered.

It would've been more fun my way, his dragon complained, watching the flaming helicopter drop from the sky.

"Jamison, keep driving, please," he said aloud, sinking back to fasten his seat belt. Stella saw him do that and laughed but did the same, as Austin closed the sunroof overhead.

"Are you all right?" Stella asked.

Damian didn't know. People in the Realms had wanted to kill him because of who he was, not what he was. Now, between the harpoon and the helicopter, it was obvious that the Hunters would never stop.

Andi was right.

"I'll be fine," Austin answered Stella, and Damian realized that's who she'd been talking to all along, and he got out of his own head enough to scent Austin's blood. "Just a flesh wound," the wolf went on, one hand clamped to his opposite arm's bicep.

"Are you sure?" Damian said.

"Yeah, yeah, go," Austin said, blowing off his concern, before catching Stella's eyes in the rear view. "How many did you kill?"

"Twenty, I think. I reloaded three times and took two out by hand."

"Twenty with the rest of the night? Or twenty more?" Austin pressed.

"Twenty on the bus," Stella said, with a roll of her eyes.

"I knew Starry Sky was a bunch of liars, but I had hopes for you, Stella," Austin tsked.

"Shove your hopes, Wind Racer," Stella taunted, before hoisting the bag she'd taken with her on the bus up to empty it. Talismans poured out, bits of bones and skins and feathers, and the dusty scent of assorted dead unearthly beings flowed out with them.

"Hmmph," Austin complained.

"Too bad you *had* to be a decoy," Stella said, sounding entirely sincere, even as Damian saw her eyes flash.

"Too bad they didn't shoot your tongue," Austin muttered, then settled back in his seat with his eyes closed for the rest of the ride home.

CHAPTER

EIGHT

For the second time that night, Andi was being driven at completely unsafe speeds in silence. She wasn't sure what —if anything—to say. She hated how comfortable it was to be around Danny again, how easy it was to fall back into old habits, how she had to remind herself continually how much she hated him —and why! So many reasons why! The lying for half her life, for taking Uncle Lee's side, for letting them do horrible things to him and for him doing horrible things to other people. How human was it to want to make excuses for him, and how nauseating was it that she couldn't turn that part of her brain off?

Andi reached for the El Camino's old-fashioned stereo dial and popped it out, then rolled the antique piece of machinery up and down the radio spectrum so she could listen to music instead of her thoughts.

"And in breaking local news, police are racing toward a freak heli-copter crash outside of town—"

Danny's hand reached over and tapped the dial in, turning the radio between them off. "What're you thinking?"

"You don't want to know."

He took a turn at speed, the El Camino's engine roaring. "The answer is five."

Andi blinked and looked over at him. "What?"

"I've killed five people. Just...five."

"Just," Andi repeated, before biting her lips, as bile rose at the back of her throat. She waited, looking over at him, and when he didn't say anything she asked, "Well?"

"Well...what?"

"Aren't you going to...I don't know...make excuses? Tell me the story? How it was them or you and you were lucky to survive?" She rolled her eyes. She was used to her slick brother Danny, who always had a reason for being late, and if he didn't, the reason was that it was your fault somehow.

"Depends. Do you want me to lie to you, or not?"

Last chance to get off the truth train before it crashed. "I think our family's had more than enough lies."

Danny nodded and stared straight ahead at the road. "All right, then. You remember when we were sixteen?"

Andi kicked off her shoes and curled up in the car seat. "The whole year, or some specific part?"

"When we started hustling people for money at pool halls, after I got us fake IDs."

"Yeah." She shrugged.

"And do you remember the third or fourth time we did it? That angry blond guy?"

Andi sucked air in through her teeth. "Yeah." The guy'd been twice her size and utterly convinced he could beat her, but it was like he'd just started playing pool yesterday, whereas she'd been playing ever since she could hold a cue in her hands. He'd kept doubling down until they gotten him for five hundred bucks; it was a lot of money now, and even more back then. He'd gotten in her face, and she and Danny had beat a hasty retreat before him and his friends could come after them.

"You remember what he said when we were leaving?" Danny asked her.

Andi paused a moment in thought. "No." She remembered the guy clearly, between his beer breath and his popped collar, but she couldn't remember a word he'd said.

"He promised he was going to come after you." Danny spared her a glance. "Not me. *You.*"

Andi met his gaze. "So?"

"So I went back that night to make sure he couldn't come after anyone, anymore," Danny said with a shrug. "Only...I didn't know my own strength. The medicines Mom was giving me...they affected me at weird times, in weird ways. It was like going through puberty all the time—"

She finally heard what he was saying and realized how come he'd made it through all those bar brawls unscathed. "Wait! You killed a guy for drunkenly threatening me? Who wasn't even an Unearthly?"

Danny blinked. "Is that what they call themselves? Not just monsters?"

Andi swept a hand between them like she was erasing what he'd just said. "No! You don't get to make this about me, Danny! I'm not the reason you killed a man!"

She saw him wind himself up to fight like they always did, then he collapsed like someone had put a pin in him. "You're right. Protecting you was just a convenient excuse. But...after that...that's how I knew I had the rest of them in me." He went back to staring at the road.

Andi watched the racing streetlights cast her brother's face in shadow, like the flickering beat of her heart. "Did Mom know?"

"No. But I told Uncle Lee. He helped me hide things. Like always." Danny sighed. "I know you're not proud of me. I'm not proud of myself, either, if it makes you feel better now."

Andi bit her lips, feeling the silence between them taking on a life of its own, a quiet wall that pushed them further and further apart. "I don't think we can come back from this, Danny," she whispered, and she knew she was crying, again. How many tears did she have in her? It wasn't fair she had to lose Damian and Danny too, although she could argue that Danny'd already been lost to her for years.

"We have to, Andi-bear," Danny said, looking at her again. "Because it's destiny...I know it—"

"How?" Andi asked, throwing her hands up in the air, burning the backs of her hands on the ratty upholstery above her. "How come you're so sure?"

He pulled his car off at the exit for her hospital. "Because Mom told me so."

"What?" she asked, wiping away her tears.

"Mom gave me all her notes, Andi. She not only did this *to* me, but she was training me to do it to other people. And her notes say that you're gonna fight by my side. Quote-un-fucking-quote."

"There's no *way*, Danny," she protested, as he turned into her hospital's roundabout, pulling on the brakes.

"Are you going to argue with a woman who lived for four centuries and turned her son into a dragon?" Danny asked her. He gave her a pointed look and then stuck his tongue out. She closed her eyes rather than watch him try to make her laugh and turned to open up the door. He caught her wrist before she could get out though. "At least let me show you her notes, Andi. She talks about you in them."

Andi knew she should be strong—*just cut the cord already!*—but she wavered.

"Tomorrow night. Just let me show you them, all right? And then after that, if you never want to talk to me again, I understand," he said, letting her go.

"I've gotta go to work, Danny. I'm already late."

"Don't answer now, just think about it!" he shouted after her, as she slammed the door shut, and wished that closing off her past could be so easy.

. . .

ANDI SETTLED herself in the hospital elevator and wound her hair up into its official work bun. She hadn't been crying that hard, had she? She wiped her eyes and straightened her shoulders. No time for crying now; she had a job to do.

She stepped out of the elevators and onto her bustling floor, heard people shouting orders down the hall, and then one of them turned to shout at her.

"Andi!" Sheila bellowed. Andi ran down the hall to her, ready to get yelled at and get it over with, so that she could move on.

"Sorry about being late—" she said.

"Devastating break up, eh? We've all been there before." *Goddammit, Sammy.* Her charge nurse grabbed the strap of her bag off her shoulder and chucked it down on the ground. "I've got just the assignment for you," she said, jerking her head back to indicate the chaos happening behind her. "There was a helicopter crash outside of town. Somehow, this guy survived it."

Andi glanced past her into the room where nurses were hanging medications as doctors placed central lines. "You're...sure?"

"Never more so. You're the kind of woman who rises to an occasion regardless of her personal life, and I'm not above abusing that when we're short-staffed." Sheila clapped her shoulder, and then stepped aside.

ANDI TOSSED her coat onto the nearest counter and grabbed some paper and a pen from her bag to start taking notes as the ED nurse— who'd wheeled the patient in—shouted at her. "Intubated, crush injury, pneumo, chest tube, you're getting a central line right now, hypotensive, levo—" Andi caught every third word while looking at the man himself, who was badly injured. "And we took these off of him. Don't ask me why, just give them to his relatives if they show up." The ED nurse swung a patient belonging bag at her. She caught it and set it aside. "Why the fuck did he have a bird skull on him?

Was he eating a whole entire chicken before they crashed? Who the fuck knows."

Andi nodded, acknowledging the weirdness of the hospital and the people drawn into it, and started taking over care.

The man was her only patient, which was good. He was on the verge of crashing. It took an hour for her to get him settled, and then he was only alive because of the ventilator that was breathing for him and the medications going in. Luckily, she had plenty of help, because surviving a helicopter crash made him a bit of an ICU celebrity, as her coworkers hoped that he was one.

"Was he a radio person?" Dominica wondered aloud. She'd come up from the burn unit to help with the dressings on his face.

"No, those people are total fakers. No one uses a helicopter for traffic reports anymore. The gas is too expensive," said Lovely.

"Plus, what kind of traffic is there this late?" Faizah said, scoffing.

"NBA player, then?" Dominica guessed.

Lovely made a sound. "Grim...but possible. Any visitors yet, Andi?"

Andi looked up from the charting she was desperately trying to catch up on. "What, huh? No." She spotted the belonging bag though and put some gloves on. If the man's wallet was inside, they could do a google search, which'd cool her coworker's jets some, until social work could hunt down next of kin come morning. She opened up the plastic bag and gagged.

The scent of burnt bone wafted out at her—worse than the man himself smelled, which was saying something. But the ED nurse hadn't been lying. Andi reached in and found a bunch of bones—including a bird skull—strung on chains. Like gruesome trinkets.

Talismans like what Xochitl and her fellow Hunters had worn.

That explained how this man had managed to survive the helicopter crash. He'd been wearing a 90's rapper's worth of magical amulets. As for why he'd been in the helicopter to begin with, it was all too easy for her imagination to run wild.

Because what better way to fight a creature that could fly than from in the air beside it? Her pulse started to pound in her ears. *What if something had happened to Damian?* Did he need her? Was he all right? Had he been injured? She'd seen Damian get hurt before—that one time with the succubus stinger, and she'd seen Xochitl's sword work on Eumie earlier in the night. And if fighting Damian had been the reason Xochitl had run away....

It was one thing for her to step back to protect him and another to think that he might be out there, somewhere, hurting without her.

"Andi? You okay?" Lovely asked.

Andi snapped the top of the bag closed. "Yeah. No wallet."

"Well, between no wallet and no face right now, it's gonna take a while to ID him," Dominica said, but she was wrong.

He was a Hunter. That was all Andi needed to know.

ANDI SHOOED her coworkers out the door so she could think and then went into the room's en suite bathroom to catch her breath. Damian had to be okay. There was no other option. Surely if he was hurt, someone else on his team would've reached out to her.

Unless they were all dead, too.

What if he was hurt somewhere...dying alone?

The terror of not knowing clung to Andi like a fog, and it wasn't something she could just push through, not like the other times she'd been emotionally messed up at work before. She appreciated Sheila's faith in her, but right now she wasn't sure she could manage her own shit, much less a dying man who'd most likely been trying to kill her ex-boyfriend.

She splashed cold water on her face in a desperate attempt to stop panicking, and then blotted herself with flimsy paper towels. She swore she saw flashes of red between blots and wondered if it was an oncoming migraine, and then felt a burst of cold air ahead of her, like someone had opened up a freezer. Andi blinked and saw a woman on the other side of the mirror that was not herself.

"Why aren't your mirrors reasonably placed?" the woman

complained after ducking through. She jumped to the floor, landing lightly even though Andi had seen a flash of heels beneath her skirt. A red bird followed the woman and started spinning in tight circles against the ceiling.

"Ryana?" Andi had only seen her after her injuries in the Realms and had never met her once awake. But she was too like Damian to not be his sister; her chin was narrower and her brow less defined, but they shared the same full lips and haughty cheekbones. She was half-a-foot taller than Andi was, though not as tall as Damian, and had the kind of generous curves Andi had longed for her entire life. She was holding a wicked looking knife with a jeweled hilt and a twisting blade.

"Princess Ryana," the woman corrected her.

Andi ignored the knife entirely. "Is Damian okay?"

One of her eyebrows arched up. "Of course. Why wouldn't he be?"

"So, that's not why you're here?" Andi pressed, because she needed to hear the words.

"Not in the least."

"Then why *are* you here?"

"Because I am a person of action," Ryana said, pointing her knife in Andi's direction. "Regardless of what anyone else thinks."

Andi backed up. "What does that mean?"

"Currently? That I'm threatening you." She looked Andi up and down disdainfully. "Common human that you are, you need to make up your mind."

"What?" Andi blinked helplessly as the other woman took up more space with her anger. Ryana's arrival had done nothing to help the already high levels of adrenaline in her blood.

"You're hurting my brother, and for what? Your pride? You think he doesn't have pride, too?"

"But...he's alive?" Andi heard herself asking softly, as if from far away.

"Yes," Ryana said, then lowered the knife slightly, as her green eyes narrowed. "Why do you keep asking?"

"Because...helicopter," Andi said, pointing through the wall behind her.

Ryana frowned. "What is a helicopter again?"

A voice interrupted them both from inside the room behind her. "Visitors incoming!" A pause, and then a question. "Andi?"

Her charge nurse shouting her name brought her back to life. Andi reached past Ryana and hit the wand to make the toilet flush. "Just emptying the urinal!" she shouted back.

Visitors meant Hunters. Ryana was here and Hunters would definitely want to kill her. And Damian may or may not be alive because Ryana didn't *know what the fuck a helicopter was.*

Andi wanted to scream, but instead she took a deep inhale to pull her shit together, ignored the knife, and grabbed Ryana's shoulders. "I need you to go back right now, Ryana. It's not safe for you here."

"I am tired of other people telling me what to do," the woman growled.

Andi danced in place for a moment, trying to figure out the best course of action. "Fine then, but whatever you do, don't open this door and don't say another word," Andi told her and then left the bathroom, closing the door solidly behind herself.

SECONDS LATER, she heard a cluster of men with Australian accents coming down the hall, talking to a coworker. "So this was a horrible tourist accident?" she heard Lovely ask them.

"Oh, yeah. We all told him it was a bad idea. There's nothing to see at night."

Another man said: "Ah, but money burns holes in some people's pockets."

"And there's always other people around to help you spend it," a third man said with a short laugh.

Andi knew who she was going to see before they reached the

room's front glass. The Australian hunter who'd wanted to see her mother's notes for himself. All three of the men were tan with close cropped hair, wearing khaki slacks and pastel polos. They looked like they'd just come off a golf course, but the man she remembered had the same strange little toothpick, no doubt made out of ivory.

He nodded at her first. "Andrea."

"You two know each other?" Lovely asked.

"Ah, no, I just saw her nametag." He gestured at Andi's chest, and then his own. "I'm Jack. Nice to meet you."

Andi didn't respond.

Lovely looked between them quickly. "All right. I'm gonna go give Faizah a break. You're on deck next, okay, Andi?"

"Great, thanks," Andi said, waving her away, as the Hunters surveyed their fallen comrade.

"He gonna make it?" Jack asked, giving her a sly look.

Andi frowned but kept her position between the men and the bathroom door. "He won't die on my shift because of me, if that's what you're asking."

The man chuckled. "Lee's right. You're too soft for that." He put his hands into his pockets. "You're going to have to toughen up when you join us."

"I'm never joining you."

"Yeah, yeah," he said, making a show of looking around, touching his friend, the bed, IV bags. Andi wanted to slap his hands down. "Consciences serve people in good stead in daylight, girl. But look at you. You live and work the night. You'll come around." He flipped the toothpick he gnawed on to the other side of his mouth and leered at her. "You wanna know if we got your friend?"

More than anything. But to announce it aloud would be to let them know they had leverage on her and would make this conversation go on longer, keeping Ryana in danger, if she hadn't wisely *poofed* herself back through the mirror when she'd closed the door. "I want you to leave. You've seen your man. We'll do the best we can."

One of the men grabbed the belongings bag, taking stock of its contents with a grunt. "It's all here," he announced.

Jack rocked his toothpick across his upper lip with his tongue, considering her. "All right, then. We're off. See you soon, I'm sure." He touched the brim of an imaginary hat as his men left, and he followed them. Andi walked into the hall behind them to watch them depart, making sure they were through the next two sets of doors before heading back into the bathroom.

Ryana was waiting inside, looking like a sea-nymph out of a Waterhouse painting, her dress and hair all aflow, only sitting on the counter instead of a stone. Her knife was tucked petulantly up underneath her chin in her hand and her red bird was on her shoulder. "Those were Hunters, weren't they." She sat up straight and her green eyes pierced Andi, sharper than the blade she held for sure.

"Yes."

"And...you didn't betray me." It was a statement, not a question. She'd been able to hear every word.

"I would never, Ryana."

"Yet you're trying to keep one of them alive?" She stared through the open door behind Andi, at her patient on the bed, and frowned.

"Also, yes. I'm not a murderer, Ryana. At least, I'm trying not to be. I know you probably think that makes me some kind of traitor, and I don't know what Damian told you, anyhow." Surely he didn't think that of her, and even if he did, it didn't matter anymore now, did it? Andi shook her head. *She'd done the right thing...even though it hurt her!* "All I know is that they were out tonight, trying to kill him, and I need to know he's all right more than I need air to breathe."

The words were out of her mouth before she could consider them, but every single one of them was true.

Ryana frowned. "Is a helicopter like that sky-weapon in *Die Hard*?" she asked sincerely.

Andi nodded helplessly.

The other woman's eyes widened and she pulled her legs up onto the counter beneath her. "I'm going back then. But you," she said, pointing at Andi with the knife, "the time is going to come when you'll to have to choose." The mirror behind her went black and a burst of freezing air came through as Ryana's frown deepened. "And if some reason Damian's been hurt—because of all your human-hunter-friends—I swear I will come back and kill you."

Andi's heart thundered in her chest as Ryana disappeared into the darkness. "I might let you," she whispered after her, as her mouth went dry.

ALIVE.

Damian typed the word into his phone to send to Andi despite the fact that it'd never felt further from the truth. After confirming that Austin would be all right, Jamison had led them on a long and strange route home to make sure they weren't followed, and Damian spent the entire trip trying to convince himself that the Hunters hadn't just gone and proved Andi's point entirely. How could he keep himself safe for her if they were willing to send helicopters after him?

"You've been quiet," Austin said.

"Just thinking."

"Hard thoughts?"

"Yes. No interstate side trips though."

"Eh, I'm in no condition to meet strangers," Austin said, shrugging his injured arm.

Damian was still lost in his own misery as Jamison parked the car remotely, right in front of his mansion's front stair. As he got out of the car, he was surprised to see his sister running for his side.

"Ryana?" he asked as she engulfed him in an embrace. She was cold—maybe because she'd changed into a dress.

"Are you all right?" she demanded to know, despite the fact that he was standing right there.

"Sure, check in on the nearly immortal dragon first," Austin said, grunting as he got out of the car. "Don't mind me bleeding out over here."

Ryana flashed him a look. "I'm not responsible for your incompetence guarding my brother, wolf-creature."

Stella sucked in air through her teeth. "Austin, which do you want first, a bandage for that wound or some ice for that burn?"

Ryana wheeled on Damian again. "Did you really see a helicopter?" she demanded to know.

Damian blinked. Maybe she'd overheard Jamison leading them in.

"Yeah, but we're fine," he told her. Her sudden concern was mystifying, but then again, he was literally the only person she trusted on Earth. Before he could address her fears, Jamison came out of the house, trotting down the stairs two by two.

"My baby," Jamison groaned, dodging everyone standing, heading straight for the car. "I knew it was bad, but...." He patted the hood with his metal hand and sighed.

"Sorry about that, Jamison," Damian said, giving his friend a nod.

"We were going to have to ditch it once they made it, anyways," Austin said.

"No, I know. It's just such an uncivilized decommissioning," he said, circling the SUV with a frown. Ryana peeled herself away to follow him and her eyes went wide. There were circular dents in the side of the vehicle where the paint had been blasted off, letting the dull sheen of the reinforced metal show through, and there was a pause where they all looked at the car together.

"I can't believe we survived," Stella said, shaking her head.

"I can't believe I got shot by a goddamned helicopter," Austin muttered.

Jamison looked down at the SUV's dented hood with a sigh. "I can't believe I'm going to have to figure out where to fit a rocket launcher into the next tour bus by dawn."

· · ·

THEIR SMALL GROUP WENT INSIDE, minus Jamison, who was already working on his new task, and Zach thundered down the stairs to meet them. "A helicopter?"

"I know," Damian said, trying to cut his surprise off at the pass.

"Are you all right?" he asked Stella next. Zach wasn't wearing a suit anymore. He was in low-slung pajama bottoms and all the tattoos across his chest were clearly on display. Damian could feel heat splash across Stella in response to seeing him, like lighter fluid on an open flame.

"Look, I'm sorry my injury doesn't rate, but can someone at least get me some whiskey?" Austin grouched.

Zach turned to his brother's side. "Austin," he tsked, at seeing all the blood, then looked at Stella again. "I thought I told you to keep an eye on him?"

She blinked in surprise, and her ruby lips pulled into a smug grin. "What do I look like, a superhero?" she laughed.

"I'm fine, I'm fine," Austin waved his brother off. "I'll heal."

Ryana left Damian's side and snapped her fingers at Austin. "Let me see," she demanded.

"Why? Have you picked up tips from Gray's Anatomy?" he snarked.

"Could I have been watching earthly medical instruction this whole time?" She sounded profoundly disappointed she'd been watching *Aliens.*

"No, no you could not have," Damian told his sister. "Do not get your medical knowledge from TV," he said, and gave Austin a glare in warning.

Ryana looked between the two of them, frustrated anew. "Well...I want to hear what happened."

"Me too, Ryana," Zach agreed.

"Yes, now that you don't look like my father, you're allowed to stay."

"Up to your old tricks?" Stella asked him, her eyebrows high.

Damian remembered how they first met, and it was Zach's turn to flush.

Damian recounted their night quickly, noting the way that Stella was perched on her chair in particular, like she didn't want to fit in. It wasn't until he told the story of their last encounter, including the way that she'd helped save them with her quick thinking that he saw her relaxing, until she caught Zach looking at her with wariness.

"Okay, well, that's enough of that!" she announced, throwing her bag of reclaimed talismans into the center of their circle. "I've gotta go."

"But," Zach began, also standing. "It's not safe."

"Hey, if you can't figure out where I live, neither can anyone else," she said lightly, backing up. "Don't worry...tonight was too fun not to repeat sometime."

Zach watched her leave with a frown, and then noticed the others noticing. "It's not safe," he repeated.

"You don't have to convince me," Austin said, shrugging his injured arm. "In any case, hooray, we survived. Damian didn't dragon out in any capacity, and I need to go wash this shit, badly."

Ryana turned towards Damian. "This is why you need servants, brother. He shouldn't have to care for himself."

"You're right, he can't. That's why he has me," Zach said low, and Ryana snorted.

"You know you *were* looking for a job, earlier," Austin reminded her.

She narrowed her eyes at him. "I only supervise," she said coolly.

Austin made a show of scratching the golden stubble on his chin before breaking into an easy grin. "Well, it just so happens, I'm a man who definitely requires supervision."

Ryana laughed, and let him lead her away.

KEEPING the Hunter alive was a matter of professional pride—nothing more—which was why Andi didn't feel bad about checking her phone at the bedside. Damian usually texted late at night, when she assumed he was finally done saving the world and going to bed, and the second it turned two a.m., she started pacing, phone out, waiting for some message to come in, which was why she saw Sammy's messages as they landed at 3:45 a.m.

I think Eumie's out of the woods. I called in sick tomorrow and I'm going to bed.

You okay?

Andi stared at her phone, her heart still beating at the same frantic rate it'd had when Ryana left. *No, I am not okay,* she wanted to text back. *And I will never be okay.* But instead, she just sent back, *Yeah,* with the world's lyingest smile emoji, and fell into the chair beside her computer.

The ventilator whooshed, the pumps pulsed, the sleeves on her patient's calves inflated and deflated, but the longer she waited, watching her phone, the more still she got. She was so filled with fear there was no room for anything else. Even her heart had quieted down, beating once, twice a minute, at most it felt like, as her dread coalesced into a physical object around her, like a cloak that was both heavy and lined with spikes.

If being away from Damian hadn't saved him, what had been the point?

Six a.m. rolled around. She was incredibly behind and she didn't even care. She could chart anything she'd missed tomorrow.

If there was a tomorrow.

How could there be if she didn't know what'd happened to Damian?

Andi picked up her phone, feeling like she faced a traitor. She typed in: *Are you alive???* and hit send.

DAMIAN DIDN'T BOTHER to shower; he just kicked off his shoes and lay down on his bed. The last several hours in the training gym had been brutal. Jamison's lasers had dismounted from the walls to join forces and walk toward him on spindly legs, like a tiny laser spider army, but he'd gotten what he wanted. His dragon was quiet at last.

He stared up at the ceiling. Sometimes, it felt like these moments, when his dragon was away, were the only moments he got to grieve properly. When it was safe to feel all that he'd lost—raw and sharp.

His phone blinked on his nightstand, and he turned to pick it up, sending the photos of Andi that he kept there fluttering to the floor. He sat up and picked them up, too, carefully aligning them and putting them back where they belonged, in a small stack on his nightstand's corner. Always present but out of reach, just like the real thing.

He glanced at his phone, expecting to find a text from Austin that said his sister had hurt him, could he come retrieve her please, when he saw a note from the number he'd been waiting for all this time.

Are you alive???

Damian realized his own message to her was sitting as a draft on his phone, unsent—he'd been so distracted after the helicopter that, although he'd typed it, he hadn't managed to hit send.

And because of that, he'd gotten his first sign of life from Andi. The first signal that she still cared and that they still had a fate. He went to text her *yes*, then realized his feelings were too big for just one word to hold anymore.

He'd been a fool to last as long as he had.

He got up instantly, grabbed a dark blue hoodie, and went for the door.

"COME TO HELP?" Jamison asked from beneath the hood of a vehicle as Damian went outside. His techmaster was inside one of the garage's bays, already working on modifying another SUV.

"No. Sorry." Damian knew what he had to do, and he only had a twenty-minute window to pull it off. He jogged for the gates and then stopped, running back. "Jamison, how did you tell Mills you were meant to be together?"

The dark-skinned man put a wrench down and dropped the car's hood. His metallic arm shone beneath the garage's fluorescent lights. Damian was painfully aware that Jamison was younger than he was and probably vastly less experienced at all things except for this— because somehow he and Mills were happy. She was even cursed too, and it never seemed to bother him.

"It's different in humans, I think," Jamison said and laughed, wiping his hands down the front of his work shirt. "But when it's right, you just know. And then you tell her everything. Because not telling her feels like dying."

"That it does," Damian sighed gently.

Jamison jerked a thumb at the vehicle beside him. "You want me to drive? I've almost got this car ready."

"No, I've got it covered." Damian shook his head as Jamison gave him an improbable look.

"After tonight, you don't think you need backup?"

"I need to do this alone. You understand."

"I do, and I know you need her, but we need you too." Jamison leaned inside the SUV's open window and popped the glove. "Humor me; take this. I promise I'll keep it one way, I won't listen in." He threw the earpiece at Damian, who easily caught it. "I'll be your eye in the sky, all right?"

Damian settled the gadget in his ear. "Thanks," he said.

"No problem." Jamison gave him an earnest smile that was almost as bright as the oncoming dawn. "Go get your girl."

CHAPTER

NINE

There was no guarantee that the timing would work out. Andi could have a meeting after work for all he knew. But he caught the bus outside the Briars and took it down into town and made the transfers so that he should be on the bus that she'd take home. He kept his hood up so that no one could see his earpiece, and rested back inside its shadows, so that hopefully no one could see him. A man tried to take the seat beside him at a stop before Andi's hospital, but the low growling sound Damian made in the back of his throat made him detour away.

And then the bus was there. The brakes hissed, the whole thing lowered, and people in scrubs got aboard. Damian's gaze flickered over each new entrant, waiting, hoping, and just as he was about to give up, the bus doors closed and the hydraulics lifted, there was a fast knocking at the glass door.

"Sorry," Andi apologized to the driver who'd let her aboard. "Long night," she said.

Damian's entire world stopped at seeing his mate again, in all her ever-so-human glory. Her long dark hair swirled around her shoulders, the way the cold outside had pinked her cheeks, her perfect, full, bitable lips, the gentle sound of her warm voice, and then she turned, and saw him.

The driver handed her her card back. "Take a seat," he said, as she let her bus card fall to the floor.

He watched her swallow and then she disappeared from view for a second, picking her card up as the bus lurched forward. Then she returned to view and slowly walked down the aisle toward him. He could see the necklace he'd given her, its gemstone nestled against her throat.

Yes, his dragon whispered, slowly uncoiling.

"Is anyone sitting here?" she asked him. Her cheeks were flushed by more than cold now. He could almost feel the reaction she was having to him, like flashes of heat lightning, all over her body.

"It's a free country," he told her, just as she'd once told him, and she sat down beside him without a smile.

Damian closed his eyes, breathing in her scent. Jamison hadn't said anything in his ear about him being in danger. He'd just been periodically reporting whether or not Damian was safe, but he hadn't tracked all the hunters on those buses last night now, had he? So Damian knew someone might still be watching, which meant he couldn't give anything away in public. He pulled his phone out of a pocket and texted her.

I have to see you.

More than this.

Name someplace safe.

He heard her phone buzz in her bag, but she didn't reach for it, she just kept staring resolutely ahead.

Was she mad at him? It was clear from her text he'd finally scared her—only not in any way he'd ever wanted. She twisted beside him, her shoulder brushing his, his knee knocking hers, and she pulled her big bag over from the aisle onto her lap, where it overlapped onto his. Another turn, another stop, and she pushed her hand beneath it, using it to cover where she touched him. He felt the outline of her hand against his thigh, timid almost, and when had Andi ever been timid in her life?

Was she going to shove him away or pull him near?

Then her fingers clawed into his denim as she made a slow, deliberate, fist. Grabbing him to her. *Taking what was hers.* The sensation rippled through his entire body, amplifying desires he'd barely tamed in her absence. His dragon surged forward, matching him, as he felt his cock thump against the restraint of his jeans. He saw the pulse at her throat jump out of the corner of his eye as he heard her breath catch.

Her fisted hand quivered against his thigh and he took a risk, seeking it with his own beneath the cover of the bag, settling his hand atop it. Her fingers slowly splayed, sending more ricochets through him, as he wound his own fingers between them, to finally hold her hand tight, elated as he felt hers hold him in return.

She was his.

It didn't matter how much time had passed, nothing had changed. He would be hers from now until he met his grave, and every moment in between would be worthwhile as long as she held onto him.

She let go at the next stop, got off without looking back, and it didn't matter. He held the memory of her hand against his like a treasure map, knowing it would lead to something more.

ANDI STOOD JUST outside the bus stop and her knees were shaking. It was like all of the blood in her body had fallen to the ground.

No, that wasn't true…it was just that none of it was in her brain. Her body had borrowed all of it. It was everywhere she wanted Damian. She could imagine his hot handprints all over her, and as she made her way to her front stairs, she pulled out her phone.

I have to see you.

More than this.

Name someplace safe.

Her heart thrilled, and then she opened up her front door to find Eumie, still dozing on her couch. Hiding out at her place because the hunters had attacked them.

"That you, Andi?" Eumie whispered, opening up an eye.

"Yeah," Andi whispered, knowing Sammy was still asleep. She made her way over to Eumie's side. "How are you?"

"So much better, you wouldn't believe." They sat up. "Want to help me go downstairs?"

"You're not opening up the bakery, Eumie."

"No, but I need to go. It's important."

Andi frowned. "You can stay here as long as you like. You know that, right?"

"Yes, but I have things I need to do."

"Who's Orthrus?" Andi asked.

Eumie inhaled. "I would say it's too complicated to explain, but I heard you talking to Xochitl—it's clear you have some history—and then I heard your story with your dragon and Sammy, besides. Plus, you got me cao wu. So, let's just say Orthrus's descendants are relatives of mine. And on the off chance Xochitl wasn't taunting me, I need to go make sure they're all right."

"But they're after you, Eumie. How're you going to stay safe?"

"I've been alive for a very long time."

"That's not an answer," Andi said.

Eumie heaved a sigh and got up. Sammy had given them some sweatpants before going to bed. "Andi. I've been hunted before, and I'll be hunted again. No one knows the danger more than me. I've lost almost all of my children to hunters over the length of my long life. Which is one of the reasons why I need to go, now. Help me get downstairs?"

Andi couldn't stop frowning, but she let the baker put an arm across her shoulders, and they made their way outside together.

Eumie paused in front of their shop to hunt for a certain rock among the landscaping and popped a latch on its back. It was plastic, and there was a key inside. They used it to open the front door up. Inside the bakery, everything was like Andi'd last seen it, weeks ago, only the Nemean Lion seemed particularly angry this morning in its fight against Hercules—or maybe Andi was just projecting. Eumie walked into the back, and Andi followed them, unwilling to let them out of her sight.

Eumie grabbed a bag and filled it full of baked goods, proffering it over to Andi, and Andi took it like the bribe she knew it was. She looked between Eumie and the mural behind her. "How long have you been alive again?"

Eumie gave her a soft smile and answered, "Very," before turning on their heels and walking down a short hall, to turn into a tiny room that Andi'd never seen before. It had a twin bed and a small TV, and it was clear that this was where Eumie'd been living all along. The girls had never pressed to visit. Usually, Eumie just came up the stairs with day old pastries, or all three of them went out.

It would have been a depressing space except that one wall of the room was stunning. It had been mosaicked from floor to ceiling and showed a pastoral scene of a time that didn't exist anymore. A warm sun hung over rolling hills which had distant caves, and in the foreground, there were shepherds and sheep and trees. Satyrs chased nymphs, and nymphs chased back. One of the shepherds was playing a pipe, and Andi could almost imagine she heard it playing, as Eumie furiously packed a bag.

She realized if everything she thought about Eumie was right—and Eumie hadn't denied it when Xochitl had called them Echidna—then Eumie'd been alive longer than her mother and uncle combined. They'd seen civilizations rise and civilizations fall, and surely everyone they'd ever gotten attached to had left or, worse yet, died. Andi was hit by a profound sense of sorrow on their behalf. "How do you do it?" she asked.

Eumie's head tilted. "Do what?"

149

"Move through life still. Even when you know you're going to get hurt."

Eumie set their bag down on their bed and came closer to take Andi's chin in their hands and stare straight into her eyes. "The only reason I'm still alive is because I *can* get hurt. If you stop getting hurt, you stop feeling, and then there's no point in any of this, honestly. If I stopped caring, if I stopped trying to involve myself in life, if I stopped looking for people to love and who might love me, then I might as well have been buried in the back of some cave, millennia ago. People who don't care don't make differences, Andi."

Andi knew it was true as Eumie said it. "But what if caring breaks you?"

"It might," Eumie acknowledged, letting her go to finish packing. "It most likely does. But when that happens, if you can keep risking it, caring will eventually give you a reason to live and put you right back together again. You're strong enough to keep caring, Andi. I know it." They zipped their bag, smiled at Andi, and then offered her the spare key. "I have to go."

"Wait...what? For how long?"

"I'm not sure, so until then, the place is yours. I've paid my lease through the end of the year."

Andi started shaking her head madly. "I don't want it—"

"I'm not asking, Andi, I'm telling. Take it. I'm not expecting you to work here. Just put up the closed sign, toss out the perishables, and make sure no one breaks in for a few months." Eumie set the key down on their bed.

"But," Andi began protesting, as Eumie waved their hand over the mosaic. The sheep on the hills lowered their heads to graze, the trees at the edges swayed with an unfelt breeze, and she thought she heard the squeal of a nymph. She was definitely sure she could hear the pipes playing now.

"See?" the baker said, gesturing to the wall. "My very own escape hatch. I've been doing this for a long time."

Andi blinked at the wall, which now seemed much more like a

window. She'd gone through mirrors with Damian. Was this the same?

Eumie leaned over and gave her a strong hug. "I'll be all right, I swear, and what's more, I know you'll be all right, too."

"How do you know?" Andi pleaded. All she wanted was one one-hundredth of Eumie's certainty.

"Because I know you." Eumie gave her another hard squeeze. "And I love you. And tell Sammy I love her too. There's a safe behind the flour bags in the back...the combination's this address. Get her car cleaned for her, would you? I know I left it a mess last night, and I know she very much cares."

"I will." Andi's voice broke, even though she was trying not to cry.

"I have a feeling I'll see you again, Andi," Eumie promised her. "And my feelings are rarely wrong."

Andi sniffed back tears and smiled. "Don't tell me it's destiny, or I'll punch you, I don't care how old you are."

Eumie laughed. "No. Not destiny. Just a hunch. But I think there was a reason we met. The gods put us in one another's paths."

"Old timey gods that I don't believe in?"

"You don't have to believe in them, as long as they believe in you." They grinned. "Now back away."

Andi did as she was told. "You'd better call me if you ever get hurt."

Eumie placed a sincere palm across their heart. "I swear," they said...and then stepped into the wall. Andi could've sworn she saw them in the scene in front of her for a second, before the image went still as the stone it was created out of again and Eumie disappeared.

ANDI WAITED FOR A LONG MOMENT, just staring. Eumie was gone. What a night she'd had last night, and then, what a morning. She contemplated just flopping down on top of Eumie's bed and going to sleep right there.

And then she remembered her phone—and Damian.

Andi knew there weren't any cameras behind her building, which was why people kept doing illegal dumping there, and Damian was alive. She needed to see him. Even if it hurt her or him or caused the end of the world. Eumie was right; she cared too much *not* to risk it. She went back into the kitchen, picked up the key and locked the front door, before opening up the back one and texting him the bakery's address.

"YOU'RE STILL CLEAR, although this doesn't seem wise," Jamison said in his earpiece, as Damian walked to the alley behind Andi's place. Every five minutes since Damian had left, Jamison had contacted him on their one-way connection, letting him know he was still safe —although he hadn't offered additional commentary until now.

Damian knew Jamison was right, after seeing Andi this morning, it didn't matter. He had no problem risking his life to see her. Not seeing her now seemed far more likely to get him killed.

And so he stood in the grungy alleyway behind the bakery beneath Andi's apartment, steeled himself, and knocked. The door opened, and Andi was standing just inside, waiting for him, just like in all his dreams.

He took a step in at once and slammed the door behind himself as she threw herself into his arms. He caught her and spun her, pressing her against the door where he could kiss her hard, tasting her again at long last, inhaling her scent, feeling the heat of her against him. The moment almost made him dizzy, and it felt like he was high, as everything he'd been denied for so long was once again inside his grasp. He wanted to hold her inside wings, with hands, with claws, and never let her go.

He pulled back to stare into her eyes. "Do I taste alive?" he growled.

"Yes," she whispered, almost pleading. Her arms were around his neck and her whole body was pressed against his, trying to apologize for so much lost time.

He moved them away from the door and navigated her backward into the bakery's kitchen. "Clothes. Off. Now." She nodded helplessly, so eager to obey, and kicked off the silly shoes that made her taller, then started stripping off her coat and scrubs. "Leave the knee-highs on," he said, when she was down to just her underthings.

Andi laughed as she took off her bra, and it was the most melodious sound he'd ever heard. "They're compression socks."

He grinned at her. "I say they're knee-highs."

"Perv." She beamed a taunting smile back, and it was like the fucking sun had finally found him. All the nights apart from her, all the ice around his heart, began to melt away.

"I remember what you like," he said with a current of threat, taking a step forward, closer to her light. "Turn around," he commanded, and she did so without question, finding herself at hip height with the countertop behind her. He leaned in, intent on her. "Time apart has made you obedient."

"Don't get used to it," she said, as she intentionally wriggled her ass against him. Heat slammed through his cock and balls, and he wanted nothing more than to take her—hard. But just because they were finally together didn't mean that he could take what he wanted now.

Are you sure? his dragon asked him.

"Touch the wall," he commanded. She looked up at him with a full pout.

"I'd rather touch you."

"You will. But for now, behave," he threatened, grabbing one of her ass cheeks.

She squeaked and stretched out—it was a wide counter, her fingertips barely touched—and for a moment he surveyed her beneath him like she was his domain. He ran his hands up and down her sides, watched gooseflesh prickle on her body—from the cold counter on her pert nipples, no doubt—and leaned over her to breathe her in, whispering low at the nape of her neck. "Have you been a good princess while you've been gone?"

She chuckled throatily beneath him. "Why do you ask, dragon?"

"Because bad princesses get punished," he said, drawing a languid hand up her outer thigh. "But good princesses get what they deserve," he said, setting his teeth against her shoulder.

He felt her shiver beneath his touch. "Which do you think I am?" she asked.

Damian rose up, looking down, and caught her twisting her head to stare defiantly up at him. Here she was, in a position of pure submission, her little socked feet kicking to find purchase beside his as his hips pressed her thighs wide, and she was still utterly, inexorably, herself. He wound her hair around his hand like a rope, pulling her head back. "Both," he told her, and started kissing down her spine.

She made small, soft sounds and writhed delightfully against him as he let her hair unspool, gliding through his fingers like silk. His mouth moved his body lower and down, until he was almost behind her, and then he knelt on his knees on the bakery's checkerboard linoleum tile. It made sense that they were here—Andi was the perfect snack. He grabbed where her thighs met her ass, rocked her up and apart, and leaned in to kiss her.

There was no preamble, nothing slow nor subtle as he tasted her like she was Eve's apple, and he wanted to take a bite. His lips parted to drink her in, and his tongue pushed against her as she unfurled, and then ran up her to rub her clit with its broad tip until she moaned.

"Oh, Damian," she whispered. Her feet had stopped kicking now. She was on tiptoe, trying to stay still for him and give her whole self over. He lapped at her with his tongue, sucked on her with his lips, and worked her with his nose and chin, reaching between her legs to pull her wide with both his thumbs, kissing the dark pink space within as she kept sighing his name.

He waited until her breath sped up and her body twitched in

preparation, then pulled back to survey what he had done. She was as wet as he had ever gotten her before. Everything about her was quivering and ready, slick and hot, and he brought his fingers up to finish her off where he could see, rolling her clit between his fingers until she whined and gave it up, her whole body thrashing, her pussy pulsing, watching her ache for him as he had spent so many previous nights aching for her.

She finished coming with a gasp and tried to press herself up. He knew because her feet lowered. "Are you done punishing me?"

"Not hardly," he said, standing. "Turn over."

"Here?" she asked, even as she did it, bringing her heels up to the level of the countertop for support, and he wrapped a hand around both her thighs, following the angry red line the edge had just cut into them.

He pushed his fingers into her because he couldn't help himself. The temptation was too great, and he felt her hips buck against him. Her hair was tousled on the counter behind her like a dark cloud, and he leaned in between her knees. His mate was perfect in every way. He knew she was his destiny, and he only had to say it—

"Princess...I," he began, as he rubbed her deep inside.

"Still clear," Jamison said inside his ear, and Damian was glad their connection was just one-way—what he would say next was just for Andi.

She pulled up, balancing on one elbow, as her hand reached for his wrist to still it. "We always fight or fuck or both, Damian. There's hardly been any in-between. Do you think you could be gentle with me? Just this once?"

His confession was swallowed by her request. He hadn't seen her in weeks; of course he'd give her what she wanted. He nodded and pulled his hand out of hers to undo his belt buckle and unzip his jeans. His cock swung out and aimed for her the second his boxer briefs were lowered, and he took his hands and stroked them down the inside of her thighs, soft as a whisper, carefully pulling her toward him to the counter's edge.

"Like this, princess?" he asked.

She nodded quietly, her dark eyes wide, and he wondered how big a part his perpetual violence toward her and around her had had in pushing her away, even if just subconsciously. If she didn't feel safe asking him to slow down ever. "Princess," he began anew, to apologize, but then her hand was between her legs again. She reached for him, touched him, and he gasped.

She pulled him closer, rubbing the head of him up and down in the line that he'd just kissed, teasing him with her slick, wet heat, listening to him moan. How had he lasted this long without her touch? He fought not to tense his fingers on her waist, to pet her body instead of pinch it, and to wait until she pushed his tip inside of her, closing her legs around his hips to draw him in. Of course she wanted him. She was his mate—even if she still didn't know it.

"Andi," he groaned, letting himself sink into her, feeling his thick cock slide halfway in like he belonged there, watching her as he did so, the way her eyes closed, her back arched, her lips parting in a sigh. She was fucking perfect and she fit him perfectly—because it was destiny, *and he needed to tell her so* before things went further and their actions swept all the words away again. "Andi," he began again, stepping back, pulling himself out.

Her eyes focused in on him blurrily. "Damian?"

"I can't do this anymore, princess."

She laughed, shaking her head to clear it. "What...be nice to me?"

"No. Not tell you what you mean to me."

He watched heat wash up her in a wave. "Damian—"

"You're everything to me, Andi. But I don't know what this is today for you. The end of a dry spell? Why do you want me here? Do I get to stay?"

She pushed herself up on the counter with both arms, her gaze turning bright. "I needed to see you; I thought you felt the same."

"I do, fucking hell. But if we do this now, Andi, we can't just stop. You can't fold me up and put me in a box and wait to play with me later." He tucked himself away roughly and pulled his jeans back up.

"I don't want that, Damian, but we both know it's not safe for us. Helicopters?" she said, her voice rising, and he took a step back as she pushed herself to fully sit up. "I saw the survivor at work last night. It wasn't pretty." She put a hand on his chest. "I'm not judging you. I'm simply scared for you, is all. I don't want to give my brother's destiny any chances. I can't have all of everything I've been through without you be for nothing." He watched her chest heave and the fear radiating off of her was almost palpable.

"What if I told you we had a destiny too?" he asked quietly.

"Damian," she said. Her shoulders sank as she bowed her head.

"Let me finish, for once," he said, grabbing and pulling her up until she looked at him, and he realized this was not a conversation he wanted to have while she was half-naked, nor while he was looming above. He picked up her coat and swung it around her shoulders, then went out into the bakery's front and grabbed a chair. He returned and put it down in front of her, and caught her holding the gemstone he'd given her protectively as he sat down. Seeing her do that, a gesture she'd clearly made a hundred times before in his absence, gave him strength.

"Andi, I know you don't want another destiny, but I'm sorry," he began, and then realized he wasn't. There were many things in his life to apologize for, but this was not one of them. "Actually, fuck it, no, I'm not. This is real to me. And I want it to be real to you." He stared up at her, her ankles daintily crossed, the curves of her body barely hidden by the coat, his gemstone glinting at her neck. She stared down at him with eyes both curious and concerned, biting her lips.

"You're my mate, Andi. Every time I ever said you were my one and only, I meant it. What we have is not just a relationship, and it's not something we can opt out of or decide to put away for good. This thing between us is timeless and endless and it echoes. And I will spend the rest of my life trying to please you, and if it means you send me away again, I'll do that, too, but please do not because life without you has been murderous for me."

And for me as well, his dragon quietly added.

He swallowed, trying to read her face as he continued, sensing all of her body flush. He could only hope that that was a good thing. In fiction, in the Realms, announcing you were mates was always a happy occasion, met with a squeal of delight and affection instantly returned, but he was on Earth now, and Andi was so beautifully human. He took her hands in his, brushing a thumb over her wrist, feeling the beating of her pulse. "Every time I see you, princess, I feel something shift and break in me. I keep changing to be a better man for you, and hell, a better dragon. I am yours. I belong to you. Say you belong to me, too."

"Damian," she whispered.

"Annnnd it continues to be clear. I feel like a weatherman," Jamison said inside Damian's ear. "Sorry, hope I'm not interrupting anything."

Damian fought down a growl and concentrated on Andi. "If you look inside yourself and know you feel that way about me too, princess...I need you to tell me."

ANDI SAT ON THE COUNTERTOP, hiding inside her coat, her hands in his, looking at Damian's beautiful face. The scent of sex was heavy in the air, and he smelled lightly of sweat, like he'd been working out before he'd met her. In the half-light of the kitchen—it was dawn outside, leaking in around closed blinds—his golden eyes looked like tarnished coins. She felt all of his concentration upon her, waiting for her to say that she felt things too.

She did. She had. This whole time. She'd been feeling things ever since she'd met him, since he'd picked her up at that first bus stop, when she'd known he'd been trouble. It'd been so easy to read the signs, even if she never could've predicted this.

"How long have you known?" she asked him.

He sat up straighter, pulling slightly back. "When we were

together in the car beneath the overpass. I was with you and...my dragon told me." She could watch him structuring his breathing, holding onto each inhale half a second longer than was natural, trying to brace himself for a possible impact.

"He doesn't lie, does he?"

Damian closed his eyes and snorted. "He is many things, but not a liar, no."

She freed her hands from his, scooting closer to the counter's edge to look down at him. "If you've known for so long, why didn't you ever tell me?"

"To tell you that night would've sounded insane."

"And all the nights since then?"

"There was never a good time. Perhaps because of all the fighting or fucking, as you said, take your pick." He sighed and ran his hands through his hair, arching his back against the chair. "And I know you're human, Andi. I had to consider that you didn't feel the way I do." He rebounded to his former position, his gaze searching hers as he put a hand on either side of her hips on the counter. "But I can't risk you not knowing anymore. If you're going to choose a destiny, choose ours."

Andi leaned forward to cup her hands beneath his strong jaw. "You impossibly hot draconic idiot. I've been trying to." His eyes widened in surprise as she went on. "Do you think I've enjoyed this time alone? Swallowing down panic every night, waiting for just one word?"

"But you said you didn't want to be in a relationship—"

"How am I supposed to make good decisions when I don't have all the information?" She let go of his face to run her hands over her own. "What the *fuck*, Damian!"

"That's not an answer," he said, his voice low.

"I don't know what mates *is*!" She shook her head, raising her gaze to the ceiling of the bakery before lowering it again to his, finding him still intent on her. "All I do know is that when I'm not with you, I want to die," she whispered and swallowed. "And not in a casual, 'oh, work sucks and I spilled coffee on my best scrubs' way, but more in a visceral, 'I wish I could stop breathing now because it would be easier than being away from him.'"

The intensity in his brow softened. "Don't stop breathing. Ever."

She hugged herself and looked down. "I had no idea how hard it was going to be to be without you until I was. I could've used a warning."

He pushed the chair he'd sat in back and stood, wrapping his arms around her. "Would it have changed anything?" he asked, his question a soft rumble.

"I don't know. Does it change anything? Does being mates make you invincible or keep you safe?" she murmured into his chest.

He took one of her hands, brought it to his lips, and kissed it. "No, princess."

Andi's stomach sank. "Then we'll have to stay apart."

"Until this is through, most likely." He tucked her head beneath his chin.

Her emotions raced in different directions, like unruly horses tearing apart a chariot. She was angry that there wasn't an easy solution and that their time together still had a timer, afraid of how right everything he'd told her felt, and on fire with how badly she wanted him. Now that he was near her...now that she could hear his heart... now that she knew it beat only for her....

She flashed back to the prior night and the accident's only survivor and looked up. "Will there be more helicopters?"

His golden eyes stared down at her and she felt herself drawn even closer to him. "Not right now," he promised.

She leaned up, yearning, desperate for a kiss now that she knew they were all counted, and his mouth met hers, tasting her gently, kissing the edges of her lips before teasing her mouth with his tongue pressing in. She ran her hands up into his hair to hold his mouth to hers so she could drink him. Her coat fell off her shoulders as he ran his hands beneath it and she remembered their first kiss on his bed when she'd been wearing a fur, when it seemed incredibly crazy to want him. But this time, she knew exactly what she was getting into—and what she wanted. Him. Damian. *Her dragon.* She pulled her head back from his, and he pressed his forehead to hers, and they were both breathing hard. "Princess," he whispered. "Never leave me again. Not like that."

"I won't," she swore.

His hands ran up her sides and down her back and he bent over to kiss her neck. She ran her hands down his shoulders as he pulled her forward to the counter's edge and she kicked her legs so that she was straddling him, her legs around his hips, asking him for more.

She knew he was hard; she could feel him grind against her, and her hands raced for the waistband of his jeans, undoing the buttons that he'd just redone to reach inside, hearing his sharp intake of breath at her touch on his hot, smooth, skin. "Help me?" she whispered, and he went for his jeans, shoving them down quickly, reaching between them to hold his heavy cock steady. He angled himself down and leaned forward as she arched her hips to let him in, her hand curling in the shorter hair at the nape of his neck as he started to push his way inside.

"Andi," he groaned, grabbing her hips and holding her steady for a thrust.

"Go slow...it's been so long," she begged, and felt him shudder with restraint.

"I'll take my time," he said, kissing down her shoulder. "I'd take forever, if I could."

She heard the sincerity in his voice, and for the first time in her life, Andi felt like forever could be an actual thing. Like there was someone on this planet who would always watch out for her, care for her, cherish her. And she enjoyed it for half a second before rocking back onto her elbows with a giggle. "Oh my God, Damian, I really am stuck with you."

He flashed her a look, and then, he laughed, too. He stood and encircled both of her thighs with his strong hands, rocking himself deeper inside her with a satisfied grunt. "Is that what it's like?"

"Kind of...right?"

"I guess," he said, and laughed again. "I've never done this before either, princess." He gave her the kind of look then that made her want to melt and hide, instead of being so ridiculously naked and exposed. She bit her lips and fought not to look away. He leaned over her, pushing himself deeper, as he placed a hand beside her head. "All I know is that we're meant to be. I have faith in our fate, Andi. Every time I see you, I feel it. Don't you?"

She knew what he wanted to hear: *yes, of course!*—but that'd have been a lie. "No."

He froze, holding himself over her. "Why not?"

"Because I don't want to believe in fate, Damian. I don't want to trust that shit with you any more than I want to trust it with my brother. I want to be my own goddamned person, not a puppet." She reached for his face again as she went on. "I know I love you and only you, and if you want to think that that makes us mates, then that's fine, but the only thing I want to have faith in from here on out is you." She was breathing roughly and he was still rock hard inside her and all she wanted was *all of him*. "Isn't that enough?"

His thoughts flashed across his face, too quickly for her to read. "It is," he agreed, kissing her, and thrust anew.

The first few strokes were slow just like she'd asked for, letting her feel all of him, both of them relishing the friction as he pulled out of her, the tension of her tight around his cock's thick head, and then the sensation of him pushing into her again, stretching her wide as she sleeved him. His cock rubbed inside at her spot, as he reached around to play her clit with his thumb. Her breath hitched and she looked up at him. "You can go faster now."

"Can I?" he teased. His hands found her waist, thudding into her once, hard, in demonstration. "Are you sure you can take it, princess?" Andi licked her lips and nodded, as he growled, "We'll see."

He lowered himself on top of her, crushing her just the right amount, making her feel pinned in place, trapped in a good way, filling her and taking her, again and again, and she realized everything she'd missed when she'd been alone. Feeling full, feeling whole, feeling wanted—feeling alive.

"Oh, fuck, princess," Damian groaned into her neck, seating himself inside her. "I don't know how I lived without this."

"I don't know how I did, either," she said honestly.

He lifted up his head to loom over her, smoothing her hair back off her face. "You don't have to. Not ever again," he said.

He didn't speed up all at once. He kept her on the edge of begging him, and she knew he was doing it on purpose, because surely he could feel her shifting beneath him, heels kicking helplessly, her fingers clawing against his back to urge him and then...and then...he started fucking her like he wanted his cock to move in, and it was all she could do to hold on.

"Damian," she gasped, throwing her arms around his head and neck, her legs laced around his back, his hips stretching her thighs wide.

It was like he wanted to demolish anything that'd ever held them back, and she was all right with that, because after this, she didn't even want to be the same person. She wanted him to fuck her until she became someone new—someone so undeniably his that there could never be any question.

"Goddamn, princess," he breathed harshly in her ear as he kept mounting her. "This is where I belong. In you. You're my everything."

Andi moaned and writhed. "Damian...I," she began, feeling all the orgasms she'd denied herself in his absence rushing up. "Damian...oh God, oh God, oh God," she whined. Her hands ran over his shoulders, her short nails ripping at his back.

"Fucking come for me, princess," he hissed, and she had to, it was his, just like she was.

She screamed, then realized how loud she was being, and bit his bicep hard to muffle herself, as the sensation ripped through her, head to toe, all of her clenching and opening, clenching and opening, trying to take him deeper and then hold him tight inside.

When she was through, she fell back with a final shudder, exhausted.

"I'm yours, dragon," she whispered, willing it to be so.

"Forever, princess," he told her, holding himself up over her, breathing hard. "Always."

CHAPTER
TEN

"Damian, you really need to leave."

Jamison's voice had become insistent, and Andi moaned as he pulled out of her. She pouted and grabbed his head, bringing his face to hers. "Why the fuck are you still hard?"

He hadn't come because he hadn't wanted to be distracted...*more distracted*. He hadn't really thought about the demoralizing consequence it'd have on her.

"The first time we get to have sex in weeks, I wanted to feel you lose yourself in me." She pressed a fist against her stomach, above where he'd just been. "I like it," she said and frowned.

His mate begging him to come inside her was, and would remain, up at the top of his long list of Things that Made Andi Perfect for Him.

"I know you do, but...." he said, turning his head.

He didn't want to leave her.

He definitely had to.

"Damian?" Jamison said, his voice spiked with worry.

"What's that?" she asked, reaching up for his ear. He caught her wrist.

"An earpiece. Jamison's been monitoring me."

She turned pale. "Can he hear us?"

Damian laughed. "No," he said, tucking himself down as he pulled his jeans up. "I'm not that perverted. Unless you wanted me to be, but even so, there's issues of consent and—"

"You're going, aren't you?" She pushed herself up to sitting again. Her hair looked like a small tornado had hit it and her whole beautiful body was covered with the marks of his love.

"I shouldn't be so rough with you."

She ran her hands down her sides as if sealing them in. "I love it. I love *you*. Are you in danger?"

He ran a hand through his hair. "Around you? Always."

"Five targets, Damian," Jamison said in a serious tone. "I can see them coming in. I don't know how it is that they're getting to you though, it looks like they're walking through buildings? Shit's making me nervous, I'm sending in a crew...."

"Stop being a smart ass," she said, grabbing his hoodie's collar for his attention.

"Andi, I don't want to worry—"

"Am I your mate or am I not?"

He snapped to. "You are," he told her firmly.

"Then is this how you're supposed to treat me?"

He glowered at her, angry—because she was right. "Hunters are on their way."

"For you?" she asked, her voice going high.

"Who else would they be coming for?"

"Yeah, you missed some shit while you were gone." Andi pushed him back and hopped off the counter to start pulling on her clothes.

He grabbed her arm. "Come with me." All he had to do was take her away from here, back into his castle with him. Him tying her up in his closet was still a valid option.

Yes, his dragon agreed readily.

166

"No," she said, stepping reluctantly back. "I think I'm hanging out with my brother tonight. He wants to show me my mom's notes."

"What?" Damian said, in far more stern a tone than he intended.

"Because it's all fate or no fate, and I'm betting on no." She gestured between them quickly. "This? This is real. And my brother? Is just a jackass. But if I participate in your fairytale ending, what's that do for his? I don't want any of it, Damian, I've told you that, repeatedly."

"Damian, they're just about on top of you...." Jamison's voice was loud, insistent.

"We have to go now to keep you safe!" he shouted at her, then managed to find restraint from somewhere as he hissed, "I'm not letting you go, Andi."

"And I'm not asking you to, this time! I can't do that again, not to you *or* myself. So," she said, taking another step back, "fucking call me or text me, like a grown-up, but don't you dare fucking die."

"What the *fuck* are you doing, man?" Jamison demanded.

It was clear she was staying behind, and he was going to have to leave her to protect her. Damian ripped the earpiece out of his ear, crushed it, and threw it against the wall. "You are killing me."

"I'm a nurse; I would know if I were." She grabbed hold of his arm and started dragging him down a narrow hall, propelling him into a strange small room, before pointing at a beautiful mosaic on one wall. It must have taken years to create. "That's how Eumie got out. They stepped through it and disappeared."

Damian grunted and frowned. "Then they were indeed Unearthly." Now that he wasn't target-locked on Andi and they were in the baker's room, he could scent something of them beneath all the other strong fragrances of the bakery. An Unearthly hiding here made sense. He waved his hand against the wall—he could tell it was magical, but it didn't respond to him. "Although that's a type of magic that I don't understand."

"Fuck," Andi said, tensing.

He scanned around the room, casting out with his dragon's senses, and felt a much cooler area behind the decorated wall. "Don't hate me," he told Andi, and then punched a hole in it. Mosaic crumbled, showing the drywall behind, which he then kicked through— finding a cement lined service closet, with a metal plate on the ground, and a faint scent of sewer. "That's my exit," he said, stepping into the much smaller room, to lift up the metal lid.

"If you see them down there, give them my regards?" Andi tried to sound lighthearted but he could read the very real panic in her body, watching him. "I need you to stay safe, Damian," she whispered, and he realized he'd never gotten the chance to explain his earlier gift to her either.

"That's why I gave you that necklace, Andi. As long as there's light in the stone, I'm yours."

She gasped as her hand rose to her throat, and seeing her standing there flooded him with fresh desire. He stepped back into the bedroom to pull her to him and give her a kiss worth dying for, the kind where he owned her mouth, sucking with his lips and pushing with his tongue, feeling her melt against him as she went weak in the knees, until he relented slowly, dragging his teeth over her bottom lip before releasing it.

"I can't lose you," she said, pushing him away with only the strength of a kitten.

"You won't. I swear," he promised, watching her swoon, before stepping away to drop down the hole.

THE TUNNEL beneath the bakery was dark, but he had no problem using his dragon's senses to navigate it. It was an access tunnel offset for a sewer somewhere. He could scent the waste, and it was barely big enough for him to get through, but it explained why Jamison couldn't figure out how the Hunters were coming for him—they were travelling underground. He heard someone's soft cough from up ahead, and another person mutter, "This is disgusting."

His dragon, who'd been close beneath his skin with Andi, hadn't yet gone away.

We're leaving her, it stated. *Again.*

Yes. But not permanently. Damian pressed his bulk against a damp, cool wall, still listening.

And you expect me to have patience. Again.

It would be nice if you could muster some, he told the beast sarcastically. *Try it, you might like it.*

I would prefer to be angry.

Damian fought back a laugh. *I had fucking noticed.*

The dragon made a thoughtful sound. *So, we cannot be with her. But we are not fully going away. And the only thing that stands between us and her are more Hunters?*

It was an oversimplification at best, but the beast was trying. *Yes.*

Like the Hunters down here with us?

Also, yes.

Can I take my anger out on them?

Damian put a hand to his chest, feeling the dragon's power blossoming inside of him, as it used its ability to sense heat, pinpointing each and every one of the Hunters Jamison had warned him about in the dark.

Dragon, be my guest.

DAMIAN WALKED into his home an hour later, after having left a large enough Uber tip for the driver to buy himself a new car. Jamison came down the stairs to see him, with Ryana close behind, carrying Grimalkin.

"Damian! What the hell happened out there?"

"Where are the others?" Damian asked, carefully taking off his hoodie. The thing was trashed which was upsetting because up until he'd had to go into the tunnel, it'd smelled like Andi.

"On their way back. By the time they'd gotten there the targets had stopped moving...which I took to mean that you'd killed them, despite the fact that your earpiece cut out. Did it break?" Jamison asked.

"You could say that," Damian said, grinning.

"Brother, you stink." Ryana's lip curled. Grim bounced down from her arms toward him, bounced back with a disgusted *mew!* then disappeared. "Even your cat agrees."

"The reason you couldn't trace the Hunters was because they were in tunnels. The same tunnels I wound up using to escape. It wasn't pretty."

Jamison's brow rose. "What you did to them, or your surroundings?"

"Both?" Damian kept smiling while he pulled off his shirt. "I think it might be easier to just burn my clothes off of me. I've got to go shower." He dodged around them and trotted up the stairs.

His shower was an indulgent thing. It felt like not only was he washing away the gross grit of the sewer, he was scrubbing off weeks of angst and pain, like he was peeling off a second skin, leaving only fresh new man behind.

The kind of man who knew that his mate loved him. He laughed, hit the wall of the shower just slightly lighter than the point at which it'd break, and whooped his joy, before getting out to dry himself off.

Coming into his bedroom, he found his sister sitting on the edge of his bed, with a hand over her eyes. "Are you decent?"

"Never," he said, laughing, moving the towel he'd had draped around his shoulders to circle his waist. "Now," he told her, and she lowered her hand.

"Somebody's happy," she told him. Her lips were fighting back an impish grin. "Don't deny it."

"I don't want to."

"Well?" She spun her hand between them, urging him on, as he went inside his closet to change.

"I saw Andi. And while technically it was a hugely bad idea, it

170

was also the best thing I've done this century." He pulled on jeans and leaned out the door. "Actually, in my whole life."

"Do tell," she said, crossing her legs and resting her hands on her knees.

"I finally told her we're mates, Ry. And while she wasn't maybe entirely enthusiastic about the concept, she loves me, and that's good enough."

"Uh-huh," Ryana said, looking smug, and Damian narrowed his eyes at her.

"Are you judging me?"

"Perpetually!" she said with a laugh. "But no. I'm happy for you. And happier still that she was receptive." She tilted her head as though she were waiting for him to say something else. His eyes narrowed.

"I'm scared to ask, but to what do I owe the pleasure of your current company, Ryana?"

"Remember how I said I'd find a place for myself if you didn't?"

Damian thought back and remembered dimly—anything prior to his recent events with Andi felt like a lifetime ago. "Yes...we'll work on that today. I think Zach's idea is excellent."

She waved it away. "Well, last night I sat around and thought, 'How best can I be helpful?' and then I thought, 'Perhaps I'll meet this Andi.'"

Damian was struck with horror. "When...wait...how?"

"Your stack of photos over there," she said, gesturing behind her. "I can use a mirror as well as you, Damian. I concentrated on finding her, then I went to threaten her last night."

"With what?" he asked, blindsided for a moment by the idea that Andi's professed feelings for him might not be true. Then he thought back to the way her blood moved through her body as she sat beside him on the bus. There was no faking that or anything else they'd gone on to do.

"Death, of course. So any minute now, you can say 'Thank you.'

Although, 'Thank you, Ryana, who is the best sister in this world and all the others,' has a certain ring to it."

Damian blinked, and then laughed, roughing his hair with the towel again. "Thank you, Ryana. But I didn't need you. Andi and I have fate on our side."

Ryana demurred with a thoughtful sound. "Did you solve anything?"

"We solved absolutely nothing...and I don't fucking care." He shrugged, pulling on a shirt. "We're mated. I know it. She knows it. Things will work out." He watched her eyebrows arch as she rolled her eyes to the heavens. "What?"

"You can't just rely on that, you know," she said in an exasperated tone.

"Why not?"

"Because. You know who else was mated? Our dad and your mom. Did things 'work out' for them?"

Damian rocked his head back, remembering. "I'm a different man than he is, Ryana."

She stood up and put an affectionate hand on his chest. "I know you are, brother. Just make sure of it."

ANDI WENT BACK to her apartment, each step feeling heavier than the next. She was worried about Damian, obviously, but it was also the increasing weight of all her realizations.

All the times when he'd told her that she was his *only*, or that *no one else could make her feel this way*, she'd assumed it was just braggadocio, words he'd said to win fights or to make her feel sexy.

But no.

He'd really, truly meant them.

They were true.

And so was he.

She rocked up on her toes and bit back a squeal of delight, before heading inside.

Sammy was in their kitchen on the other side of their short breakfast bar, munching on a bowl of cereal, looking worse for the wear.

"What're you doing up?" Andi asked her.

"No reason," Sammy chirped, despite her apparent exhaustion. "Is Eumie all right?"

"Yes, but, about that...they took off, for their own safety." Andi set the spare key down on the counter. "We might not see them again for some time."

Sammy blinked in disbelief. "For real?" she asked, and as Andi nodded, she went on. "That fucking sucks." She put down her cereal bowl slowly, stunned. "And I didn't even get to say a proper good-bye."

"You helped save their life, Sammy. They told me to tell you they loved you. And also they left money behind to help clean your car."

Sammy frowned. "They could keep their money, if it meant they'd stay," she muttered.

"I know they wanted to, but it's just not safe."

Sammy took in a deep breath and sighed. "It's just sad, is all."

"I know. Good-byes are not actually ever good." Andi sat across from her on a barstool because she might as well tell Sammy everything right now. "And, I've known Danny was back for a while now. It's just that he's in some things, deep—"

"Of course," Sammy snorted.

"And I didn't want you to get involved. Or me, for that matter." Despite the fact that, according to Danny, it was inevitable. She wondered what Danny was going to try to show her tonight. She imagined him pulling out one of the folded paper fortune tellers kids used to use in the back of the bus. Or maybe they'd play a rousing game of MASH. She did know someone who had a mansion, after all.... "Anyhow, if you see him, stay away from him, please."

"Oh, obviously," Sammy said, sounding offended that Andi even felt she had to say something. "Does he still owe you money?"

"Yep." Andi had finally turned the cash Damian had given her into Danny's bail bondsmen, so at least they were off her back, but it was the spirit of the thing. Danny'd gone and left her high and dry, completely unsurprisingly.

She kicked off her shoes and felt all her energy drain away, except for a tickle of pleasure of knowing she was *with* Damian. "Anyhow, Sammy, we can talk more later, but I really need to sleep now."

"Yeah, I'm heading back to sleep myself," Sammy said, giving her cereal bowl a desultory rinse in the sink. "Uh...I don't know how to say this, but...just in case you're gonna do that again?" she began, gesturing downward. "You should know that Eumie was absolutely not kidding about the walls."

Andi felt herself turn bright red. "Oh my God," she said, sidestepping toward her room. "I just turned invisible, bye!"

Sammy laughed indulgently. "I'm telling you as a friend!"

"You can't see me! I'm not here!" Andi called from the safety of the darkened hall.

"You didn't sound invisible earlier!" Sammy hooted after her, as Andi closed her bedroom door.

WHILE THE MOST hygienic thing to do would've been to take a shower, she didn't want to. She could catch whiffs of his breath in her hair, and she was sure she smelled like exactly what they'd done, but it was good. It felt like reality. *Love* and *fates* and *mates* was nice and all, but on some level, because she wasn't used to it, it felt unreal.

Whereas this? The satisfied soreness running through her body, the air that smelled like sin? She *had* this—and he'd *had* her.

She kicked off her shoes, flopped into her bed, and basked in how badly he'd wanted her—to the point of distraction, if not release.

She didn't think she was dozing until her phone buzzed and she found out that she had been. She fumbled for it, quickly, and found one word:

Home.

Really? Andi texted back. *Just, 'home'?*

I could ask you what you're wearing.

You already know what I'm wearing. I'm tired and very lazy.

All right then, princess. Go to sleep.

Andi glared at her phone. He wasn't *wrong*, but he also wasn't right. And just because he was the boss of her when they fucked, *sometimes*, didn't mean he got to order her around in daily life.

Would you like a bedtime story? If you haven't already turned off your phone, that is.

Andi bit her lips and stared at her phone, not touching the keys.

Perhaps I will tell you one, regardless, and if you have turned off your phone, like a good and tired princess should, you can read it when you wake up.

Andi turned onto her side, propping her phone beside her on a pillow, so that she could see its screen, tucking her arm up beneath her.

Once upon a time, there was a particular cat who loved cheese more than anything in the world. So much so that he talked his beloved owner into buying him cheese from Serbia, despite the fact that the export restrictions on said cheese made it highly illegal to do so.

Andi laughed so hard the phone fell over. She picked it up and put it into her scrubs breast pocket to save Damian's story for later, relishing the feeling of it buzzing periodically as she drifted off to sleep, like a tiny mechanical heartbeat.

DANNY STOOD her up that evening.

She hadn't precisely been looking forward to seeing him, but she didn't want him to treat her like she didn't matter, either. Andi didn't know why she expected anything to be different now; he'd essentially taken her for granted her whole life, but it still hurt.

She'd held off on texting Damian back because she knew his opinion on her brother and didn't want to hear it, but she'd read the entire story about his efforts to procure illegal cheese for his magical Siamese cat when she got up. She wasn't sure if it was real or if he'd made it up; it didn't matter. It delighted her.

Around ten o'clock though, when it became clear that Danny wasn't showing—or that if he did, she was only going to flip him off —she settled in with Sammy on the couch, to watch *Investigation Discovery*, and texted Damian first.

Hey.

He didn't text her back for three hours, by which time she was sprawled out on her bed, reading book review blogs on the internet, but when he did, at least it was longer than one word.

Hey, I'm in trouble, because my brother's done something bad again, or just a normal, casual, hey?

The last one. Also? That was a really nice bedtime story. It made me laugh. It's been awhile.

Me too and you're welcome. What's going on?

She knew what he wanted to know. *Danny ghosted me. Surprise, surprise. I...uh...don't suppose you had anything to do with that?*

It took him longer to respond than she might have liked. *When I do fight your brother, I'll have the decency to let you know.*

Sorry. Just had to ask.

I understand.

And just like that, her brother was messing with her dates again, when he wasn't even in the room.

A new text came in from Damian: *Are you sure you're all right with this?*

She frowned at the screen. *I thought it didn't matter, because we're fated, right?* she texted, immediately followed by three ironic eye-rolling emojis.

I know you don't believe me, he sent, and she could see he was still typing. *I'm trying to be kind.*

Hard for you, eh?

I am half-reptile.

She snorted. *So was that what this morning was? The story, not the sex. An effort to be nice to me, before you kill my brother or fuck my brains out again?*

There was quite a long pause before he sent his next message. *Why do you insist on being so prickly, princess?*

I'm half-nurse. We don't get fairy tale endings at the hospital. I distrust them implicitly.

And another, longer, pause. *Explicitly as well, it seems.*

Andi set her phone down to rub her forehead with her fingers. This wasn't going how she wanted at all. She was just taking out her anger with Danny—and worry for him, too, if she were completely honest with herself—on Damian. The easiest way to make things better, if he were here, would be to kiss him, which was the exact kind of cheating she was attempting to avoid.

Her phone buzzed. She picked it up and was flooded with a wall of text.

We each have our burdens, Andi, and neither one of us can escape our pasts. But I refuse to believe that our chance at happiness is over. There has to be a forever for us, and I'll do anything to make it happen.

Even if that means being nice, sometimes, to you.

Even when—not if—you make it hard.

Andi tapped her finger on her phone. *I make it hard...???*

It's nice to know I'm not the only pervert.

Trust me, no normal girl would sign on for this.

Nor would I want to have her, he sent her. *And speaking of, I heard you met my sister.*

*And you think **I'm** the prickly one? I'm generally unarmed.*

That's not true. You always disarm me.

Andi felt herself start to flush. *Want to hear the whole sordid story?*

Of course.

Andi typed in an abbreviated version of what had happened with Eumie and Xochitl at the theater the other night, up through Danny, and the helicopter survivor, and Jack too. Damian didn't say anything until she finished.

So that's that. They're gone now, which makes me sad , and now I have a key to the bakery with a tunnel to...Hades? Where did it go, anyhow?

He ignored her question. *You were in DANGER AND YOU DIDN'T CALL?*

He didn't need the all-caps for her to know that he was shouting. *It was pretty live-time, Damian. I didn't have a chance. Besides which, I survived. Faaatteeeeee?*

It's too late to try to use that for cover now. She watched the typing dots swirl. *And your baker friend was* **the** *Echidna?* Damian followed his text up with a mind-blown emoji, which made Andi snort, because she knew he used them only under extreme duress.

Yeah. Although they'd never told me. I wouldn't have known, except for the crazy lady fighting them.

The Echidna? he pressed again. *That just seems so highly unlikely, Andi.*

You're telling me, she thought as she typed. *I know you never met them, but you know I'm not lying—and you punched through their magical wall!* She sighed as she typed the next bit. *Before they left they might have implied it was 'meant to happen.' You already know how I feel about that, but I did save their life. So, who can say?*

Interesting, he said, and she heard it in his rumble.

They also said we might meet again.

I hope to be there when you do.

Andi squinted at her phone. *Wait...how does a Prince of the Realms know about Greek mythology?*

I'm a dragon. I like heroic tales. Go figure.

Which begged the question: *What does your dragon think of all of this?* She meant...everything. All the fate stuff, Andi pushing him away, Andi pulling him near. She couldn't blame the beast if it was angry with her.

That we're insane. Then he amended. *No, that I'm insane.*

Not me?

No. He always takes your side. And he also always thinks he's on your side, even when we're fighting. He thinks he knows you better than I do....
He's a bit much, if you ask me. Andi smiled, as he went on. *But monstrous as he is, Andi, he would never, ever, hurt you. He loves you.*

Andi's mouth fell into a tiny 'o.' *And you? You haven't said it yet, you know.*

I will, princess.

When? She pouted softly at her phone.

The next time I get to see you in person.

THE NEXT THREE days passed the right kind of slow. She spent an hour or two texting with him each night, before work or her bedtime. He told her about how Ryana had seen Austin's favorite movies and now probably thought that humans were half-metal, hiding aliens inside, and when she'd pointed out that Jamison was part metal, he pretended like he'd never noticed that before. He told her strange things about the Realms, like how they celebrated birthdays: outside, under a moon—out of three! they had a lot to choose from!—and your loved ones threw handfuls of dirt on you while someone played a flute. She wanted to believe that that was made up, but Damian swore on his dragon that it was true.

And she woke up to some vignette from his life each late afternoon. The first time he remembered Grim. How his dragon had once tried to help his sister fly. What dawn looked like over the sarcoplex, the cemetery for royalty in the Realms where his father was interred.

She didn't ask hard things, like about his curse or the Heart, and he never once mentioned her brother or uncle. It wasn't because they were hiding anything; it was because they already knew those things were *there*, swinging overhead like dangerous trapezes. What they were doing now was weaving a safety net. They'd acknowledged the dangers above and were trying to build something to catch themselves below.

"Oh my God, just make out with it already," Sammy said, leaning over on the couch, shoving her phone at her face. Andi fought her back with a laugh. "Jesus," Sammy teased.

"Look, not all of us get to see our men in person, all right?"

"How am I supposed to rest secure in the knowledge that you're going to be able to protect me from freaking murderers, if we don't pay attention to the show together?" Sammy said, gesturing to the TV.

Andi shook her phone. "I know someone who knows someone," she said, like a mobster. Sammy rolled her eyes.

Andi knew her roommate didn't quite believe her about Damian...but she also didn't quite disbelieve her either. Sammy was biding her time, and Andi knew if Sammy ever *did* see Damian again, for once her first question was not going to be about the Pagani— she'd want to see his dragon.

"I'm gonna go take a nap," Andi announced, getting up, no matter that it was already eleven. Time worked weird when you were nightshift, everyone knew that.

"A 'nap,'" Sammy said, with air quotes, turning off the TV.

"Shush," Andi told her, walking back into her bedroom.

ANDI STRETCHED out on her bed, staring at her phone. Damian had last said something about food and so she knew she had a moment before he returned. She liked that he had the same weird schedule she did; it was nice not being lonely at night, for once.

Except in all the ways she was.

Texting was nice and all...but....

Visit me? she messaged him.

Almost immediately the dots of his words started spinning. *You want to hear the words that badly?* he teased. *No. Despite your uncle's promises, I don't trust my being there to not put you in danger.*

Jamison had told Damian, who'd told her, that her apartment was under perpetual surveillance now. Probably for Eumie's return, but....

Can I come to you? There was more than one decent sized mirror in her house.

That's not safe either, Andi.

Why not?

Because if you came over here I might not ever let you go.

No, really, Damian, she sighed.

You know how many ropes I have. You think I'm joking?

Andi's heart skipped a beat. She never knew fully if he *was* joking when he said things like that via text. She also wasn't sure if she wanted to.

Turn your mirror around, princess.

What, so you can see me? she asked, looking over at the mirror that'd been turned around since the night they'd flown. *How do you know I need too?*

Don't ask.

She snorted and ran into the bathroom quickly, to make sure she looked presentable in a tank top and pajama bottoms. The temptation to put on something more alluring was high, but she had limited time before he'd tease her about it, as they both knew she wasn't going out again tonight. She leaned forward, fluffed her hair, swiped on lip gloss, and returned.

Don't make me regret this, she texted, then turned the full-length mirror across from her bed around.

No promises, he said, as she sat down in front of her bed, cross legged, then bent her head to text him.

I feel silly. He was going to get to just sit and watch her text...hooray?

You shouldn't.

Andi rolled her eyes at her reflection, and then typed out, *We could just video call, you know, like normal people do,* quickly.

And make your poor roommate hear? His reply was almost instantaneous.

Hear...what?

He ignored her question. *Come closer to the mirror, princess.*

Andi licked her lips, and did as she was told. Their texts so far had been flirty, but neither of them had ever taken things further, and up until right now, Andi didn't think they ever would. But as her phone buzzed again, she started to hope....

I often wonder if you know how beautiful you are.

Andi read his text and then felt herself grow red. *It's not fair for you to put me on the spot, just because you can see me and I can't see you.*

When have I ever not pressed an advantage?

She stuck her tongue out at him. *I could turn the mirror back around.*

You won't.

You sound so sure.

I am.

You realize when you act like this it just makes me want to defy you?

You realize when you want to defy me it just makes me want you more?

Andi closed her eyes. She didn't need him in the room with her to hear his smug laughter.

And also defile you, he went on.

She gave her reflection a challenging look. *How?*

Take off your top, princess.

This is so unfair, she complained.

If it makes you feel better, I'll take off mine, too.

I won't be able to see.

No, but you know I'm not a liar, Andi.

Andi's hands bunched at the bottom of her tank top. Everything about this was ridiculous, but she wanted to see where it would lead. She yanked her top off with a burst of energy, and threw it at the mirror.

So feisty, he teased, and she remembered what it felt like to hear him rumble. *Lick your fingers, Andi.*

She tilted her head up. Either she was going to fight him at every stage of this game or give up and play along. She batted her eyes at him, and pushed two fingers into her mouth, sucking on them meaningfully before pulling them out.

And now you're plotting something. I like that, too, he told her. *Take your fingers and trace them over your perfect breasts for me.*

Andi did as she was told. Her nipples perked as she brushed them gently, one by one, pebbling under her own attention, and then she picked up her phone. *Okay, well, that was fun, now I need to go do some online shopping....*

He sent her a string of laughing emojis. *Yes, well, before you start shopping, I think you should know that I'm very, very hard.*

Hmmm...then that begs the question...how hard are you? she asked, before giving her reflection a mischievous grin.

Hard enough I could break both our mirrors, easily.

Andi lay back perpendicular to the mirror and held the phone overhead. *What a sad thing it is to waste a raging erection.*

Oh, I won't be wasting it, princess. You can go ahead and shop, but I'll be over here, stroking myself, thinking of you. With the mirror, or without.

What if I told you not to?

You love me. You would never be so cruel.

Andi turned her head toward the mirror. The temptation was to impetuously demand abstention—an obedience she could never prove—just because she could, to fight him.

But then, again, he was right.

How badly do you need me, dragon? she asked, then reached out to the mirror with a delicate hand.

The dots danced as he typed. *I wake up aching without you. I go to sleep, if it can be called that, burning for you every night.*

I wish we could solve all of our problems, somehow.

I wish we could, somehow, too.

Andi rose up then, rising up to her knees, and shimmied her pajama bottoms and underwear off. She felt very silly to be in front of the mirror with just herself there in the nude, but she heard his pain. She felt it, too.

She crawled over to the mirror on her knees and then knelt in front of it. "If you were here," she said without sound, just mouthing the words so he could read them, and then spread her knees.

She set her phone aside and ignored it, she didn't need to know what he wanted anymore. She licked her fingers again and played them in broad strokes around her breasts, one by one, then tugged on her nipples the way he liked to with his lips, pinching them as if he himself were there, lifting them up and then letting them drop.

"Dragon," she mouthed. "Is this what you want?" she asked, as she sent her hands over her ribs, sliding slowly down. She sank them lower then, pushing them down her thighs like she was pushing down stockings, until she reached her knees, only then to rake her fingertips back up, leaving soft pink lines behind.

Her phone didn't buzz again. She hoped on his side he was entranced and touching himself—because that's what she was going to do. She rested one hand on the mirror's frame and pushed the other between her legs, entering herself, pulling the wetness that she found there out to rub her clit with, and she closed her eyes.

What if he were behind her, taking her again? Or what if she were on top, astride him, riding his cock—or riding his face as he lapped at her? It felt so raunchy to be touching herself like this in front of him with him not there, which was silly. He'd seen her touch herself during sex what felt like a hundred times. But now that she was putting on a show, she made herself open her eyes and look up so that he could see her, and saw her own reflection—the way he must see her when she was getting close. The way her jaw was dropped, her hot short breaths making the mirror glass mist, how her hips bobbed as she wound. Her dark hair brushed against her skin like it was strokes from his fingers, and sometimes she pushed her fingers in to rock against, and it wasn't like he was there, but it was still good, and she knew he wanted her to come. In fact, she knew he wouldn't come till she did. She leaned forward, one hand moving fast, the other clenched against the frame, biting her lips to stay quiet as her orgasm built.

"Come with me," she whispered at the mirror's glass, and then cried out silently, breathing hard as she did, shuddering and quaking until she was through, slowly pulling her hand away from herself before leaning in to smear her mirror with her juices and give its corner a chaste lip-glossed kiss.

After that, her phone didn't buzz for quite some time, and she wondered if he'd been called away. She laughed at the thought that he'd missed her performance, but no, her phone vibrated just after she'd pulled her pajamas back on, and she picked it up to read his text.

They were back to one word again, but this time it was, *Incredible.*

CHAPTER

ELEVEN

The next day, Damian had what felt like half the contents of a sex shop delivered to her door. She started opening up packages on the couch unwittingly in front of Sammy, then stopped when she realized what was inside the first anonymous brown box.

Sammy took the box away and looked inside, and for possibly the first time ever, Andi got to see her unflappable roommate go pink. "Wow...that's...."

"Yeah, it is," Andi said, surveying the other boxes. Then she started giggling uncontrollably. There were ten more to go through, and the thought of carrying all of them into her bedroom on multiple trips was just too silly. She tossed a box at Sammy. "Help?"

They went through all the boxes then, snickering at all the suave yet cheesy packaging, playing with toys like they were swords.

"I'll give your man this, he's confident." Sammy laughed when they were through.

Andi looked at the array of implements. It was true, she'd seen Damian's green room, she knew he wasn't shy. "This is weird, but do you want some? Like, I think there's three of these," she said, setting some of the objects Sammy's way.

Sammy gave her a wicked look. "Does he know how many vaginas you have?"

"Sammy."

"Maybe dragon-ladies have three vaginas. I'm just saying!"

Andi picked up a toy at the same time as Sammy ducked. Andi would've thrown it at her, only it wobbled in a disconcerting way. They watched it wiggle and then laughed until they were in tears.

"Oh my God. I can't breathe," Sammy gasped. She picked up the toy and made it wriggle again. "I'm breaking."

"Stop, stop," Andi begged her, taking it away—which meant holding it herself as it flopped between them, sending them cackling again.

Her phone buzzed and she laughed even harder, imagining herself explaining this to Damian. It wasn't his fault even. Non-erect dicks were inherently hilarious, even if they weren't made out of silicone. She saw plenty of them at work. There was no mystery to them. Damian's was fantastic, yes, but a large part of that was because it was attached to him.

"Don't pick up!" Sammy warned, still tittering.

"Shh, it's just a text, I'm fine," Andi said, swiping her screen on.

It was...but not from Damian.

Yo. Andi-bear. I'm on my way.

Andi suddenly sobered. Danny was on his way over, and he hadn't even bothered to ask her if she gave a shit. But maybe there was an opportunity here. Maybe she could persuade him to stop this foolishness.

At seeing her, Sammy got serious, too. "I know that face," she said. "I spent eight months making it."

"Danny's on his way over here to see me." Andi set her phone down and frowned.

Sammy looked down at their couch and coffee table, now

covered in sex toys. "Guess we'd better put the plastic dicks away before the living one shows up."

DANNY DIDN'T COME up the stairs; he just honked outside when he got there like a bad prom date. Under normal circumstances, Andi would've just waited him out, but she didn't want to irritate her neighbors, plus she didn't want him to come up and start something with Sammy, besides.

The only thing holding her up was whether or not to bring her phone. She wanted it, like a safety blanket, just in case she needed Damian.

But going out with it didn't seem very smart. She knew Jamison made sure they weren't spied on when they texted—although she didn't know how—and also somehow made sure her apartment was bug free, something Andi hadn't even considered that the Hunters might have done until Damian mentioned it to her.

But if the Hunters got her phone as a physical object and somehow traced it back to him.... She shoved it in between the cushions of the couch to wait for her return.

She jogged down the stairs to meet Danny, already irritated. "Could you not?" she asked, as her feet hit the pavement.

"What was that?" he asked her, cupping a hand to his ear. "I just got the horn replaced!" he said, hitting it again.

"Stop it," she hissed, walking over to the El Camino's passenger side, listening to him laughing. "I have neighbors, you know."

"Eh, they're all right, it's not that late," he said, leaning over inside to unlock her door for her. "Saddle up."

She reluctantly got in. The seats were different now, their leather intact and clean, and all the chrome parts inside shone. "You stood me up."

"And you didn't text to see if I was alive." He was dressed casually in jeans and a Nike T-shirt.

"I got used to thinking you were dead when you skipped bail."

Danny chuckled. "So we're even again, then, right?"

"No. Not now, not ever again," she said, flashing him a look.

"Pshaw," he said, then he took a deep inhale and sidled his head back and forth. "So...since I'm taking you to my secret lair and all... I'm afraid I've got to ask you for some favors."

"Oh, God."

"Nothing major," he protested. "I just need to see your bag." Andi rolled her eyes but handed her small purse over and watched her brother rifle through it, not all that unlike when they were kids and he was looking to steal cash. "Where's your phone?" he asked.

"I left it inside."

"All right, that works." He reached under his seat, and pulled out a bag made out of some kind of velvet with a drawstring, like a Crown Royale bag, but bigger. "I'm gonna need you to wear this."

"You're kidding."

"Nope. Not about the super-secret lair part. I can't have you seeing how to get there."

"Dannnnnnnnny," she groaned. If Damian knew she was even vaguely contemplating this he'd be flying over already. But if she hung out with Danny, there was a chance she could get him to cut this shit out. Her brother had always had the attention span of a goldfish; maybe there was something else she could get him to latch onto that wasn't murdering people.

Failing that, maybe she could find out something that would help Damian.

"Come on." He shook the bag at her. "Daylight's burning."

"It's already nighttime," she said, but snatched the bag out of his hands.

THE GOOD THING about letting Danny drive her around with her eyes covered was that she couldn't really judge his rate of speed. The bad thing about it was that each time he turned, it made her nauseous.

"If you ever kidnap anyone else, you need to upgrade to cotton," she told him, holding onto the door with one hand, and her seat belt with the other.

"I'll take that under advisement. So...how've you been?"

"Oh, you know, the usual. Living, working, taking care of helicopter crash victims."

She heard him snort. "Pretty intense, eh?"

"It wasn't fun." That Hunter was still intubated and in the ICU. "Maybe your friends should've left some of the magic gizmos behind for him. I've had more than enough patients in with scapulars on before."

"Eh. They're not my friends."

"Just coworkers you share pieces of your skin with?" Andi snarked. She couldn't see him react with the bag on, but the silence between them stretched uncomfortably long. Andi thumped her head back against the headrest. "I'm sorry, but why the hell are you letting them do such a horrible thing to you, Danny? It's not like you." She wouldn't have believed it if she hadn't seen the one piece on David at Rax's casino. Danny had always been a selfish bastard— it was entirely unlike him to share anything, much less *that*. She fought not to shudder.

"I won't pretend it's fun."

"What's your dragon think of things?"

"He's not happy about it, but he doesn't get a vote." Suddenly Andi was glad for the hood, so Danny couldn't see her arched eyebrow. It didn't sound like Danny's dragon got an opinion— whereas Damian's very much did. "It's just...never mind. How did you even meet a dragon, anyhow?" he asked, taking them through a tight right-hand turn. "Had to be at work."

"Why?"

"Because you never go out, otherwise."

"I'm very popular," Andi said lightly, defending herself.

"Yeah, with librarians."

She snorted. "Does it matter? I met one."

"And....?" He prompted.

The bag was even better now; it hid her furious blushing. "And *nothing*. I'm not going to tell you a thing. I'm just here to see Mom's English notes."

"Uh-huh," he said. "How many times have you seen it?"

She put a hand to her mouth and pressed the velour to her lips. Was it safe to answer? "Twice."

"What was it like?"

"You know," she said.

"No...I don't get to see mine on the outside, remember?"

Andi wove her head. "Awe-inspiring? And...scary. Even though I know they wouldn't hurt me." She caught herself before she gave Damian's pronouns away. "It's just not a thing you expect to see in everyday life. So it's always a surprise."

Danny made a thoughtful sound. "What's it like for them?"

She remembered telling her story to Damian's dragon on the helipad, how intelligently the creature had listened, and how focused it'd been on her, then the thrill of their subsequent flight. "Are we there yet?" she asked Danny, trying to change the subject.

"Almost," he promised. "Come on."

"I don't know." She kicked off her shoes. "I don't ask too many questions."

"Andi Ngo, you are such a fucking liar," he said with a laugh.

She groaned inside the blindfold and licked her lips. "You know, if you stopped this shit, you could meet them and ask them yourself."

Danny laughed. "It's not that easy. And how do you know you can trust them, besides?"

"Because I don't have bad taste in friends like you do."

Her brother snorted derisively, to let her know what he thought of that. "Oh, yeah? Then why did I have to come and save you at Rax's? Where were they?"

Andi caught herself before she gasped. She'd forgotten that Damian and Danny had ever overlapped, but they had. Did Danny really not remember? He'd been in such a state that night, so intent on taking vengeance out on David. "The only reason I was there was because of you. Rax said he had information, so technically, that night, you were the one who put me in danger, in the first place. You and Uncle. What even happened that night? What were you doing?" She wished she could look at him. "How did all of this happen to you?"

"Some combination of Mom and Uncle." Andi felt the car decelerating, take a sharp turn, and then bump over a low curb into a parking lot. Moments later, they parked. "Hang on," he told her, and she undid her seat belt, while waiting for him to come to the passenger side. She heard her door swing out and felt a gust of fresh air as he put his hand on her arm and helped pull her up, putting a protective hand above her head so she wouldn't hit it getting out.

"Thanks," she said, standing. "Now?" She reached for the hood.

"Once we're inside," he said, taking her arm and pulling her forward.

"I don't like this game," she muttered, but went with him regardless.

They padded across a parking lot. Danny warned her to step up onto a sidewalk, and then continued. "Mom started working on me when I was twelve, because by then, Dad was pretty much out of the picture. Stand here." She stood where he told her to, listened to something beep, and then heard the opening of a sliding door. "And one night, around the time I turned fourteen, she took me out with her."

Andi frowned. There had been a period one summer, after Dad had left, when their mom had "cleaned" nights. She remembered struggling to be the woman of the house during the day when her mom slept and Danny apparently fucked off, trying to hold things together, answering the phone, the door, going to the Asian market around the corner so their mom could cook when she got up.

How had she never known?

He pulled her forward again, and now she was on carpeting, and she heard his voice echo like they were in a hall. "We went out, she introduced me to some others, and we fought this thing. I didn't even have words for it at the time. I couldn't have explained it to you if I'd been allowed. It had wings and teeth and seemed like it was half made out of slime." He paused them again, another beep, another door. "It was insane. And...you should've seen Mom. You know how we watched all those kung fu movies as kids? All of a sudden, it was like she could've been in one of them. But better. She was stronger and faster than she had any right to be. It was like she was an entirely different person."

A person Andi had never met. She bit her lips beneath the hood.

"We're here," Danny announced. "You can take that off now."

Andi reached for the hood, pulling it up and feeling her hair static along with it. They were underneath fluorescent lights in a cavernous room that held a cage the size of a basketball court. "Danny," Andi whispered, knowing immediately what it'd been for.

It was dragon-sized, after all.

"Yeah, yeah, I know. It's dangerous though, Andi. You wouldn't understand."

"How does your dragon stand it?" she asked, stepping up to the bars. Strange objects had been strung from the struts above, things that looked like jeweled skulls or artifacts from other times and other countries. A carved horse covered in beaten gold, a silver spoon holding a dollop of stone, a tiny pot that had a tiny plant growing in it, and more. The whole roof of the cage looked like it was a nursery mobile made by an inpatient committee at a sanatorium.

"The objects of power help," Danny said, jerking his chin at the weird art installation. "And I tell myself to be cool about it, as best I can. Come on," he said, leading her to the next room.

This one was just as large as the first, but the cages lining one half of the room were more numerous and normal—complete with cots and toilets. Countertops holding scientific instruments with cabinets above them occupied the room's other side, making the space look half-prison and half-Stanford, with a side of Ikea, and... inside the cages were people.

"Elsa?" Andi asked, naming her uncle's secretary. She recognized the woman's blonde hair, even though her back was to her, laying on a cot.

"What?" Elsa snapped, turning around. "Oh. It's you," she said flatly. They had the attention of all the people inside the cages now, many of them had come to stand against their bars to see their visitors.

"Danny, what's going on?" she asked, shrinking back.

"I remember how I was back then. Mom had no business letting me be outside. This way's safer for them." He waved his hand at the people. "This is my sister, everyone. Uncle Lee wants her here. It's all right."

Several of the people grumbled and wandered off, picking up the books or tablets they'd discarded to come see, while others kept staring disconcertingly.

"What on earth are you doing to these people, Danny?" Andi asked, looking around. Danny walked over to a fridge and opened it —there were multicolored jars of reagents inside, clear glass tupperwares full of tree-bark-looking-stuff, and Diet Coke. He pulled one out to offer it to her. "See? Your favorite, I remember."

She waved his offer away. "I'm good. Start talking."

He cracked the can open and used it to gesture at the people behind himself. "I'm making a dragon army."

She waited after that, for him to go on, like any normal person would—to laugh, or to apologize, or in some way indicate that they knew what they'd just said was insane. "Don't tell Uncle though," he continued.

"He and I aren't on speaking terms right now," Andi said, frowning. "Just what the fuck are you doing to these people, Danny?"

"Exactly what I said. I'm using my skin and skills and Mom's notes. Uncle's off gallivanting around the globe, building up his Hunter network, all worried about the Joining. He wants everyone to be prepared. It's going to be some kind of epic massacre—natural disasters, monsters pouring out of the sky. Well, this was my idea;

it's how I'm helping." He downed half the can of soda in a gulp, and he burped just like they were at the high school cafeteria again. "I mean, if dragons come through, I'm going to need more help to fight them, right?"

Andi put her head in her hands. "Again, you do realize, that some of those monsters are people? Just like you're a person?"

"Ehhhhh," Danny said, tilting his palm between them in midair and rocking it.

"So, it's okay for you to make a dragon army but not okay for there to be people out there who are born part dragon? Or part wolf... or part whatever?"

"Yep. Because when you start off human, you already know what side you're on."

Her lip curled in distaste. "You kinda sound like all the racist kids we knew growing up."

Danny rolled his eyes and huffed. "There's a difference between stupid human categories and fucking creatures from other worlds, Andi."

Andi felt the eyes of all the people in cages on her and knew if she glanced over she could see them. The whole scene here was giving her major zombie movie vibes and raising her hackles. "Whatever. Just show me her notes already, all right?"

"Sure, sure," he said, pulling her back into the hall. She felt immensely safer once the door was closed behind her, and more so when she heard it lock. "You've got to put the hood back on."

She double blinked. "What?" Not with a hoard of pissed off half-dragon Hunters at her back she wasn't.

Danny waved her down. "I'm going to take you to where the notes are. It's a different location. You think I keep them in there with all those fools?"

"Danny," she exhaled in a rush. "No."

"You'll be safe," he said and laughed. "I mean, come on, being by my side is like the second safest place in the city for you."

"Where's the first?" she challenged him before she thought it through.

Danny chuckled. "You tell me," he taunted, and she pulled the hood back on before he could see her flush.

SHE WAS quiet all the way back to the car. She hadn't even made a dent in his self-righteousness; if anything, she'd pissed him off and made him double down. She concentrated on not tripping, got in the car, and sighed inside the hood.

"I can't believe any of that," she said after he got in and started the engine. But being in the hood wasn't helping. There was nothing to distract herself with—just darkness and the memory that her completely irresponsible brother was keeping people in cages.

"They all volunteered, I'll have you know," Danny said.

That part...well...yeah. She remembered talking to Elsa once. The woman'd seemed very keen on advancing her Hunter "career" and what kind of promotion could be higher than becoming part-dragon? Or...all dragon? If their mother's notes were to be believed?

"It's just crazy, is all," Andi murmured to herself.

"Yeah," Danny agreed.

Andi sighed inside the hood. "So, what else happened that first night?"

"Big fight. Mom was a bad ass. And then, when we were done, everyone cut up the body."

"Don't make me puke in this hood."

"It wasn't a person, Andi," Danny tsked. "Not when we fought it, at least. And it wasn't like it was screaming for help—it was more making Chewbacca noises. It almost killed Joshan. Mom saved his life."

"The same guy that Uncle killed?" Andi asked, putting two and two together.

"Yep. Too bad...I liked him. But Uncle had to make a point about your safety, and Mom'd already given him an extra ten years, so hey."

The hood did make it easier to not hyperventilate when she panicked, at least. "So, what, then they had a bar-be-que?"

Danny snorted. "Kinda sorta. But don't worry, I didn't eat any of it. Don't start thinking I was being noble, though," he said, as she felt them turn left. "After what I'd seen, I would've gladly taken a bite, after watching all the fighting. Only Mom wouldn't let me. She wanted me to stay pure."

Andi curled a lip. "I'm really disgusted, but I also want to make a virginity joke."

"Uh, yeah, no," Danny laughed. "Even then, she was worried I'd introduce variables into her experiment. And, after that night, she and Uncle Lee pulled me aside and asked if I'd sign on board. They didn't exactly force me, so much as told me I needed to try, for humanity's sake. And, shit, man, the only thing I'd actually read up until that point were comic books. What the fuck else was I supposed to do?"

Andi bit her lips inside the blindfold and realized they were making yet another left-hand turn. "Was she sure it'd work?" she asked softly.

"No. That was the kicker. She'd try one combination of things, and I'd feel stronger or whatever—she didn't dare let me play any sports—or invincible, but it wouldn't always last. And I couldn't ever change into a dragon...until just recently."

Andi wondered if her brother's feelings of invincibility was what had led him to all his brushes with the law. "What changed?"

"Near as I can figure, I did. After Mom passed, I took some time off. I couldn't manage trying anymore. It reminded me too much of her. But after a while? I missed it. I didn't want to feel normal again. What was the point? I never had been. So Uncle Lee set me up with funds, and help. He added that David Argento dude to our team. You saw my workspace, it's nice, and I still had all Mom's notes, mostly, so...."

"Why didn't you ever tell me, Danny?" she asked, as they took another left-hand turn. "After Mom was dead?"

"Would you have believed me? You already thought so poorly of me, Andi, don't lie. If I'd come to you before this, before you met your dragon *friend*, you would've thought I was insane."

They took another left, and she sighed. "I know you're just circling the block now."

"So what if I am?" he said lightly, but then she felt them make a ninety-degree turn, probably into another parking lot.

"I don't understand why you had to drop off the face of the Earth, Danny. And Rax said you were kidnapped...."

"We just did that so there'd be a reason I was gone, on video and everything."

"Did it ever occur to you just how much you'd worry me?" She yanked the hood off because she needed to see his reaction. She looked around. They were in the rear parking for a place she remembered from their childhood—Skeeters. One of the first bars they'd hustled at. Shit, she remembered their dad taking them there on weekday mornings in summer to play pool, early enough that the bartenders didn't care that they were far, far underage. She threw the hood at her brother. "You asshole."

"Hey! I'll show you her notes, I promise. I just wanted to hang out with you some, first." He tossed the hood on the dash. "I mean, when's the last time you played pool?"

More recently than you know, she thought, and shook her head. "No, Danny. Answer my question first. Did you think at all about what it would do to me that my twin brother and only living relative dropped off the face of the Earth?"

"Yes. Just...not a lot." Danny whipped a hand through his hair. "It was a dick move, all right? I acknowledge that. One hundred percent, Danny-grade dickery. It's just that once the dragon-thing started to work, I needed to be in a cage, and not the actually-in-prison kind."

Andi frowned. "And when you called me scared? From Argento's phone?"

"And that was when it was starting to work. The dragon...." Danny began, staring out at the back porch where several of

Skeeters's more colorful patrons were power-smoking cigarettes to get back to their beer. "He needs to be in a cage. He's me...but he's not like me. And changing back and forth...it's hard."

She could see the pain of it, written on his face. In their former lives, this moment was exactly when Andi would've given him a hug. But she couldn't do that now, knowing everything she did. And he knew it too. She saw the lonely truth of it in his eyes when he next looked at her. "Wanna go inside? Drinks on me? For old time's sake?"

Andi took him in. She knew he was asking for forgiveness of a sort. And while she could never offer that to him...she felt sorry for him, for what he'd become, too. All those times he'd acted sketchy in high school and she'd thought he was on drugs. *God...how much* easier would his life had been if he'd just been on cocaine? It was like her mom had asked her kid twin brother to become a super-villain... and then given him absolutely no other life skills.

She closed her eyes and heard herself say, "Sure."

SKEETERS WAS EXACTLY as she remembered it inside. Torn posters along the narrow hall getting in, the walls underneath more graffiti than paint, and she already knew she didn't want to see the bathrooms there ever again in her life. The main bar still had the same poorly-lit-so-you-can't-see-the-grime thing going for it, facing a decently sized room with tables, chairs, and two pool tables along the back. Honky-tonk was playing overhead, but Andi knew that might change at any moment, depending on the bartender's whim, and blessedly, no one was on the small stage. No one was here for the music on a no-live-band-night. Tonight, it was only a bar for serious drinking.

Andi let Danny lead her over to one of the pool tables. "I'll be right back with beers."

"I'll rack."

"Don't cheat," he said and grinned at her, before departing. She watched him as she placed the pool balls into the triangle, and from his attitude and body language, she could tell he was shamelessly flirting with the bartender, who was old enough to be their grandmother.

Well, maybe not their *actual* grandmother.

"Gross," she said when he came back.

"Whatever," he laughed. "It doesn't hurt me to make an old lady's day."

"Don't let her hear you say that."

Andi set her coat down on a nearby chair and tucked her purse underneath it, then chalked her cue, all business, and Danny eyed her. "What, you think you're gonna speed round me and get out of this?"

"I'd like to, yes."

"Well, just so you know, it's the best two outta three, already."

She shrugged. "I can beat you twice."

He leaned over to stage-whisper. "I'm a freaking dragon."

"Strangely, I don't think being a dragon makes you good at pool." She took the white ball and lined it up. "If we were playing frisbee, maybe. Football? Then, yeah." She took her aim and broke the rack, sending the balls flying, and she and Danny both took a second to stare at the table and do their personal calculus. "Let's play to sixty."

"Ooooh, and here I thought I was only going to get you for fifteen."

"Nope. See, if I win, you give up this turning people into dragons shit."

Danny laughed. "Fuck no. You think I'm stupid?"

"Do you really want me to answer that?" she asked, as innocently as possible.

"Man, when I'm not around you, I forget how mean you are sometimes."

"Mean, right, same difference, really."

He rolled his eyes and leaned over to prepare his shot as she took a sip of her beer. They were just going to get one point per ball in, and not bother with the solids or stripes, until the first one of them hit sixty, less than half the length of a tournament game. "So, what's your dragon friend like, anyhow?"

Andi wiped the foam off of her lip. "Ah ha. The real reason we're here arrives. Get me competitive, liquor me up, and hope that I'll talk."

"We both know that just one beer is not gonna get you drunk. Asian red, maybe, and I'm not above us using that to help us hustle, but we'll both know the truth." He shot her one of his charismatic smiles. "Just answer the question?" His eyes stayed on her as he made his shot—and the ball sliced away.

"Ooooh. Too bad there're no re-dos." Andi lined her next shot up and made it, then she stood, surveying the table. Was there anything about Damian that was safe to tell Danny? Without thinking, her hand went for her necklace. She'd taken to rubbing her thumb across its stone in thought at work, and glancing at the light inside it all the time. Then she saw Danny's eyes, following her gesture. She dropped her hand and straightened. "They're a good person."

"Even though they kill Hunters?"

"Don't start. They don't go out of their way to kill you, like you do them."

"Uh, except for that were-girl we spared for you. And all the other ones on vengeance trips. Uncle Lee's still catching heat for letting her go for you. The Australians went to a lot of trouble to bring her in. Plus there's been a lot of fighting recently."

"Well, maybe if you didn't use helicopters, you wouldn't have to get fought so hard," she said with a frown. "I mean, if all of you left town, I don't think it'd continue."

"No one's leaving town now. Not now that dragons are involved."

Which was what Andi was afraid of because if she didn't get to touch Damian again soon, she might die. "What's it like?"

"To be a dragon?"

"No, to be the world's worst brother."

Danny snorted softly. "The changing is the best part." He lined up a shot, took it, and missed, and it occurred to Andi that he was missing so many shots so that their game would last even longer. "You'd think it would hurt, right? But it doesn't. It's like stepping into a suit of armor that was made for me. When it happens...I feel so amazing, Andi, you have no idea. I'm so strong and so powerful...." She was about to call him on his shit and ask how he thought it felt for dragon-shifters, but the expression on his face made her pause as he went on. "But then, what comes afterward." He blew air through pursed lips, and then took a sip of his own beer. "He's really angry all the time."

"Because you keep him in a cage, Danny." Maybe if Danny let the beast out—*and let it fly!*—then he'd have more empathy for other dragons.

Danny's eyes went wide and he gave her a look. "Are you kidding? Do you know what would happen if he got out? He'd go on a rampage for sure."

Andi frowned, not understanding. "Can't you just talk him out of it?"

"No. There's no one to talk *to*. He's me. All me." He stared at her. "He's like all the angry parts of me sewn together like Frankenstein's monster. It's not like it's another person, and we're all, 'can you pass the ketchup?' inside. It's like me, amplified to ten thousand and built like a tank with wings. What are you not getting about this?" He squinted at her, then his eyes widened again. "Is it different for your friend?"

As far as she knew, Damian was one of a kind—his dragon embroiled within him because of his curse. "They do fight with their dragon some," she offered, non-committal. "But they can take theirs outdoors, at least. Maybe because nobody's trying to skin them." Andi had never wished more than now that all that 'twin connection' bullshit she'd heard about as a kid was real. If it was, then she'd use it to download just a fraction of her empathy to her brother. "If you treat it like an enemy right off the bat—no wonder it's always pissed off, even if it is you."

Danny's eyes rose to the heavens. "You're such a sucker, Andi."

"Being nice isn't a crime, you know."

"Which is why you're nice to everyone else but me?" He jerked his chin at the table. "You're up."

Andi frowned at him, then scanned the table for opportunities. Her next shot was far away. She leaned forward to make it and her necklace swung out. She was hyperaware of it now, but knew Danny would notice if she tried to take it off.

"So, has he been a dragon his whole life?"

It was her turn to miss; her pool cue went wide. "How do you know it's a he?"

"No ordinary person gave you that necklace, Andi-bear. And, nothing personal, but knowing what that is...I'm assuming it came from a man."

Andi fought a blush and ground her teeth. "You shouldn't make assumptions," she said, covering the stone with a hand.

"Nah. I remember when we took molly at Elia's party, and you whispered and made out with Elia half the night. Afterward when I asked you about it, you were all, 'boobs are fun and all, but it's probably dicks for me.'"

"Thus ending my thrilling career with the truth-telling drug that is ecstasy." She stared at him. It was unfair that they'd been so close —at least, she'd thought—for half their lives. Danny still knew more about her than anyone else—more even than Damian did. She and Damian were working on that finally, but it would just take time. "I love you, but also, sometimes, I fucking hate you," she said, and it was true.

"Yeah. You deserve to," Danny agreed and shrugged, as though this were an acceptable thing. "But whoever gave you that...." his voice drifted as he looked back at her necklace. "They couldn't hate you if they tried."

CHAPTER
TWELVE

Damian stared at his phone. He'd texted Andi two hours ago with no response, which was unlike her, because ever since they'd started texting at will, she'd never been apart from her phone once. He had just sent her an ostentatious amount of sex toys though.... Was she pissed at him? Or arranging them into what he hoped was a shrine around her mirror?

He snorted at himself and gave her fifteen more minutes before heading down to see Jamison. He went to knock on their door and found it open.

"If it's not an emergency, give me five?" Jamison was in the rooms he shared with Mills, its mancavey-ist part in one corner, immersed in some sort of full body game play experience with wires and multiple screens.

"Sure," Damian said, even though he wasn't. He sat down on their couch and looked around at the rest of the décor, which was far more Mills's doing, and looked for all the world like high-class cottage witch. Intricately patterned rugs were on the walls and floor, bunches of drying herbs hung from the ceiling, and almost everything was made of wood or stone, but nothing looked old or was dusty. Even the things Damian knew were old, like the broom on the wall gifted to Mills from her great-grandmother, were shiningly oiled and clean.

Damian waited a patient three-minutes-and-thirty-some-odd-seconds before clearing his throat. Jamison laughed. "Okay, okay. Sorry, just had to save." Jamison unplugged himself and his seat swiveled around. "I'm not sure how much more relationship advice I have, man, although I'm honored you'd ask twice."

Damian would've gotten angry on that point, but he could sense that Jamison really meant it, whereas if he'd had the same conversation with Austin, in every subsequent one the wolf would insert a tease. "Thank you, but no. I need to know where Andi's phone is."

The obvious reason she hadn't responded was because she'd broken it somehow and lost his number.

"Why?" Jamison asked, rather than do as he was told.

"I sent her a message." *Asking what she was eating for dinner.* He was hopeless and he knew it. *Still.* "She hasn't responded."

"Is she busy?"

"It's been two hours and I know she's not at work tonight." If Jamison couldn't find her phone, maybe he'd have him hack the hospital....

"So, to be clear, we're stalking your girlfriend," Jamison said, in a tone that let Damian know what he thought of it.

"No. What is happening right now is that you're stalking her, with my permission. This way I don't have to cheat and use a mirror." But it'd now been two hours, seven minutes, and thirty seconds with no return text.

"Tom-a-to, tom-ah-to," Jamison said with a frown. "Normally I'd fight you harder, but, given the circumstances—"

"That I'm a dragon with a temper?" Damian gave him a meaningful look.

"No, that even more Hunters are in town.... Never mind." Jamison closed his eyes and pulled one of the screens he'd been playing his game on over. It floated out on a metal boom and then showed a map of their city from far overhead before zooming in to one red dot. "There. Her phone's at her house."

Damian squinted at the dot. It wasn't as satisfying to see as he had hoped.

"But," Jamison went on, slowly, "it hasn't moved in two hours. I don't know what that means...."

"Grim," Damian called out. His cat appeared immediately. "I need a mirror large enough to step through."

"Damian!" Mills called his name cheerfully as she walked in. "What's going on?"

Damian ignored her, as Grimalkin did his bidding, creating a mirror to hover in the middle of the couple's living room. "Show Andi to me." He waved his hand and demanded.

It was only afterwards he realized that if she *had* created some sort of shrine with all the sex toys, immediately showing her to everyone else in the room would be awkward. But the mirror he'd summoned fogged and then resolved into a blurry image. Whatever he was seeing Andi's reflection in was quite dusty, but it was clear she was not at home.

She was with another man.

"Oh, dear," Mills said, sitting on the couch beside him.

"More mirrors now, Grim," Damian demanded with a snap. The cat did his bidding and a panoply of mirrors appeared. Damian sent his magic out in a wave and now everything even vaguely reflective near Andi was reporting in. They saw pieces of her from glasses, lamp shades, the shine on some kind of ball, and from piecing together all the images, it seemed she was out at a bar.

"Where. Is. She."

"Working on it. Not sure of the ethics of this whole situation though," Jamison said, giving Mills a panicked look.

Mills went to stand in front of the biggest mirror, blocking Damian's view, considering. "She looks happy," the witch announced, and Damian started a low growl.

Then someone took pity on him and set something decently

reflective nearby—an empty beer glass—and he could see it too. Andi laughing. Without him. She had a pool cue in her hand.

He watched her bend over the table beside the strange man and he about flew through the ceiling, especially when the man leaned over and said something to her, jostling her as she took her shot. She swatted at him with what looked like affection and Damian felt his dragon rising as quickly as his temper, ready to cut its way free, when she and the man both stood as one to look over at something.

The man wasn't that much taller than her. And, once the mist on the beer glass had dried, the reflection crisped and he could see the resemblance between the two of them.

"Danny," he murmured. *Even worse.* His fists clenched.

Danny whispered into her ear, and Damian saw her eyes widen. She casually grabbed her necklace and spun it so that the stone was at her back, behind her shirt and hair, just as other people showed in the reflections. They were talking to Danny. He clearly knew who they were, so Damian assumed they were other hunters.

Damian channeled more of his energies into the mirrors and more points of reflection reported in, a veritable kaleidoscope of images, showing even fractional views of Andi.

"You use much more power, Damian, and they'll know," Mills warned.

"Jamison?" Damian asked through gritted teeth.

"Got it! Skeeters. Dive bar downtown. Want me to get the SUV?"

"Yes," Damian hissed. He stood. He needed to go there now and rescue Andi, but he was also transfixed.

"And just what will we be doing there?" Mills asked them both.

"Saving her," he answered.

"Why?" Mills pointed to the largest mirror. "She's already with another dragon."

The other men, wearing polo shirts and khakis, were talking with Danny—and at her. He saw one of her shoulders drop and knew she was rolling her eyes. Then her brother went to rack up a game. Damian slowly sank back down as they began to play.

Can we not just go kill him? his dragon asked, watching the mirrors as intently as he was.

In front of her?

He felt his dragon thinking. *Is behind her back any better?*

He made a sound of discontent as the men surrounding the pool table watched Andi play. It was unfair that they were near her, breathing her scent, within arm's reach of her waist, and he was forced to watch her from afar.

She cleared the table against them, much as she had the night at Rax's, and Damian watched Danny tell the other men to pay up. It was clear that they were pissed, they hadn't even gotten in a shot, and one of them got into Andi's face—probably to accuse her of cheating—but Danny talked them down and Damian snorted as they handed over money.

New terms were arranged, and this time Andi's turn was last. She waited nearby, leaning on her cue, watching the table intently, and then, as she bent over to line up her shot, the hand of one of the men in khakis reached to goose her ass. Damian growled as Danny saw the motion and the other dragon clocked the man's jaw without hesitation, hitting him before his fingertips managed to touch her. The struck man spun back half a turn to collapse artfully among the nearby chairs, hitting several on the way down. The other three men rushed at Danny.

Damian felt his dragon in him straining. If he changed here and flew there, he might still reach her in time, but Andi's brother had the situation under control. He pummeled each of them in turn while holding some of his strength back so he didn't kill them. Damian recognized the technique. Andi had jumped to the side with her back to the wall and she looked scared—and WHY DIDN'T SHE HAVE HER PHONE ON HER—but she wasn't running away, and she could have.

Once all the other men were on the ground, Danny stood straight, offering her his hand, and she took it to gently step over one of the Hunter's bodies, before they walked for the door.

Mirrors went black as she walked out of range, and Damian fractionally relaxed. He supposed the second safest place in the city right now was at her brother's side, even if the man had shit choice in company.

Surely, she was going home now, and surely, she'd be messaging him shortly. His teeth ground against each other though.

The mirrors caught up again when she and her brother were sitting down, having a spirited conversation inside of a vehicle. It looked like she was yelling at Danny.

"Damian," Mills said, putting a hand on his knee. "I think you've seen enough."

"Bah," Damian said, but waved his hand, turning all of the mirrors off.

Jamison cleared his throat. "I don't know if this is a good or bad thing, but I've finally got his car." The screen he'd shown her phone's location on earlier flashed an image from a security camera of a dark green El Camino pulling out of a parking lot.

"Let me know when he's alone." Damian stood up, staring at the screen. "And just so there's no confusion, yes, I am stalking him now."

ANDI FOLLOWED Danny as they quickly made their way to the back porch and his car. "Just like old times!" he crowed.

"Yeah, just what I'd been missing in my life—bar brawls," Andi said, keeping a protective hand over her face in case anyone else was watching. Luckily, Skeeters didn't seem like the type of place to draw hospital administration.

Danny whooped, throwing himself into his car with a thump. "I wouldn't have had to kick his ass if you'd just played along. You're supposed to let them think they're going to win a few times first, remember? We could've gotten them for so much more!"

"You wouldn't have had to kick his ass if he hadn't been about to touch mine. Don't think that I didn't know it. Girls have radar." She'd been thinking about sliding her cue back to knock the guy in the balls if he'd followed through, but Danny had beat her to it. "Doesn't anyone teach Hunters manners?"

"Jack's crew has some top-down issues. He keeps his team all men. Feels challenged by strong women."

"Well, speaking of, I'm not wearing that mask again. I don't trust you not to take me to an entirely different pool hall." She crossed her arms.

Danny laughed, and then gave her a meaningful look. "I just wanted one more normal night with you before I gave you these."

"This has been a normal night?" she asked, rolling her eyes, as he leaned over her lap and hit the button for the glove box. The thing sprang open, revealing what looked like all sixty years of car registrations tucked inside.

"Normal enough." He yanked the papers out and handed them over. "I've got my own copies transcribed, don't worry. But I thought you might like to see the originals."

It took her a moment to switch gears and realize what she was holding. The papers were old and scrawled with her mother's particularly particular handwriting, the English that she learned to write with long-long-long after learning Chinese.

Danny started the car. The interior light went out and he drove away from the streetlight they were under before she could protest. "Danny!"

"It's okay. They're yours," he said, pulling onto the highway. Andi's fingers reflexively tightened as he went on. "I know you don't have much of her stuff."

"It's hard to get attached to stuff from Walmart."

Danny snorted. "Mom never did like spending money."

Andi looked over at her brother, his profile backlit by streetlights, and realized that he knew far more of her mother than she did, and probably had more of her belongings, too. Like the photo album he'd given her. Her uncle had managed to accrue all sorts of belongings throughout the centuries, so surely her mother had had her own talismans to give to Danny, if nothing else, and the thought made her slightly jealous. It wasn't that Andi wanted pieces of old bone. She just wanted the chance to *not* want them. Even if it didn't make any sense.

Danny glanced over at her. "Just promise me you'll check them out, Andi. It's okay if we still disagree afterward. I mean, we've been disagreeing on things our entire lives," he said and shrugged. "I think when you read her notes, you'll know. Also, there's a big one at the end that says I'm always right about everything. Just a heads-up."

Andi's hand reached for the stone around her neck and threaded it back forward again. "Even if there was, and I know there's not, I don't think it's going to be that easy, Danny."

"Nah. It will be." He gave her a familiar wicked grin, then twisted his attention back to the road.

DAMIAN HAD an earpiece in and a balaclava in his pocket and was driving his Pagani at absurdly high rates of speed into town. Jamison wanted to send a crew with him, as did Mills, but he was worried about losing the element of surprise with too many people, and certain things, you just had to do alone.

Like murdering your mate's twin brother.

"Damian, I still think you should wait," Mills said in his ear. She'd wanted to give Danny a day, to see where he went, if they could find out more about his people and his habits.

But Damian was fresh out of patience. He'd used it all up on Andi, and now there was no more. Danny and his so-called destiny were the only thing standing between him and his dragon's future happiness. He and Andi were fated. All he had to do was sweep Danny off the board. And then, surely, Andi would forgive him. She'd have to, wouldn't she?

Yes. We are meant to be, his dragon hissed, as his hands wrung the steering wheel.

His phone beeped. He picked it up, reading a text from Andi.

So sorry! Just getting up from a nap. Had the strangest dream!

Damian threw his phone down in front of his passenger seat with a growl.

"It could be a trap," Mills said. "And you are in the world's most recognizable vehicle. Her brother is into cars, remember?"

He grunted over the line. According to Jamison, they'd driven back to Andi's, and now Danny was off driving someplace else, presumably to his own place. Damian followed a few blocks behind him, well out of sight, until Danny started twirling up into a parking garage and parked. Damian followed, parking on a lower level, trusting in Jamison to wipe the tapes.

"Damian...whatever you're about to do," Mills began in warning.

"I'll do alone," he told her, taking the earpiece out and setting it on his dash. He spared a glance for his phone where messages from Andi were still coming in—wondering where he was, no doubt. He pulled his mask on, got out, and slammed the gull wing door shut behind him.

The garage's concrete structure was too dense to see heat through, and the open walls meant that wind washed away any scent, so Damian was on high alert, especially after he spotted the empty El Camino, two flights up near the stairs. He looked up the empty staircase, and had a feeling, running up the next eight floors until he was on the garage's roof.

There were only two cars up there, and Danny was leaning against one of them. Actually, Damian saw, he was looking inside of it.

Probably figuring out if there was anything inside to steal.

Close. So close, his dragon hummed and urged him to clear the distance between them and pounce. A million and one ways he could finish Danny unfolded in his mind's eye. He could grab the back of his head and whap him into the side of the car he was by, crushing

213

his face before breaking his neck. He could tear him in two and throw the pieces over the side of the garage. He could eviscerate him by hand and strew his innards out over the gritty asphalt like unwound yarn. His childhood in the Realms had prepared him to consider every death imaginable, and he would give all of them to Danny if it meant finally having Andi at his side.

"I know what you're thinking," Danny said, standing up. He turned and looked at Damian. "You're thinking, 'What's the fastest way to kill this asshole?'" Danny gave Damian a so-come-here gesture with his fingers. "Hurry up."

Damian paused. Mills's warning that it might be a trap echoed in his mind. "What's the matter?" Danny taunted. "Dragon got your tongue?"

Damian raced up on Danny, and the other dragon didn't twitch. He engulfed the smaller man's throat with one hand and sent him reeling back into the car behind him, setting off its alarm, and leaving a Danny-sized dent in its door and roof.

Danny didn't even raise his arms to defend himself, and Damian stopped, panting, not with effort but with emotion.

What are you waiting for? his dragon snarled. *We are of the Realms!*

Damian uppercut Danny, same as Danny had the Hunter earlier in the night. Danny's head snapped back, his entire body rising up into the air with the force of the blow. When he landed, his torso dropped. He grabbed hold of his knees, catching himself, but he didn't raise his hands.

Damian held his fist in midair as Danny slowly stood. The other dragon rubbed his chin and spit out a wad of green blood. "Fuck, man, you're real."

Damian didn't respond. *Kill him! Now!* his dragon howled. His blood rushed like static in his ears. He wanted to. He wanted to see this small human's blood spattered over the next three parking spots, as he wiped Danny's smile out on the cement wall behind him, but at the thought of actually doing those things, all he could see was Andi's tearful face.

"You know you can't kill me," Danny went on.

"That's a lie," Damian snarled.

Danny chuckled nastily. "You're pretty strong. So, yeah, maybe you could. But you won't, not tonight."

"And why is that?" Damian asked, voice low.

"Because Andi and I haven't had our destiny yet," he said. Damian made an inhumane sound without thinking, twisted and tortured and true, and Danny fell to chuckling even more. "You hate it, don't you? The fact that she and I share a past and have a future." Danny stepped up to him and poked a finger at his chest—Damian only barely resisted the temptation to snap it off. "I know her better than you ever will; it doesn't matter what jewelry you give her." Damian growled and kept growling as Danny went on. "I know you have feelings for her. Otherwise, I'd already be dead, or we'd be giving downtown a kaiju show."

"Then you know I'll never give her up. Leave town, and I won't follow you."

"Fuck no," Danny spat. "How about this, instead, you let me win?"

Damian laughed harshly. "At the expense of what? The lives of all of my friends and my own hide?"

"Guess we can't help each other then." Danny shrugged and shook himself like a dancer about to go on stage, like he was finally fully inhabiting his body. "It's my job to save the world, asshole. And I'm not going to let you—or my sister—get in the way of that. You can take a few more shots if you want, but it's not going to change anything. You don't have the balls to kill me and Andi and I are bound by fate."

Damian took a menacing step forward, his dragon trying to take control of him, burning in every single cell of his body. All he'd have to do was lose control, his dragon was waiting *right there* singing a song of violence to him, coiling around his bones, spewing venom into his blood.

He and Andi had their own fate. Their future was guaranteed and fuck this smug punk sideways. Damian brought his fist back and shifted his weight, preparing to punch Danny into next week.

Find out if his heart is crystal, his dragon hissed.

Danny laughed at Damian's anger. "See, man? We're just the same!"

Damian reversed his arm's course and swept it up instead, catching Danny beneath his chin, yanking him up in midair. "No," he said. "The difference between you and me is I know I don't deserve her. So, take my name out of your goddamned mouth."

He dropped Danny, who landed with preternatural grace and then gawked up at him. "I don't even know your name," he said, sounding pissed for the first time that night.

"Keep it that way," Damian said, and turned around.

DAMIAN RACED HOME on empty streets. He could hear Mills asking him questions periodically, via the earpiece on his dash that he did not put back in, and he could see his phone flash in his wheel well with occasional messages from Andi. He wanted nothing to do with either of them right now; he was too pissed.

Why? his dragon asked, as they drove away. It only asked once—unlike the women, it was sure he'd heard it.

Because he'd snarled back. Because he couldn't face Andi knowing he'd taken her brother down. She was right, and that hesitation was going to cost him or his friends someday. The problem was no longer about her choosing between the two dragons. It had ramifications beyond that. If something happened to him, what would become of Ryana? If the Hunters murdered one of his crew, what would that do to their group? Michael's death had been hard enough, but at least his dying at the hands of an unearthly that'd come through a rift felt like an Act of God. Horrific, but plausible.

Not like losing someone because their boyfriend couldn't bring himself to act quickly enough.

And there was no way he could get Danny to stand down. He'd

sounded like a true believer. Who the hell tells their child they're going to grow up to save the world?

Ruling the world, like he himself was raised...that's one thing. It's a doable task, given the right firepower and magic.

But *saving* it?

That had spiritual connotations.

They were vastly different situations.

Right?

Damian pulled in through his gates and parked the Pagani in his garage. He knew Jamison would've been tracking the car, even without the earpiece in, so now everyone inside knew he was back, but what they didn't know was how impotent he'd been.

He'd been right there. His dragon had wanted it. He'd wanted it —no, he wanted Andi—and, "Fuck!" he shouted, pounding his fists against the steering wheel the way he hadn't on Danny earlier.

He was tempted to just leave his phone behind in the car and let Andi helplessly message him all evening, but in yet another stunning example of how he couldn't do anything *right,* he leaned over and picked up the phone, just as another message came in, and he glimpsed the most recent messages he'd missed.

Where the fuck are you Damian?

I need you!

You'd better be alive!!!

HIS MOOD and his magic flickered to the rearview mirror. He opened it up to see her and found a view of Andi from her bedroom mirror that she hadn't yet turned back around. She was sitting in front of it in the middle of a small hurricane of papers and, oddly, an open leather case. She was moving papers from one stack to another while she...cried? He could read the anger in her body from here—but also there were tears streaming down her face. He was sure of it.

He reined in his anger and exited the car.

· · ·

217

Mills and Jamison were waiting for him as he came inside. "Danny's still alive," he announced, without looking their direction. "And he has no idea who I am, other than another dragon."

"Damian," Mills began, as he shook his head.

"Not now. Feel free to be mad at me later, but right now I'm occupied." He took the stairs two by two and started looking at his phone as he stalked down the hall.

So sorry! Just getting up from a nap. Had the strangest dream!

Oh wait, it was actually a nightmare where my brother came and got me.

He's got other Hunters in cages at some weird lab where he's trying to turn them into dragons. And then we went to this shitty bar from our childhood and played pool against some Hunters and kicked their asses— in more ways than one—and then? He gave my mom's notes to me.

It's like really them, Damian. I recognize her handwriting.

The timestamps of the messages started spreading out as he got closer to his door.

I just read everything.

And everything Danny ever said was true. I can't believe it.

Before I saw these notes, there was a chance that all of this was just a shitty story. Something Uncle Lee and Danny whipped up to make excuses for themselves and what they'd done.

But these all prove it's really her.

She lied to me all along.

And the things she did to him, Damian!

I can't believe she wrote them down!!!

What kind of mother does that to a child???

*Oh my God, Damian, **it gets so much worse.***

Damian slammed his bedroom door shut behind him and walked straight for his wall of mirrors.

CHAPTER
THIRTEEN

A ndi couldn't believe that she'd asked Damian for help. But then maybe she was fated to? Why the hell not? Everything in her life had apparently always been a lie.

She'd never had a choice.

Right down to her relationship with Damian.

After Danny dropped her off, she'd come upstairs to read her mother's notes, sitting on the couch after she tossed her keys on the kitchen counter.

It wasn't until the first few pages were done that she realized she was sitting like she did when she and Sammy watched something particularly awful on TV. She was curled up in a defensive ball, her hands tight on the papers, her eyes squinting as if not seeing well could somehow help the horror.

First off, her mother was completely unapologetic. She knew exactly what she'd done, and was proud of it, even. There were formulas of medication in there, things that Andi knew were poisonous, lists of applications, injections, bitter things Danny'd had to hold for hours underneath his tongue before spitting out, stinging insects that her mother had left cupped against him. Her mother wrote down what didn't work, striking them through with a precise line, and then underlined the things that seemed to have—treating Danny like he was a test subject the whole time.

He was never "Danny" in her notes. He was hardly even there. Just a series of dates, trials, outcomes. Was she trying to avoid judgment, by not calling her brother "the child" or even "the patient?" Trying to divorce herself of the familiarity of their bond?

Or trying to deny that bond entirely?

Because what kind of mother would boil up homemade medicines and inject them between her child's toes where authorities would never see? Or confess to tying him down to put eye drops in his eyes? Cupping scorpions against his skin? Cutting him afterward to see how fast he would heal—or if he'd suddenly somehow gained scales underneath to protect him.

As he grew, her notes got stranger and more urgent—and Danny finally became *the boy.*

The boy is moody.

Yeah, no shit, Mom, you're torturing him.

The boy fought again and won. The scorpions are working.

The boy tried to start a fire at school, but does he have the fire we need inside?

And then the notes reached the point where Danny broke off to do his own thing when their mom's cancer hit her, and Andi knew she started in on chemo. Her handwriting got a little more loopy. Her thoughts were more scattered and she turned her eye on her legacy and the notes became more like her diary.

HAVE I done enough to prepare him?

Where is the dragon hiding?

Some days I swear I can sense it, just underneath!

. . .

AND THEN THERE was a longer gap during which Andi knew the cancer had been winning.

CLOSE TO THE END NOW. My flesh is winding down. There's no point in fighting, the doctors won't even use Huang Qin Tang—although if they did, Andi would throw herself in front of me. She has such faith in the medicine she uses...little does she know what she could do if she knew more.

"THANKS, MOM," Andi muttered, smoothing a creased page down, before reading the next.

ALL OF THIS effort and I'm still not sure of the outcome of my life's work. I feel sure I have changed something inside him, summoned some beastly part of him more near, but I do not think I will get to gaze upon a dragon again in this lifetime. I can only hope I've done enough.

AND THEN, the last page:

I AM, and have been, the luckiest mother alive.

I have raised two spectacular children, each in their own way: Andrea to be a creature of empathy, and Daniel to be a creature of action. My heart and my liver, and I love them both.

I have the same dream every night now, as the end grows near, and I have dealt in magicks long enough to know it means something. It is a vision of the future, of Danny and Andi fighting together, protecting one another. And while I am dismayed that they must fight, I know that I have done everything within my power to prepare them for the battles yet to come.

Most importantly, I'm leaving them each other.

. . .

ANDI HOWLED WITHOUT THINKING. It was something guttural inside her, like a scream she'd been holding back for months—maybe years. Maybe ever since she first realized she was going to lose her mother and that she was going to have to stay strong because nobody else in her family could fucking be trusted to—not her brother who was running off to God-knows-where or her uncle who was off doing God-knew-what. That first scream that she'd entirely swallowed when she realized that she was abso-fucking-positively alone. It came out of her now from someplace in her soul, for the span of an entire breath, and then when it was over, she inhaled and did it again, and again, because fuck this and fuck everything and how could she hurt so bad again? Why didn't it ever stop? Would it ever stop? Had her mother really thought she could just point and shoot Danny off, like a wind-up-soldier, and her find out about it, and that she'd be the same? That she'd be *okay?*

She loved her mom. She missed her mom.

What the fuck had her mom done?

When Andi next caught her breath, between screams and sobs, she realized that just because Sammy was out again didn't mean she'd stay that way. She grabbed up all the sheets of paper quickly and ran to her room.

And three steps inside her room she tripped on her rug and fell sprawling to the ground, her mother's notes fluttering down like butterflies, knocking the wind from herself.

She lay on the floor for a long moment. It was easier to feel like there was ground when you were on it—a lesson every drunk person inherently knew.

Her mom...and her brother...and her mom....

She twisted her head to get away from her past and saw the pile of things she'd shoved under her bed in her Ambien haze weeks ago —her stuffed animals, her mother's photo album, and the case for her old pool cue, the one given to her by her father.

She reached out for the leather case and tugged it away from all the other stuff. At least playing pool was pure. Their dad may have been an abandoning asshole, yes, a disappointment, absolutely, but he hadn't had an ulterior motive during their childhood. There was something clean in that. Because *very-sarcastic-HOORAY.* She was empathetic? Wow, what's that get you these days, a Diet Coke if you toss in a buck fifty? *Thanks, Mom, for helping me to meet the basic minimum standards of participating in society. I get to be a good person and you turned my freaking twin brother into a KILLING MACHINE?*

Andi slowly got up, pulling the case out with her. If she'd had her own pool cue with her tonight, she'd have dispatched those Hunters even faster. Ironically, in hindsight, the only times she'd ever been really "bad" was with Danny—participating in the hustling, witnessing the fights, drinking on their fake IDs. She wondered what, if anything, her mother knew about their escapades, or if her mother chose to turn a blind-eye toward the only brother-sister bonding they ever got to do, seeing as there was a gulf between them in every other way.

She'd moved around to the front of her bed, pulling the cue and the papers with her, preparing to show them to Damian whenever it was he got back, arranging them into timeline order again in front of her as best she could, and then she opened up the case for old time's sake.

Her cue—the last treasured memory of her father—was gone, and her first instinct would've been to assume that Danny'd stolen and sold it, were there not even more tightly rolled papers in its place. She pulled them out and carefully unfurled them to read, her heart dropping as she realized what the words meant.

She texted Damian in a panic, trying to hold on to the world she thought she had, while knowing it was too late.

The destiny she'd been fighting all along had still caught up with her.

And no wonder Damian had fallen for her, and she for him.

She'd been a fool to think she'd ever had a choice.

. . .

"ANDI?"

She heard a rustling from her bathroom just as Damian emerged. By then she'd picked up all the notes and had them in order again, and she knew she'd done the wrong thing.

"Go back," she said, running for him, pushing him back into the bathroom. "None of this is real, Damian. Just go back."

He stood firm, looking down at her with stern concern. "What happened?"

"It's not safe—"

"I'm not leaving you," he growled.

Andi stopped shoving him. "No. Of course you're not." She gave a bitter laugh.

"Princess," he began.

"You want to check me for strings, Damian?" She spun around in front of him. "Or maybe you can insert a rail somewhere to whip me off of, like those little race cars Danny used to have. Just shoot me off at a preordained target, like a fucking missile."

"You're not making sense."

"It doesn't matter if I make sense. In fact, nothing fucking matters at all." Andi ran her fingers through her hair, sitting in front of her bed by the piles of notes as Damian looked worriedly down at her.

"Did they poison you at that bar?" He put a hand on her forehead and she slapped it back.

"No. That was the best part of the night. For a moment, I felt vaguely free."

"I don't understand...."

She picked up the nearest pile and shook them at him. "You don't need to. Someone wrote everything out for me, years ago. You ever wanted an Andrea Ngo instruction manual? Well, here it is." It was one thing to be trapped—and another yet to know it. Why wouldn't the room stop spinning? Her whole life had been leading up to now!

Damian slowly sat down beside her. "I saw your texts, Andi," he said, his voice a bass rumble. "I'm sorry your mother is not who you thought she was. I understand that that's traumatic."

"Yes, but," she said, finding the last note in particular. "You didn't see this." She held it over to him and rocked back, to read it in reverse as her nightlight shone through the thin page.

ANDI.

This is just for you.

I know you will find it when the time is right.

So much in this world is predestined, whether we know enough to understand it or not. And if it is your destiny to throw this case away without opening it, I am willing to take that chance.

I am sure I succeeded where your brother is concerned. It's only a matter of time now. I know he will continue, although I no longer have any time left.

I know you will feel betrayed, reading this without me. Knowing what you likely do now about me and my people.

I just wanted you to have a choice, my sweet heart. I have protected you all this time. I just wanted to give you a chance to live your life. To see where it would take you.

But if you have opened this case now, and you are reading this with full knowledge of what I mean, then it is time to choose.

You and your brother are one of a kind, born of a woman who ingested dragon magic for centuries. The circumstances surrounding your birth are utterly irreplicable—there is no point in trying.

*But because of that, **both** have dragons in you. Daniel, I experimented on. Whereas I left you my blank slate. My formula to summon yours is on the next page.*

It will never work on anyone else but you.

Tell no one this formula exists. I will take my secret to my grave, and you might very well take yours, too. I have no judgment for or against that

—the world doesn't need you to protect it. I have already given it Daniel. Isn't offering up one child to destiny enough?

I just thought that you should know. My heritage did not skip you, my gentle girl, nor did I leave you without power. Protect yourself—with or without using it. Pass on my legacy. Make a family, have a home, fill them all with love, and remember me fondly.

Your mother,

Mei Li

DAMIAN KNEW Andi was watching him read, and he also knew she'd say something the second he was done. *Fate, or familiarity?* He didn't dare smile as he set the page down.

"This is why you love me, isn't it?" she challenged him.

One of his eyebrows rose. "I haven't even said it yet."

"You don't have to. I'm not an idiot."

"Well, if I say it now, you'll say it was predestined. And if I don't, you'll say that was predestined too." His brow furrowed. "This is why I hate prognosticators."

"We didn't meet by accident, Damian," she protested. "It wasn't a meet-cute, you hiring me. You knew, or fate knew, and all this time you've only wanted me because I'm part-dragon. Even if you didn't know until you read that page. You didn't get a choice, either."

He watched her get all worked up. "Even if that were true— which it isn't—would it be so bad?" he asked, trying to calm her.

"Yes! Because if this nonsense is all true, then the thing with me fighting by my brother's side is probably especially true, right? Don't deny it."

Damian nodded slowly, with a sigh. "I saw your brother tonight as well."

"Did you kill him?" she asked, although she could already read the answer on his face. "No. Of course not. You couldn't. We still have destiny. So it's not allowed." She put her head in her hands and he knew he was watching her second-guess every decision she'd ever made.

Damian put one hand on her shoulder and used the other to lift up her chin. "I don't give a damn about destiny anymore, princess. I just want you."

Her expression was haunted. "Even if it's all a lie?"

"If you're a lie, then you're the sexiest lie I've ever seen." He slid the hand on her chin up against her cheek. She fought the temptation for a moment because his mate was a fighter. That's what she did. Then she leaned into it and he knew that everything would be all right. "I know what it's like to run from destiny. I'm a prince of a place I hate, remember? But now, knowing that you and I are mated, did I hate it because it was the right thing to do, or because hating it brought me here? Who can say?"

"You've told me enough stories," she said. "It was the right thing to do."

"I agree," he said softly. "Especially after meeting you." He reached for her and she let him pull her to nestle safely against his side. "The more I have to deal with all this Andi, the less convinced of anything I become," he admitted. "I'm inclined now to think that what we do becomes our destiny. And all I want to do is be with you."

"But don't you get it, dragon? All of this is just a game. None of it is real," she said, looking up.

He kissed her forehead and willed it to flow through to her overheated mind and then chucked her chin over so that she was looking at the mirror they were reflected in, showing him wrapped around her. "This is real, princess. I don't care if I'm fate's plaything, as long as I'm at your side."

He saw her give him a bittersweet smile in their reflection, and then she looked up with a gasp. "Damian...all those people my brother has in cages...they're in there for nothing! It's never going to work!" She paused and her eyes went wide. "And they're skinning my brother for nothing, too," she whispered, horror at the thought of it racing across her face.

"You don't owe those Hunters or your brother anything, Andi," he said, squeezing her protectively. "They made their choices, and so be it."

"That's heartless," she complained with a frown.

"Guess you're still more human than dragon, it seems," he said, nuzzling against her. "And thank goodness for that. Someone has to be the beautiful one without scales." He gently kissed her forehead again, then pulled back. "It's really not safe for me to be here, Andi. If I were a Hunter with any kind of sense, I'd be watching this building with heat vision right now, and as we both know, I am very hot," he teased, and she punched him lightly as she groaned. He chuckled, stroking her arms with both hands, happy to feel her against him once more. *How had he ever gotten so lucky as to win her love?* "Really, princess, are you going to be all right?" he asked. Her eyes were still puffy from crying, and he could scent her past tears in the air.

She took a shuddering inhale. "I don't know. I mean, technically, I guess I have to be, seeing as I still have a date with destiny."

"Just as long as no one else cuts in line," he said, with mock ferocity.

She boggled at him then laughed, shaking her head as her fears finally melted. "I just got so scared, Damian. You know how I am. I keep waiting for things to break. It's hard enough to trust in other people when magic isn't involved. And...I want to be my own person. Always." She leaned even closer to him and held on. "So being with you, like this, it's like standing on the edge of a cliff and knowing I'm going to jump. Oh, hell, I've already jumped, and now I'm just scared of the landing."

"Princess, you don't ever have to land when I have wings for us," he told her, and meant it, holding her tightly back. "I would fly with you anywhere, and never let you fall."

She gave a soft gasp and looked up at him, the dark brown of her eyes soft and inviting, like the richest fur. He couldn't help but kiss her—nor she him, he knew, as he felt her leaning up.

Their lips met, tentatively at first, and it was such a bad idea, but when she pulled back to whisper, "Quickly?" how could he not respond? His hands went for her waist in answer, as her mouth came back for his. She kissed him deeply as he furiously worked the buttons and zippers of her jeans down, his hands chasing her hips, already rocking in invitation. He wrapped an arm around her and slowly lowered them both to the floor, holding himself above her, as her hands wound in his hair and against his scalp to hold him there, finally kissing her back, pressing his tongue into her mouth like it belonged there. One of his hands sank just below the denim of her jeans to stroke the soft cotton of her underwear against her and feel her wetness already soaking through.

"I want to taste you," he moaned.

She curled up and grabbed his shirt, peeling it up his back and off. "There's no time," she said, as her hands chased down his naked chest to land on the waistband of his own jeans. "Hurry," she pleaded. "I just need you in me. Now."

He growled without thinking. Her words provoked a reaction in him—like he was a fuse, and she'd just lit a match. "Yes," he agreed quickly, his voice rough, raising himself up to help push his own jeans down, as she shifted gears to wriggle out of her shirt beneath him, squirming her way out of her pants. His hard-on swung out just over the level of his jeans for her.

"I want to lick you and suck you and do all sorts of things, but...." she began.

"That's my line, princess," he said with a laugh, leaning over her, sliding his fingers underneath her underwear this time to push in. "But I think you can take me now," he said appreciatively, then grinned. "I've trained you well," he added, clearly teasing.

Andi laughed below him, trailing a hand down his chest. "Don't get used to it."

"I promise I never will," he said, pulling his fingers out. He used her juices to slick his cock and then held himself over her, arching his hips to bring himself into position as she rose up on her own to take him in. The thick head of his cock pushed against her and he started stroking forward. "Andi," he hissed, her heat enveloping him. She was his mate—now and always—and fucking her would always feel this good.

"Go faster, Damian," she whispered, wrapping her arms around his neck and breathing in his ear as he landed. "I don't need to come; I just need you to finish this time. I want to feel you so deep in me I know no one else could ever pull us apart." Her hips moved in his time like proof of her words, and she moaned as he thrust again. "Fuck destiny, Damian...and fuck me."

He made an inhumane sound and took her at her word. He needed her. He was her mate, and she needed him. He was risking everything right down to his life right now to fuck her, and if that wasn't love—an insane and perverted kind of love, but love none-theless—he didn't know what it could possibly be.

"Oh, God, yes," she whispered. Her breath was hot against his neck when he wasn't devouring her with kisses. His hands cradled her head from the floor so that he could maul her shoulder and jaw, licking up her neck in broad stripes that made her shiver and her nipples ache. He knew because she reached between them to grab and pull them and everything was speeding up, and he was taking her faster still. He felt like a ticking bomb and he knew if he didn't come in time he might explode. "Come for me," she panted.

"Is that what you want?" he growled in her ear.

His mate nodded helplessly. He knew why she liked it, because feeling him lose himself, coming for her—those were the only times she knew she was in control. That somehow, she—a human girl still, who didn't want to be anything else—had somehow tamed his beast.

"All right," he agreed, pulling himself out of her, moving up her body to kneel on his heels above her hips. He'd touched himself in front of her before, but he'd never used her solely for his pleasure quite like this. He crouched forward and wound his hand in her hair, bending her neck to make her look. "Watch me, princess," he said, and started to stroke himself fast in front of her. "See just what you do to me."

She flushed red beneath him, undoubtedly knowing what was coming. He knew it probably felt dirty, which was half the fun, but he wasn't going to disrespect her without acknowledging it. "I wouldn't do this if you hadn't asked, princess."

She was breathing hard between his thighs, her breasts rising and falling, and her jaw was dropped as her eyes flashed up at him in challenge. "But I did."

He growled and leaned forward, so fucking close. No one else in his life had *ever* made him this hard.

Did she control him? *Yes.*

Was he hers?

Utterly.

He felt his orgasm surge up as his balls tightened. "Princess, I'm going to," he warned her with a grunt, and then he was coming, lacing her neck and breasts with hot silvery ropes, again and again until he finished, stroking himself through the final twitches and dragging the head of his cock through the cum he'd spattered on her cleavage, before dismounting to her side with a groan.

She swallowed and looked up at him as he let go of her hair, her brown eyes wide, innocently horrified now. Yes, well, he was still a monster, he supposed, and then he watched her draw a finger through the mess he'd made and push it between her perfect pillowy lips. Fresh heat sank in him and he knew he could've taken her again in a moment, if only they had time.

"Goddamnit, princess," he whispered. "Every fucking thing about you turns me on."

"It should," she said with a pretend pout. "Being that it's destiny and all."

"Now you believe?" he said with a snort, before pulling his jeans

CASSIE ALEXANDER & KARA LOCKHARTE

up, then he paused to look down at her disarray. "I feel like an asshole, leaving you like this, without making you come."

"You can make it up to me later, as long as you stay alive." Andi rolled up onto her knees and kissed his jaw. "Besides, someone got me all sorts of playthings to spend time with while they're away."

"Hmmm, yes, as long as you use some of them in front of your mirror." He reached behind her for his shirt.

"No, leave it here." She grabbed it on her side and tugged. "I want something that smells like you."

He beamed at her then. It didn't matter what kind of filthy things he did with her, her heart was always pure. "Andi...I—" he started, but then they both heard it, the sound of someone rushing up the stairs outside.

"Go!" she shouted, shoving him in the direction of her bathroom. He hesitated, wanting to protect her. She knew it too. "I'll be fine—as long as you are," she said, shoving him again.

He placed his hands beneath her chin and brought her up on her tiptoes to him, kissing her one more time, before releasing her and running backward, diving through her bathroom's mirror glass.

DAMIAN CAME THROUGH HIS MIRROR—SHIRTLESS and still high from the contact with Andi—and into his bedroom, where Mills, Jamison, and Ryana were waiting.

Mills took a quick step up and slapped him across the face. "Are you done being an idiot who works on his own?"

Damian cupped his cheek as Jamison gawked at the witch. Ryana looked between the two of them, vaguely horrified that someone had had the gall to put a hand on Realms royalty, and then her eyes narrowed and she asked Mills, "Should I hit him too?"

"Is everyone against me?" he asked, running a hand through his hair. He still smelled like Andi. He should've taken something of hers in return. Or just her, entirely, bringing her over here against her will.

"No," Mills snapped. "We're all *with* you. We've been *with* you this entire time. But you keep running over all our very reasonable boundaries, and for what?"

"I need her, Mills. You wouldn't understand."

Mills rose up to her full height in front of him and her braids began to ominously unwind. "You were there when Jamison and I got together. When I had to stand up against my entire coven. So, try me."

"All right, maybe you do, stand down." Damian glowered at her. The illicit thrill of being with Andi was fading under the witch's judgment. "I feel like all I do these days is apologize," he complained.

"Well, maybe if you acted in a more team-oriented fashion, you wouldn't have to apologize so frequently," Mills said, and Jamison wisely coughed instead of laughing.

Damian attempted to stare her down, but she didn't retreat. As he was still in a good mood, he had to smile. "Fine. Is there a reason all three of you are standing in my bedroom?"

"Yeah, we needed Ryana to operate the mirrors, because we were fairly sure you were walking into a trap," Jamison said.

"Well, I didn't." He gave all of them a cocky grin. "Once again, I was successful. As I am at everything I do, by and large."

"I can hit him just for fun, you know," Ryana offered.

He rolled his eyes at her, still pleased. "What kind of trap?"

"Hunter activity has increased at the ports. They've gotten in more shipments of nets and harpoons," Mills said and started pacing.

Damian groaned. "When will they give up?"

"Never, it seems," Jamison said. "And all their weapons caches have become increasingly well-guarded, past that early night."

"I assume we're tracking helicopter flight paths now?"

"Of course. There's been no movement on that front, though."

Damian looked around his bedroom, now too small to pace in what with all the others present. "Everything's going to have to come to a head eventually." His current situation chafed intolerably.

He didn't just want to scent Andi when he was lucky enough to get the chance. He wanted her permanently by his side. "What if I lured them out? Exposing myself and then we handle them, once and for all?"

Mills shook her head. "I'm tracking two hundred separate Hunters right now, Damian. That's a lot. Even for you."

He suddenly understood why she'd been so stressed. "Time to call in reinforcements? Other wardens owe us favors."

"This is true. I just hesitate...because what if the Conjunction happens while they're here, and they've left their home territories undefended?" Mills chewed on the inside of her cheek in thought. "They'd never forgive us; most of them have strong local ties." She stopped suddenly, deciding. "In any case, it's not a problem we need to solve tonight. Now that you're safe, we can see what paths the Hunters take and work on reasonable plans that aren't you taking on two hundred of them all at once."

He laughed. "All right."

"But in the meantime, no more risking yourself, Damian." The witch glared at him. "We are a *team*."

Damian put a hand on both her shoulders. "I know."

DAMIAN WATCHED them leave his bedroom, his sister turning back to give him a pretend uppercut with a snicker. As she was part dragon, it might actually hurt if she punched him—whereas Mills's slap had just been a surprise. He'd been self-absorbed lately, yes, but after everything he'd been through with Andi, who could blame him? And she'd needed him tonight, even if she wanted to pretend she didn't.

He sprawled out on his bed, thinking about Andi's letter from her mother. It changed nothing about his feelings, of course. But Andi's pain had been written all over her body when he'd gotten there. He supposed all his life he'd assumed he had a magical destiny. When you were royalty, almost everything felt preordained. But it must have been quite a surprise for her to find out that she had had one, too. One of her own, no less, not contingent on anything Damian or Danny could offer.

Is it true? his dragon asked him.

It'd been quiet when he'd been with her, surging forward only at the end when he was mounting her, then receding right after he'd come, but he knew it'd been paying attention the whole time.

Is there really a dragon trapped inside her? it pressed.

I don't think her mother would lie to her. She knew she was dying and felt that Danny's "experiment" had been successful, so...yes. He felt the creature grow pensive inside him, as if it were having a dream. *What do you think about that?*

It pleases me more than words can say, and Damian felt it, the deep rush of its pleasure, like there were a million extra nerves inside him and all of them were happy to be alive. *But,* it went on, *if she were as we are...they would hound her as they hound us, would they not?*

Damian exhaled. *They would.*

Then...I do not think that she should change. Damian felt the beast steeling itself, and all of the joy and feeling of expansion he'd been suffused with disappeared, like a full sail suddenly gone slack. *Some skies are too dark for safe flight. Let the beast inside her slumber.*

Damian agreed, of course, but he'd been given all his dreams with Andi. He realized his dragon's decision came at a much higher cost. *Thank you.*

His dragon didn't respond. He felt it disappear inside himself, to mourn its loss in silence, as his phone vibrated and he pulled it out, finding a text from Andi.

It was just Sammy, you know. Which means you could've stayed. Or... you could come back.

I can't, princess. It's not safe, and I've been informed that if I risk myself thoughtlessly again, Mills will kill me herself to save the Hunters the trouble.

Don't let her! Andi texted back with a laughing emoji.

I won't. But I do need to be more considerate. Apparently, the world is still an awful place.

Damian watched the dots on his phone twirl as she kept revising what she was sending, and then words flooded the screen. *When will all of this be over, Damian? I don't want you to do anything foolish, but I don't know how much more I can take.*

He stared at the screen, unsure how much more he could take, either, so he answered her truthfully. *Soon, princess. Soon.*

CHAPTER

FOURTEEN

After being thoroughly teased when she ran half-dressed out into the hall to find Sammy coming inside—"You're not supposed to use all the toys at once, Andi," Sammy had snarked—Andi retreated back to her bedroom to do a better job of cleaning herself up, setting Damian's shirt aside in particular to wear after her shower, when she'd texted him.

Was "soon" good enough? What if something she told him egged him on into danger? Then she realized she could spend the rest of her life being nervous about playing into the hands of some fucking puppeteer—or she could just live, giving up. (Which was maybe what she was meant to do? Oh, fuck it, did it matter?)

Andi pulled Damian's shirt on to sleep in. It was soft and it still smelled like him and she crawled beneath her covers. She hadn't even been using her Ambien lately because she'd been feeling like she had things to look forward to—like talking to Damian—and that helped her to go to sleep on her own. And now, with his shirt on, it was even easier for her to pretend that he was here. She pulled her blindfold down, closed her eyes, and drifted off into a mostly dream-less slumber....

Except for the one dream.

It was her, Danny, and her mom and dad and they were all out at the zoo. It was the day their father had taken that photo of them, all together, the one he wasn't in. She remembered the day vividly, how her face had been smeared with pink from cotton candy and how Danny had gotten a bag full of the wax mold creatures you could buy outside each area for quarters, a yellow wax alligator outside the reptile house, a purple gorilla in front of the apes. She could feel how hot the day had been and taste how delicious the sugar was, but it wasn't as sweet as the way their father had looked at their mother, nor the way she in return had doted on him. For one crisp moment, everything had been perfect.

"They don't belong in cages!"

She and Danny were both leaning over a wide cement berm, still many feet away from the lounging tigers, with a high wire fence in between them. She remembered hoping to find a long stick to poke them with, wanting the tigers to do more than just pant in the shade with the heat, whereas Danny had found some rocks to plink over the edge.

"They don't belong in cages!" she heard again, and it was Danny's voice. She realized he wasn't aiming for the animals at all; he was throwing the rocks at the cage on purpose, upset that it was there, that the tiger wasn't free.

"Yeah!" she said, and he looked over, seeing the light of agreement in her eyes. Almost as one they decided that he would push her up and over the berm, and then maybe she could reach the cage and climb over it because surely somewhere there was a lever and—

Their mother had come over and whisked them away, as if sensing the chaos in their hearts....

And when Andi woke up, the sun was shining brightly around the edges of her blackout curtains, and her blindfold had been knocked off sometime the prior night. She reached for her phone, out of habit, and also to figure out what time it was.

Three-thirty. She'd slept way in, for her—or not quite late

enough if she was working tonight—but she was off, right? She sat up in bed, confused about the time and date in the way that only night work made you, when you didn't know if you were coming or going and the days threatened to become a gray slide except....

There was a text from Damian. She swiped her screen on.

Princess?

Are you there?

I just wanted to check on you.

Andi smiled at her phone and texted back. *Sorry, I was sleeping.*

His reply was almost instantaneous. *I know.*

You looked??? She gave herself a brief glance in the mirror and saw the kind of bedhead that came from sleeping on wet hair.

Yes. Briefly.

Andi groaned. *Damian, I expect to have some privacy.*

I've seen you sleep before. Nice shirt, by the way.

Shut it, Mister, she typed with a grin.

She cast her phone aside and went to her desk to fish the photo of her family out. Her dream had felt so real, her emotions so genuine and warm. She wished she could rewind everything and get back to that point with Danny, back when they plotted with one another, instead of against, before their mother had pinballed them off in different directions.

I had the nicest dream, she texted, returning to her bed with the photo.

Was I in it?

Don't take it personally...but no. It was about this trip we took to the zoo as kids. Danny and I hatched this scheme to release the tigers. We were convinced they wanted to go into the air-conditioned reptile house with us. It was a hot day, you had to be there, and it'd help if you were twelve....

That sounds charming.

It was. Andi gave both her phone and the photo a soft smile. *Sometimes when I remember the good stuff, it's hard to remember the bad, Damian. And I know, that's 100% what someone who was abused would*

239

say, so don't come at me with that. It's just that...it wasn't all bad, you know?

I know, princess, he agreed.

She set the photo down and turned her smile just to the phone. *Thank you.*

For what?

For not being mad at me. For not expecting me to just cut him out of my life completely. I know he's no good, Damian, and I know everything he's done, but he's still part of me. And I know you're going to have to do what you have to do eventually, no matter how much we try to avoid the topic, and I'll still love you even after that, I'm sure...but...it's going to hurt me.

Oh, princess. I am so, so sorry.

Andi hugged a pillow to her chest. *It's okay. It's not even your fault. I mean, they're not going to stop until you do, so....*

I wish I were there with you right now.

Me too.

She stared at the phone disconsolately, willing Damian to say the right thing, even though she had no idea what that might be. *Princess, I apologize deeply, but I have to go. Mills is calling a meeting.*

The thought of that snapped her to attention. She knew Damian's group always had meetings before going out. *Be safe?*

For you? Always.

Andi reluctantly set the phone down and picked the photo up.

DAMIAN JOINED the others in the conference room and was surprised to find everyone else present and somber. It was clear Mills had sent Grimalkin to call him last. Max was wearing all black and leaning forward with his head in his hands, and Ryana had her wings hidden and a deep frown. Zach was in one of his tailored suits and his arms were crossed, while Austin looked rumpled in jeans and a flannel and had that look in his eye that said he'd rather be anywhere else but here. Stella was the only one who seemed as clueless as he was, again in her motorcycle leathers, and with her helmet sitting in front of her. He guessed she'd just arrived.

"Everyone here appears to be alive, yes?" he said, making his way to his familiar seat at the table's head.

"For now," Mills said with a frown. She was in jeans and a tight death metal T-shirt, like she'd been thinking too hard to get dressed for the current occasion, whatever it was. She gave Jamison a meaningful glance. His techmaster lit up the wall to Damian's right.

"The Hunters are taking their armaments to Cyclo Arena," Jamison said. He was in one of his usual tank tops and had his wrist plugged into the technology beneath the table. "They've been shipping trucks in and out all day." The screen flickered between still shots of nondescript dressed men and women moving boxes around with dollies.

"Well, then, I'll make it a point not to go there." Damian shrugged.

Mills nodded. "That's well and good, but...there's a car show starting there this evening."

Damian smirked. "Did someone enter my Pagani without me?"

"No. It's a vintage thing. And there's one Daniel Ngo and his fully restored 1970 El Camino registered to attend," Jamison said. "The car show opens tonight at seven, but earlier for participants."

Damian rocked back, as realization washed over him. The closest the Hunters had gotten to hurting him was the night with the helicopter—a trick they hadn't tried again. So, it seemed in their frustration that they'd adjusted their scope.

Because if you couldn't kill one dragon...perhaps another would do.

"Let him die, Damian," Ryana said, the quickest to speak. "In this case, the enemy of my enemy is indeed our friend, and if they take him off the board, then your hands are clean. It's perfect."

"I agree with Ryana," Max said. "This is a Hunter problem. Let Hunters deal with it."

Damian looked to Mills. "How sure are you?"

"It's the only thing that makes sense," Mills said. "Although he has his own people to protect him, surely, and they're fools to think they won't come after him."

"Not if all of his people are currently in cages at an undisclosed location trying to become dragon soldiers." Damian spoke through gritted teeth.

"What?" Stella said, snapping her head to look at him.

"Danny took Andi out last night and showed her his lair. It includes people in cages, apparently, waiting to become draconic. He thinks he needs an army against the Conjunction."

"Well, poor planning on his part then," Mills murmured.

Damian looked to the other wolves. Zach shook his head. "I'm out on this one. I have opinions, but I don't think you want to hear them."

"I always want to know what you think, Zach."

"Then, in that case, I'm aligned with Ryana and Max. My heart says you should intervene, but the man who wears this suit," Zach said, tugging at his cuffs, "says fuck him."

Damian grunted. The man who "wore" Zach's suit frequently looked like his father, and that was indeed something his father would say. "And you, Austin?"

Austin leaned forward with a heavy sigh. "You're boned, D. You can swear all of us to secrecy, and we'll give it, but if Andi finds out you just let him die...." Austin's voice drifted as he shook his head.

"Is there a way to help him that isn't also a suicide mission?" Stella asked, looking around the table in hope.

"There is one way," Jamison began. "I've gotten Danny's phone number from Andi's phone. He doesn't leave it on too often though, which makes it shit for tracking, but there's a number he contacts regularly. It's not programed in—he has it memorized—and if I were a betting man, I'd guess it was his uncle."

"So, you're going to call a leader of the Hunters and ask him for his help?" Zach's tone conveyed just what he thought of that idea.

Damian considered his options quickly. "I can't call Danny; he wouldn't believe me. I know that from last night. And telling Andi to tell him would only put her in danger, I know, and he probably still wouldn't listen, besides. So, yes, I'll try calling Lee, and ask him to rein in the others. It's the least bad idea in the bad idea barrel. Grim?" Damian called, and the cat appeared. "I need a balaclava and a burner phone."

The cat sat down just out of reach on the table, blinked, and both items fell from the ceiling.

"I'll never get used to that," Stella murmured as Damian pulled his mask on.

"What's the number?" he asked Jamison, who projected it on the wall behind himself. Damian backed up so that no one else would be visible and called on video. Jamison projected that so the others could see too, although Lee would only see Damian's masked face on his screen.

Lee was a slightly-past-his-prime Asian gentleman with a tidily trimmed beard, and Damian could see the slight resemblance between him and Andi, in the bright intelligence of their eyes, which narrowed on the screen. "Interesting," he said, at seeing Damian. "Speak, or I'll hang up."

"I'm calling on behalf of the Ngo twins."

Lee made a thoughtful sound. "I'm listening. Be quick."

"Danny...Daniel...is in danger."

Lee sounded amused. "Is that so?"

"You left town, left him on his own and left other Hunters, hungry. They're planning an attack on him tonight."

Lee's eyes narrowed. "You presume to know much, stranger."

"I know that other Hunters are planning to murder Danny."

Lee laughed once, harshly. "My people will protect him, as if he were me."

"Your nephew, in his infinite wisdom, decided to turn your people into a dragon army. They're all currently in cages," Damian informed him. He could sense the far older man's reluctance to believe. "Find out for yourself," he said, hanging up. He set down the phone and pushed the mask off his face.

"I like how he doesn't disagree that his people are capable of killing his nephew, so much as he thinks they'd be too scared to," Zach said, one eyebrow high.

"He knows who they are," Damian muttered, then looked around. "Max, start adding fuel to the Forgetting Fire. If we're going to do something this public, we're going to need a fucking river of it to cover up the damages."

"It sounds like you've made up your mind regardless, Damian," Mills said. "Have you?"

If he'd left off with meeting Andi's brother in person last night, maybe things could've gone a different away. But after being with her last night, and texting with her earlier—while someone else might get frustrated with her for not choosing—he understood. He knew it took a big heart to love himself, flaws and all, as he knew he had a lot of them. He was temperamental, he could be cruel, cold, imperious, demanding, and there was every bit as much blood on his hands as there was on Danny's, even if he liked to think it more cleanly earned. If Andi was able to still love him, in spite of himself and his problems—and even with his curse!—then it was no wonder some small part of her still loved her brother, too.

And knowing that her brother had been murdered in cold blood by his "friends" to be eaten for his magical properties was not something his gentle mate could so easily return from.

So, we've decided then? his dragon asked him. *To help this other dragon?*

For Andi's sake. Do you agree?

He felt his dragon thinking free of him. *There will be a lot of carnage?*

As many Hunters as there are drops of rain, sounds like.

Then I go where you lead. The beast flexed inside of him. *As long as we always lead to Andi.*

Damian looked around the table at each of his friends, and none of them looked away. "I realize I can't ask you all to come with me. If Mills is right, which we all know she is, then we'll be walking into a firefight with several hundred well-armed Hunters, all of whom would like to see our blood."

"Yours, in particular," Ryana reminded him. Her frown was unchanged.

"I know," he said, and the phone rang. Everyone present looked at it and then looked to Damian.

He pulled his mask back down and answered it, Jamison projecting Lee's image on the wall again.

"There appears to be truth to your words."

"Can you help him?" Damian asked.

"No." Lee's jaw tightened. "And you must have known that when you called." Lee's expression became more menacing as he leaned closer to his phone. "So who are you?"

"Someone willing to try to save him."

Lee looked puzzled. "Daniel cannot possibly mean that much to you. What is it you want?"

Damian stared down into the phone and let the impassive wall he used to keep his dragon at bay overtake him. "I want carte blanche," he said coolly. "I want permission to murder every Hunter we find there, without retribution later."

"Very well," Lee promised. "Do not let a single traitor live." Damian heard his sister snort, as Lee went on. "But what on earth could possibly cause you to risk your life for Daniel?"

"I'm not doing it for Danny, Hunter. I am the dragon that's in love with your niece." Damian reached up and pulled off his mask, as Mills gasped and Zach started wildly shaking his head across from him. "I'm not saving Danny for you or for him. But for Andi, I would do anything—and finding out that men like you slaughtered her brother will break her." He threw the mask on the table.

For the first time a genuine emotion, amazement, penetrated Lee's stern facade. "A dragon. In love with Mei Li's girl." He stroked his beard as he mused. "Truly, fate is unpredictable."

Damian gave Lee a withering look, and let some of his magic echo out in his voice, while allowing his dragon to ride just beneath his skin. This would be as much its fight as it was his. "You wanted to know what ties would bind me to earth, human," he said, his voice like gravel. "Andi has chained my heart."

Lee took a sharp inhale and licked his lips. "Go then, Andrea's dragon. Win," he said, and Damian hung up the phone.

ANDI HAD JUST EATEN LUNCH, if you went by the time of day, or breakfast, in that it was her first meal of the day and that it also had been cereal, when her phone buzzed again.

Hey, you know how sweet my car is, right?

She would've known who was texting her without seeing the name. *Debatably, yes.*

Her brother sent over an eye-rolling emoji. *Well, I've got it entered at this car show. They've got free early entry for participants. Wanna come check it out with me?*

She squinted at her phone. Her life felt like it was getting more complicated which, at this point, was entirely unfair. But...she did have to tell Danny to let those people out, somehow, without letting on how she knew that his experiments would never work on them.

I'll buy you cotton candy, he went on, and she smiled at her phone.

Diabetes on a stick? You'd do that for me?

Yeah, I think there's probably 75 cents still stuck inside my car somewhere.

That car's so old it's probably seven hundred fifty dollars now, with inflation.

Another laughing emoji. *Actually, the Elky's already at the show. I dropped it off yesterday. Can you bus in or uber to Cyclo, and I meet you at the doors at five-fifteen to get you in?*

Her eyebrows rose in bemusement. At least if she took the bus in, she wouldn't be treated to Danny's driving, and there was no way she could accidentally wind up at a pool hall. *Sure.*

Sweet. See you soon.

Andi went through the rest of her "morning" while Sammy was still at work. She combed out her hair, hit it with a flat iron just because it'd been ages since she'd gone out, and put makeup on for the same reason too. She and Sammy had redone the blue streak not that long ago, back when Damian had been in his "alive" phase, so she was particularly pleased with the color, and planned her entire outfit around showing it off—dark blue jeans, low gray ankle boots, and a tight white T-shirt that made her hair and features pop. Then she took the shirt off and replaced it with Damian's because she wanted to, and she could.

His shirt was more appropriately a nightshirt on her, like she'd worn it the prior night to be, but eff that. She tied the excess fabric in an off-center knot at her waist, cropping it up. She was going to a car show; she could show a little skin.

And then at four-thirty she caught the appropriate cross-town bus to Cyclo, getting off it at precisely five-fifteen. She hadn't figured out what or how to tell Danny in the meantime, but she knew she'd think of something.

"You made it!" Danny announced, seeing her walking up.

"I'm the on-time one, remember?" Andi told him.

"See also: judgmental and one most likely to drink haterade."

"But also most beautiful and smart," she corrected. "The haterade makes my skin glow."

Danny laughed. "Come on in," he said, gesturing her over with a ticket.

"So you're going to explain what we're looking at to me?" she said as they queued in line for wristbands. It was a hot day; she'd been wise to leave her coat and purse at home and just load up her pockets.

"All our childhood, all those cars, and none of them stuck?" he asked, reaching over to tap her head as she ducked.

"No, nursing school pushed all nonessential information out of my head. What's your name again?"

"Oh, that's low," he said, grabbing his chest and looking pained before rebounding and giving her a look. "So, what, like, now that I know about your man, you're just flaunting him at me now?" His eyes indicated her shirt.

Andi inhaled sharply. "Would you believe that nursing school also pushed out the fact that dragons can smell other dragons?"

"Sure," Danny said with a shrug, shaking his head before giving her a lopsided grin, half-poisonous, half-pure. "Why not."

Once inside, the arena opened up, and the entire floor of it was parked full of all sorts of vintage cars. There weren't too many people yet, and she guessed most of the owners gravitated toward their own cars for quick inspections. She followed Danny's lead and he took her over to a neon green car, which had a square of paper underneath a windshield wiper, announcing it was a 1970 Plymouth Duster.

Andi looked at the car. It was a car, just like any other car, only greener, and then looked at her brother, who'd ditched her to peer in the windows and make out the smaller writing on the tag. She pulled her phone out of a pocket and turned around to snap a desultory selfie with the car over her shoulder and started texting Damian.

Danny was back at her side in an instant. "Who're you texting?"

"You know very well who I'm texting."

"Should I be in the photo?"

"Probably not. Besides, he'll see the cars and know I'm out with you."

"What does he think about that?" Danny asked, frowning, as she finished typing the words to go along with the photo—*just gotta tell him about the cages is all. wish me luck*—and hit send.

"I don't know. It doesn't make him happy. But he's also not a controlling jerk, so...." she said with a shrug, as they walked to the next car. "He cares about me."

"So do I," Danny said.

She raised her hand between them just like he had his the prior night, rocked it, and said, "Ehhhhhhh."

"Look, I don't have to be around you all the time. Not when we have history."

"Well, that part's true." She made a show of looking in the windows of the car they were beside, even though she didn't know what she should be looking for. "I was just remembering that one day at the zoo with the tigers. When you were so pissed off they were in cages."

Danny laughed. "I about had you over that guard rail. If Mom hadn't come by when she did, oh my God. That shit would've made the evening news for sure. And do you remember after that? All our plots?"

"Oh my gosh," Andi said, putting her hand to her mouth. "I'd forgotten." They'd spent the rest of that summer formulating plans to get the tigers out. They were going to smuggle in ropes and they stripped an umbrella of its fabric and struts so that they just had the extendable pole to help them reach the buttons. "We were so serious, weren't we?"

"Deadly so! I don't know how Mom handled us, frankly. We were kind of jerks when we teamed up."

Andi snickered and sighed, biting her lips. "Danny...you can't let them put you in a cage again."

"What, because I'm a tiger?" he asked with a glint in his eye.

"No, because you're *you*. And you've got to let all those other people go."

"I'm doing science, Andi; it's not safe," he scoffed.

"What if your 'science' never works? Or what if something happens to you? Then what happens to all them?"

"Like what?" he laughed. "I'm fucking invincible, Andi."

"You don't know that for sure," she said with a head shake.

He took a fast step closer. "What're you saying, Andi-bear? Is your man coming for me?"

"No. He would never," Andi protested, and then Damian materialized beside them. He was wearing an all-black outfit that clung to him, outlining every tensely flexing muscle, his strong arms and his broad chest, wrapping around his thighs like a hug. The outfit's color matched his hair, the stubble on his square chin, and his mood. He'd brought his storm with him; she could read it in his bearing, and his gold eyes shone like distant lighting.

She knew he wouldn't be here if there wasn't trouble, but at seeing him, she'd never felt safer.

"Both of you need to take one of these, now," he demanded, holding two marble-sized spheres on his palm. Andi remembered them from their night in the hospital, how they'd allowed them to get away safely without being seen. She took one without hesitation.

"What the fuck," Danny seethed at seeing him.

"You're in danger, asshole. I'm here to save you. Take this so you can hide," Damian said, shoving his hand farther out.

Danny picked the sphere up, held it up for inspection, and then crushed it like a grape before flicking it aside. "Fuck you."

"Danny!" She immediately got between them. "I'm sure Damian has a reason!"

"He does, and I'm looking at it," her brother growled at her. "Step aside, Andi."

"Don't change!" Damian shouted. "That's what they want!"

"Who?" Andi asked of him.

"The Hunters that've lined this arena with weapons," Damian answered, looking only at her brother. "They're coming for you. Other Hunters." He stepped closer to them both. "If you stay between Andi and me, our spheres can cover you, we can keep you protected until we get out of here."

"My people would never—" Danny began.

"The other Hunters don't give a shit, and your people are in cages," Damian growled.

Danny's eyes narrowed in on her. "You told him? Is that why you wanted me to free them? You felt guilty for playing along with his trap?"

Andi gasped. "Danny...no! There's no trap here! Damian would never lie!" She reached for him as he stepped back into a clearing. She heard the sharp report of a distant gunshot, followed by a scream.

Damian intuited what Danny was planning before she did, and started talking fast. "My people are up there, taking out Hunters, risking their lives for you because I asked them to. Don't do this, Danny. Don't waste their efforts. And don't put her in danger." Damian placed himself in front of her. "I am begging you, as a dragon, and a man. Do not do this. Please."

Danny shrugged and shook his head. "Nah. This is all your fault. Although, I suppose we both knew it would come to this, didn't we?" And then he spread his arms wide, threw his head back, and Andi didn't see what came next because Damian picked her up and ran.

ANDI YELPED in surprise and struggled against Damian, not to fight him, but because she had to see. She pulled herself up to peek over his shoulder and saw that Danny wasn't Danny anymore. He was a dragon now, slightly smaller than Damian's, four legs and two wings, and beautifully, dangerously, sinuous. Instead of gold, he was a deep army green, almost the color of his Elky. Screams started up behind them on all sides.

"Oh God, Damian." She didn't bother to ask if his story was true. Of course it was. "How many Hunters are there?"

He set her down inside one of the cement alcoves that lead to the arena floor. "A lot." He looked over his shoulder at Danny, then gave her a haunted look. "Andi—I don't want to fight him. You have to believe me."

"I do," she said, and meant it. He stood up straight and became invisible because she wasn't inside a sphere anymore. "Shit!" she cursed. "I dropped mine—" It'd gotten jostled from her hand when he'd grabbed her.

"Take mine," Damian said, planting his into her hand.

251

"No!" She shook her head quickly, trying to give it back. "The Hunters—they know who I am. They know not to shoot me. My uncle would—"

"I don't think we can risk your life on them being afraid of him right now." A herd of people were running down the hall behind them, none of them sparing them a glance inside their bubble of magic, although Damian was having to shout to be heard above their screams. "I need you to be safe, Andi. I can survive anything as long as I know that you're all right," he told her, and she realized he was leaving.

She stood straighter and slammed both her fists against his chest, finding it rock hard, like his dragon was waiting, just underneath. "You have to come back to me!"

Everything about him softened, just for a moment, and he leaned into her hands. "Of course, princess. It's fate," he said, then pulled away and ran into the crowd behind them, going against the flow.

DESPITE THE FACT that all his dragon wanted to do was change and wrestle Danny, Damian knew that wasn't very smart. His crew kept reporting in via earpieces. No casualties so far, but the tide of Hunters hadn't slowed, and a few of the Hunters had talismans that let them see through the spheres's magicks, so clearing them out wasn't going as fast as they had hoped.

He ran back into the arena and up a set of stairs, knowing that Danny could likely smell him, but he needed to make it to the second level quickly because Jamison was in his ear shouting out the location of the nearest harpoon.

"Second floor, section C, behind the sound station!"

"I see it," Damian grunted, running flat out.

It would be faster if we flew, his dragon complained, likely because he himself wanted to change.

And give them two targets?

They are mere humans, his dragon sniffed.

Who still managed to orchestrate all this. Damian was nearing the Hunters now. There was a group of them still trying to get their weapon in place.

The harpoons were heavy and unwieldy and they hadn't gotten to bolt the launchers into the ground so they had them wedged in between steep rows of seating, and they were aiming it as a group. One of them saw him nearing but then ignored him entirely, likely thinking that he was just some lost car aficionado, racing up out of fear, until he reached them and started throwing the men and women there aside like rag dolls, not caring how they landed or if he hurt them. When he was done, he pulled the whole assembly free, yanking out the harpoon to bend it against his knee, before stomping a dent into the launcher's barrel. "Next?" he demanded.

"Same spot, two floors up!"

Damian looked up at the wide shelf of concrete above him. "Fuck."

Now? his dragon asked, waiting, longing to go back to Danny.

No. Not yet. We have to take these fucking things out first.

Why?

Because! Damian shouted at it, but then they both saw their answer. A harpoon sailed out from above, aiming at Danny, who had been pacing the arena floor with his bulk. It missed, landing just beside him, but it exploded still, and suddenly Danny's dragon turned, looking at where it'd just been shot from. Danny's dragon hurled itself into the sky, hovering, before coming straight at them.

"Duck, duck, duck!" Mills shouted in his ear, but he didn't. Damian was pinned in awe. He hadn't seen another dragon in flight since his father had died, he'd forgotten how glorious their passage was.

Danny's dragon reared its neck back sixty feet overhead, and then spewed out fire. Two floors below Damian was still buffeted by its heat. He knew all the Hunters above were dead, and he heard the sounds of the rest of the munitions there exploding.

And then Danny's dragon turned to look at him.

"We're on the same side," Damian bellowed, wondering if it could hear him. But before he could find out, another harpoon shot across the arena and hit Danny's flank, exploding and shoving him sideways. The dragon howled and whirled in midair, turning to chase this new assailant down.

Other harpoons popped off, their nylon tails stretching behind them like streamers, like the car show below them was being decorated for a particularly bloody prom. Not all of them hit, and not all of them were explosive, but they were harrying him, and soon Danny's green-scaled bulk was dotted with harpoons, making him look like a toreador's bull at the end of a fight. Damian felt his own dragon sink in on itself internally, finally understanding.

"We took out half of them Damian, but there's just too—" Jamison began on his earpiece.

"I know," Damian cut in, racing for the railing to watch what was happening below. Danny's dragon had been knocked back to the floor of the arena, where it was picking up cars to hurl at the people that shot at it. It shrieked defiance with each new blow, writhing itself left and right, casting about itself in a circle of fire. Its wings were so shredded, they'd take too long to heal, so it couldn't fly again now if it tried. He hoped like hell that Andi'd gone, as he cupped his hand to his earpiece to shout, "Tell everyone to keep going!"

ANDI WAS ENTIRELY sure she should have left but she just couldn't. The rational part of her brain had taken the first bus and was half-way home, but the rest of her, the things that made her *her*, all her emotions and guts and blood, kept her pinned here, hiding just inside the cement alcove where Damian had left her, watching her brother fight.

And...lose.

It didn't matter that he was a dragon. He kept healing, but they kept fighting him, shooting him with horrible things that looked like spears. Oh, God, fucking *harpoons?* They'd already knocked him out of the sky and now massive metal nets were dropping down, the size of a basketball court. He kept burning things and thrashing and throwing cars, but there was nothing he could do. The hunters were too far away to attack and they were pinning him to the ground.

All of that power he'd been imbued with, all of the torture that he'd tolerated, and it was going to end here for him. Like this.

Alone.

Or not...because she started running for him. It was the absolute stupidest thing she could do, but she couldn't listen to the dragon—*her brother, Danny!*—howl in pain and not respond. Not as a nurse... and not as a sister.

"Danny!" she shouted, so he would know she was coming for him, running around the wreckage of burning cars, trying to see him through the smoke. "DANNY!"

She saw his grand head raise, trying to see her, straining against the nets. A harpoon speared out of his neck, and she could see the spurting green of his blood. "I'm here, Danny!" she cried, racing up beneath him, getting splashed.

But his eyes wouldn't focus on her and he was looking around wildly.

"I'm here!" she shouted. His head fell to look directly at her, his wide nostrils taking monstrous inhaling breaths, and she realized he couldn't see her with the sphere, only smell her, and she smelled like Damian. "It's not a trick! It's me!" She threw the sphere away, revealing herself, and Danny bent his head to acknowledge her with a sorrowful sound.

He didn't sound human anymore, and she didn't think the Hunters would stop now, even if he did.

"Step away from the dragon, girl," someone with an Australian accent told her. She turned to see Jack there, with his omnipresent ivory toothpick, and a beautiful Latina woman by his side.

"At this point, why save her?" Xochitl said, unsheathing her bone sword.

Danny snaked up a protective paw around her, and flapping the remnants of his wings against the nets that pinned him ineffectually. Andi struggled to bring one of his claws down so that they could see her speak. "You don't want to do this," she warned them.

"Andrea, we're not afraid of your uncle," Jack said with a rough laugh.

Andi stepped onto Danny's lowest claw to gain more height and shook her head. "That's not who's coming."

CHAPTER

FIFTEEN

Damian had forced himself to wait for the last possible moment as Danny roiled, trapped on the ground. The more Hunters that were drawn away from their caches of nets and harpoons, the better. Mills reported in that they were leaving their stations in droves, each of them so eager to get a knife into Danny's side.

But then he'd seen Andi, running for the other dragon.

Of course, she hadn't left him.

He should've known there'd be no way. The second Danny was injured, her path had been set. By fate or destiny—take your pick—she was going to fight by his fool side.

Just as he was destined to do anything to protect her.

"I know what you're thinking, brother," Ryana said, panting from exertion, over their intercom. The only reason he'd let her come on this mission was because if things went south, there'd be no one left at his castle to protect her. "Don't."

A wave of Hunters reached the arena floor and were racing for Danny as one.

Damian leapt up to the cement railing in front of him. "Ryana, if you're lucky, someday you'll also be mated...and you'll know I never had a choice." He pulled out his earpiece and let himself *go.*

His dragon rose up and overtook him, and for a brief moment they were one and the same. He felt the expansion of its wings, felt the glory of its strength, and heard himself trumpet a challenge with its throat, until he was compressed back inside to the place he stayed when it ran wild.

It launched itself off of the railing, soared briefly overhead, and then landed purposefully in the midst of the Hunters running in, roiling its tail to swipe whole herds of Hunters sideways, flapping its wings to knock down more and building up fire in its throat.

Damian didn't need his dragon to tell him that it was happy, as it shoved at the nearest burning car with its paw, sending the hot metal skidding back into another row of fighters. It was in its element, using all its senses, tracking and triangulating, as it waded through the attacking Hunters. Bone swords chipped at its scales, and talismanned daggers pricked, but he was a dragon, a mighty beast, and there was nothing that any human could do to stop it. He roared flames at them, catching even more cars on fire, and he would kill and keep killing until Andi was safe.

"No!" he heard her shout, and then she wailed.

His dragon snapped its head in her direction and ran forward on all fours. A woman with a bone sword was there, plunging it into Danny's side, and Andi was trying to get free of her brother's claws to fight her.

"Stop!" Andi shrieked, and Damian would never fully know what had happened next, only that he was not himself. He blew out gouts of flame, instantly vaporizing the Hunters on both of Danny's sides, and then raced up on the hobbled dragon, whipping the woman away from Danny with his muzzle, getting a close up look at her unlined face and the rime of green around her mouth from Danny's blood as he tossed her back thirty feet.

Andi didn't stop howling. She was free of Danny's claws now, and she ran for his side where the sword was still embedded, jumping up to grab hold of it and pull it out. "Danny!" she screamed, and he could scent the salt of her tears as she threw the sword away behind her and sobbed against Danny's scales, ineffectually trying to wrap her brother in a hug, as the dark green dragon's body went slack.

Damian was conscious of the fight still continuing around him—his people fighting Hunters, Hunters trying and failing to fight him, but everything narrowed down to this one moment, witnessing the thing he'd been trying to stop from happening this entire time.

Danny was dead.

Andi stumbled back from her brother's side, holding herself, deep in pain, moaning, taking gasps of air in like she might never breathe again.

His dragon shoved him forward in an instant, knowing that she needed him on a human scale, to be touched by human hands. The men who'd been fighting against him lurched forward as their opponent disappeared, and he ignored them, running through piles of smoking debris to get to her side.

"Princess!" he called for her the second he was near. She stumbled back to standing and ran for him, falling against him, sobbing.

"Dragon," she whispered. "You were too late." She shuddered with tears. "He's gone."

"Oh, my princess," he said, soothing her, stroking her back and hair, feeling her wet tears fall against his naked chest. And beyond all the chaos, the sounds of things catching fire and exploding, and the ever-diminishing screams, Damian heard a familiar sound.

The crackling of Forgetting Fire.

The battle was through. Mills must have called it, and now it was Max's turn, and before they'd left his castle, they'd upgraded the bear-shifter from lantern to a flamethrower. He saw gusts of bright orange flame past Danny's body, returning the arena to what it once was prior to all their magical damage—and the confused look of any remaining Hunters trapped in its path, who'd just had all their knowledge of what'd happened taken from them.

"He's gone, Damian. And now it's just me." She looked up at him with an expression of pure sorrow, and it was like he could feel the very breaking of her heart. It made his break for her.

"Andi," he whispered, holding her tight. He could feel the heat of the Forgetting Fire at his back, and turned them so that it was at hers instead, bowing his head to touch hers, saying words only she could hear. "It's not too late to fight your destiny, princess, and I can take away your pain."

She blinked up at him, eyes red with tears, eyeliner smudged. "How?"

"The same as I first offered you in the pond. If you turn around and stare into the Forgetting Fire, it will be as if none of this ever happened. You can forget the nature of your brother's death, your uncle...and me. All of this will go away. It will not bring him back, but at least you won't carry the burden of these memories. And I'll understand if that's your wish, although it will destroy me." Damian felt her gasp as he continued. "But if you can manage it, princess, then you should know that I will be at your side forever. And you will grieve, yes, but I will make sure that you are happy, too."

She stared up at him and ran her hands into his hair, trapping his face to hers. "Do you really think that I could ever choose to forget you? No matter how bad things got?"

"No," he said, giving her a soft, sad smile. "But I didn't want to just trust in fate, Andi. I wanted to have faith in you. I love you with all my heart."

His hand rose up to dry her tears, and she kissed his palm as it neared. Then she closed her eyes, ducking her head against him as he lifted her up, cradling her in his arms to walk her away from the worst of it, while casting his gaze around. "Is everyone safe?" he called.

Ryana piped up first. "I saved his life!" She leapt on top one of the magically restored vehicles and Damian could see several tears in her wings as she pointed wildly at Austin.

"Just the once," the werewolf grumbled, stepping out between other cars.

"Stella...stop!" they heard Zach shout, and everyone turned. The weregirl had her gun trained on a kneeling man. He had khakis on and a mint green polo smeared with ash. A toothpick jutted out between his lips.

"I know him!" Stella shouted back, as Zach strode up to press her gun down.

"But he doesn't know you," he growled at her, pointing at the pool of urine growing by the Hunter's knees. "Not anymore. They've all forgotten."

"I don't care. He killed my brother," Stella said, her voice like ice.

"I didn't! I swear!" the Hunter pleaded, his toothpick falling to the ground.

"Shut up," Zach and Stella both told him at once, and then glared at one another.

"He is not innocent, and I will never forgive him," she swore.

"I'm not asking you to. I'm just saying don't murder him in cold blood."

"You're not in charge of me," she growled, but Zach stood his ground. She reholstered her weapon and pulled out her earpiece to throw at his feet. She then stalked for the nearest exit, abandoning their team. The other werewolf watched her go.

Max walked up with his flamethrower. "Everyone alive has been wiped except for us. But I still have a ton of clean-up to do."

"I've been diverting the authorities as best I can," Jamison reported, with the glazed look he had when he was communicating with technology. "I can give us at most another fifteen minutes, but then the cavalry's gonna hit here, hard, so we need to get out of Max's way."

"We've got a real 'call me Ishmael' situation happening here, Damian," Austin said, coming closer.

"Is this where I say yippee-kai-yay?" Ryana asked Austin, and Austin chuckled.

Andi squirmed and he delicately put her down as Mills came up. "Andi...about your brother."

"I know," Andi whispered, and Damian realized she hadn't yet turned back around. "I was here the whole time. You all did the best you could. Thank you for trying, I know it was dangerous." She held herself and Damian wrapped his arms around her, trying to shoulder some of her burden. "I just wish he'd believed me."

Damian watched Mills's eyes widen at something behind him, and whirled, crouching defensively.

"What if he did?"

ANDI WASN'T sure she could believe her ears. Because the person she'd heard sounded an awful lot like Danny, right down to the cocky tone of voice. She turned right after Damian did, and there was her brother, smeared with green, one eye swollen shut, holding a scrap of upholstery leather over his crotch.

"Danny?" she asked, her voice going high.

Her brother looked past her at the rest of Damian's crew. "Man, you guys are like a well-oiled machine."

Andi shoved Damian aside and walked up to him. "You're alive?"

"No, I'm totally a ghost dragon now."

"Fuck you," she told him, as she wrapped him up in a hug.

He grabbed her with his free arm. "Fuck you too," he said back, laughing.

When their hug was over, Damian loomed near. "How," he demanded.

"Well about the time you started shouting we were on the same side, I realized you were right, but it was too fucking late for me." Danny looked around them and Andi saw his eyes light on his car with relief. He started angling there and she followed. "By then the only way I could help was to let them capture me, so that they wouldn't be manning those harpoon launchers against you." He jerked his chin at Damian, and she heard Damian grunt. "The only way to get them away from those things was to play on their greed, and nothing makes a Hunter lust more than the thought of tasting dragon."

"I wouldn't know," Damian said dryly from her side.

Danny was in front of his car now, looking at it from all directions. "What happened to your keys?" Andi asked with a snort.

"Since when has a lack of keys ever stopped me?" He gave her an eyeroll, switched his loincloth to his ass, and bent over to do something with the side door. It sprang open, and he pulled out a set of clothes inside. "Give me a second. I can't take myself seriously hanging out all au natural like this dude."

Andi covered her eyes while her brother changed, while noticing that Damian never once looked away. He didn't trust her brother in the least...which was probably for the best.

"And," Danny went on, now in another Nike shirt and jeans, "I knew Andi was still going to fight beside me. Which meant that you were going to fight for her. And likely save my sorry ass in the process." He shrugged with his entire body and then winced. "I trusted in fate, pretended to be struggling more than I was for a little bit—distracting many of the Hunters from you, by the way, and you're welcome...and now I'm fine."

"I saw her stab you, Danny," Andi said.

"But was it a dragon bone sword? No." He shook his head. "I mean, it hurt like hell, don't get me wrong, but we both know I've been through worse."

Andi knew he meant everything their mother had done to him. His entire separate and painful childhood without her. "Danny, would you change all this, if you could?"

His gaze softened on her and he took a long breath. "Not if having this happen to me stopped it from happening to you," he said, and Andi knew he meant it. She was and would always be his Andi-bear.

"Daniel," Damian said. "We need to know where your other people are."

Danny tore his eyes away from her to look at the other dragon. "You're going to make them forget, aren't you."

"It's the only way to keep you safe from them...and us," he said, putting a protective arm around her.

Danny shook his head and closed his eyes. "But I'm so close—"

"No, Danny, you're not. Mom left me some letters too. I found them when I got home last night, inside my old pool cue case. Right where somehow she'd known I'd look, at just the right time. She told me that you and I are the only people that can become dragons, Danny, because we were her children. Those people at your lab, you're really just torturing them."

"Screw them. You can become a dragon too?" he asked, his eyes wide.

"Yeah, but I don't want to," Andi said, shaking her head quickly.

"Can I see what she left you?"

"No. I burned them." Andi felt Damian tense in surprise beside her.

"How do I know you're telling the truth then?" Danny said, advancing on her.

She placed a hand on his chest the moment before Damian would've intervened. "If you don't trust me after all this, Danny, you really are an asshole."

Danny stared her down for half a second more, and then laughed. "All right. Fine. You win. Here's where the lab is," he said, rattling off an address. "Wipe them clean, and I'll start over some-place else."

"With Uncle Lee?" she asked.

"Most likely." His gaze lifted up to Damian's. "But I know I owe you, and I want my sister happy. You disappoint her though," he said, looking back at her, "and I'm always just a phone call away."

"I will do my best to keep her happy for the rest of her life," Damian promised.

Danny inhaled, gave a still-naked Damian a look up and down, and Andi started blushing furiously. "Yeah, 'cause you're like the whole package, huh? Emphasis on package?"

"Oh, God...Danny, I love you. Be safe, but just go away." Andi grabbed Damian's hand and started pulling him back as Danny laughed.

"I love you, too, Andi-bear," Danny called after her. "Make sure he wears a condom!"

"Fuck you," she called out over her shoulder, flipping him off with her free hand without turning around.

"Your family relationship is really strange," Ryana informed her, coming over to her side, before looking up at Damian. "Mills says we need to leave now, and she called your car."

"Good and thank you," Damian told her. "I'll see everyone at home."

"Damian, I killed so many people," his sister went on. "I was like the Terminator! Max is so proud."

Andi bit back a chuckle. "As well he should be," Damian told her, and she could hear his grin. "You can tell me all about them later on. At home," he reinforced.

Ryana turned to her. "I'm Ryana, by the way," she said, like they'd never met before, giving Damian a devilish grin. "I'm an *actual* princess."

"Ryana," he growled in irritation, and she laughed, running away from him.

"Is it really over?" she asked him now that they were alone. The arena had recovered in the same way her hospital had, everything that'd been magically imbued or damaged was gone...which actually left a lot of bodies and nonmagical harpoons behind. It looked like two angry gangs of roving whalers had done the MMA version of *West Side Story*. She didn't envy the police who were going to have to sort all this nonsense out. Who knew, maybe in a few years she and Sammy would be watching it on *Unsolved Mysteries*.

"It is," Damian told her, as they were nearing the exit. A limousine with the darkest tinted windows she'd ever seen was waiting right outside, its door already open, driver safely back in his seat. Damian strode for it like he knew it was for them, and had the graciousness to let her get in first despite his lack of clothing, pulling the door firmly closed behind himself. "The next start-up I invest in is going to be a fleet of these," he said, knocking his hand against the door. "Pay enough money and you can order up a no-questions-asked limousine, with a no-questions-asked driver. They won't mind bloodstains, sewer smells, or casual nudity."

Her eyebrows rose. "Wouldn't it just be easier to just avoid all those things?"

Damian gave her a baffled expression—on purpose, she could tell. "What would be the fun in that?"

She laughed as he leaned in to kiss her, and threw her arms around his neck, sliding up against his body. He tasted good. He tasted free, and Andi was going to spend the rest of her life making out with him...and other things....

"I bet I can make you come three times before I get you home," he murmured, the next time she came up for air. His hands were at her waist and she was already straddling him, albeit with her jeans still on.

"We are downtown, and it is rush." She cocked one hip and an eyebrow.

"Hmmm, then five," he promised, twisting her down against the limo's wide seat. "Aren't you going to bet against me?"

"Why the hell would I?" she laughed. The limo stopped, and Damian pulled himself on top of her.

"Princess," he began.

"Dragon," she teased, pushing his dark hair back.

"I want you to hear me say it. Free and clear."

Andi smiled up at him, winding her legs around his waist, pulling him to her. "Okay," she told him.

"I love you," he said, the corners of his lips curling into a smile. "I've loved you since I saw you at that bus stop the night I hired you.

I wouldn't have been able to admit it, but I saw you and I knew my life was changed."

She brought her fingers down to trace the edges of his lips. "You do realize the only reason I needed that money was because of Danny, right?"

He nipped at her fingers lightly. "So what if we're bound? Just because we're fated doesn't mean it's bad. But I have given you all the freedom that I can stand, Andi. From here on out, I need you near."

The part of her that was always afraid people were going to run away thrilled to hear it and even dared believe. "I need you near, too, Damian," she whispered.

He made a satisfied sound above her, and then animalistically licked up her jaw, before bending back and lowering his hands to her waistband.

She moved to help him. It wasn't fair that she was still in clothes when he was already all skin. She kicked off her boots and wriggled as he tugged, freeing her, and once he'd done so, he caught her nearest ankle and kissed it. She made a soft moan and sighed, as he started kissing up, and she pushed herself back on the seat so that he had as much room to lay down as she did, trailing his kisses up the inside of her calf, her knee, her thigh, giving her time to anticipate what was coming until he was finally there, his mouth buried between her legs, tongue swiping, chin grinding and she was crying out with one hand in his hair.

She'd always given herself over to him completely, holding nothing back, but now, knowing that he loved her and that this was real, everything was hot and heady, as she moaned and kicked her hips up for him, one foot arched behind him on the shoulder rest, the other on the limo's floor.

"Damian," she whispered, and she saw his ass clench in return, grinding himself against the seat, and then he pushed fingers inside her and started rubbing and she felt so good and full. "Damian," she whined his name, lifting her hips up high, his mouth following her, his gaze watching her, watching him make her come. "Oh, Damian... yes!" she shouted and thrashed, curling up as spasms took her, and he kept licking until she was so sensitive, she couldn't take it anymore. She whined again and twisted and he raised his head up from her hips to wipe his lips against her thigh.

"I have to have you, princess," he warned her, and all she could do was helplessly nod, as he crawled up her body, aligning his hips with hers, sheathing himself inside her in one bold stroke. She moaned as he landed and then caught her breath as he held himself over her, stretching her tight. "You're mine now, and you know it."

"I do," she breathed, looking up at him, running her hands up his chest and down his shoulders, kneading the muscles there.

"And the things I am going to do to you," he promised, in a tone that made her shiver.

"I don't know if I should look forward to that or run away."

He chuckled low. "I would like you running away, consensually, of course, to catch you very much. It's a predator and prey thing."

Andi swallowed, suddenly realizing just what she'd willingly signed on for and feeling ridiculously small.

"Don't tell me you're scared now, princess," Damian teased, holding himself higher over her to give her more space. "Unless you truly are, and then I want to know."

She shook her head. "Not scared. It's just...this is real now. I don't think I've ever had anything real before. Oddly, you are far less frightening than the thought of being happy for the rest of my life."

Damian tilted his head and licked his lips thoughtfully before speaking. "Reality isn't perfect, Andi. No matter my good intentions, I can't promise infinitely happy tomorrows. You know that."

Andi nodded. *His curse.* "I do. But...you want to try, Damian. And I've never had anyone want to try with me before."

He gave her a soft look. "I'm not sure if that's due to fate, princess, or that every other man in your entire life you've ever met has been a fool. But either way, yes, I do want to try."

She reached up to touch his face. "Because you're my mate," she whispered, and she felt him gently nod.

"I am. And you are mine."

She moved beneath him then in a way that she knew he'd take to mean he should keep going, and he did, slowly pulling out of her only to slowly push back in, and she made the soft sounds she couldn't help but make and that she knew he loved to hear. He held himself carefully over her, kissing her between each thrust, taking his time, as she kissed him too and ran her hands up and down the strong muscles of his back. It was like they were kindling a slow fire between them, the kind that would go out if either of them blew too hard, but if they moved just right, timing things perfectly, they both knew that it would eventually catch flame.

"Princess," he growled in her ear after kissing just below her earlobe, as she wound a hand into his hair. "Andi," he named her next stroke, starting to move faster as she moaned. "My love," he said not long after that, as Andi felt her hips begin to wind and her pussy grab him tight, as he ground his hips against hers. She heard him rumble and he mounted her deeply, so hard and arrow-straight inside. "My mate." He claimed her, and she was on the brink, moaning beneath him, so close to coming, she just needed one more stroke to rub her right, inside and out. "My mate," he purred again and ground his hips up, as if knowing what she needed.

"Damian," she warned him. She wanted him to come too, she needed it inside her.

"Yes," he promised, as she came for him with a shout of release. His hips followed hers through her spasms with strong strokes and then pressed in, keeping their seal tight as he grunted, and then his hips shuddered as he pumped himself inside her still grasping pussy, making hot groans of satisfaction in her ear. Their bodies moved as one, rocking against each other, perfectly matched, perfectly mated, just like he'd told her.

They both lay there afterward, breathless and mirrored, until he nuzzled her neck, breathing her deep. "My mate," he said reverently, then prepared to push up.

Andi wound her arms around him in an instant, holding him to her tightly. She wasn't ready to be through. "My mate," she whispered in his ear, and felt him shudder in response, at being claimed.

She was his, and he was hers.

For as long as they had.

He kissed her neck and slowly pushed himself up. She let him go, until she could see his eyes again. Damian often looked open after sex, but now, his expression was boundless. Pleased, satisfied...and hopeful.

It made her hopeful, too.

She bit her lips to stop from smiling. "I don't know if we're going to make it, Damian," she told him in a serious tone.

He blinked, focusing immediately. "How so?"

"If we keep making love instead of fucking, there's no way there's going to be time for three more orgasms before we get back to your place," Andi said and giggled as she blushed.

Damian laughed aloud. "That's rich, princess, but you assume I didn't think of that." He jerked his chin over his shoulder. "I'm paying this man an ungodly amount of money to circle downtown until I tell him not to."

"Cheater!" Andi gasped.

"Please, princess," Damian said, sounding affronted before laughing again, and beaming down. "You know when it comes to you, I'll never play fair."

EPILOGUE

Damian was at the end of an exceptionally long hallway where all the doors looked the same and were evenly spaced, and Damian knew he'd never seen a single one of them before. "It's no fair if you collude with the cat," he shouted, loud enough for her to hear.

Grim appeared out of nowhere to sit beside his feet. "Why not? I like this game."

I do too, his dragon told him.

"Both of you shush," Damian said aloud. Grim sniffed and disappeared again—likely to do more of Andi's bidding.

She'd moved in not that long ago, and while there were some adjustments to be made, things were going well so far, he thought. She seemed happy and the others liked her and she liked all of them too.

Even Grim liked her.

Which was why they got to play this game, which had been a lot more fun for him in the original lay out of the house, until she'd convinced Grim to help her cheat. Hide-and-go-seek that wound up in her running away, with squeals of fear and delight, followed by sex in unexpected places. But now with the cat helping her to hide... well, there had been the time Grim had also created an entire tree-house for her, behind one of the doors, and Damian had gotten to eat her out as she sat on a railing with what seemed like a hundred-foot drop into a forest below. Or the time she'd been hiding inside a scarf factory of some sort and he'd gotten to use reams of silk to tie her up, stringing her from the ceiling, raising and lowering her entire restrained body by a rope to suck on his cock.

All in all, Andi had a rather active imagination. He just wished she wasn't so good at hiding. This hall had at *least* ten doorways, and Grim had made all the walls thick enough to block his heat vision, and by now, she'd lived here long enough that everywhere had something of her scent—or Grim erased it for her.

Utter cheating.

You should try being more patient, his dragon told him.

You try being patient with a three-carat ring in your pocket.

I don't have pockets, it said, and broke into the dragon version of laughter.

Damian thought back, *Fuck you,* and then groused. It was stupid to be nervous. They were already mated, and he'd already given her his necklace. What was just a ring?

Then he laughed at himself. His mate was in here somewhere, waiting for him to pounce, and no matter what surprises she had in store, he was sure his was slightly better.

"Ready or not, here I come," he shouted, as was apparently traditional on Earth. He stormed into the first room and found it empty except for Andi, dressed simply in jeans and a T-shirt, and sitting cross legged on the ground behind a candle.

"There's not a trapdoor between you and me, is there?" he asked from the doorway.

She laughed. "No, but you really shouldn't give me any ideas."

"I take it back then," he said, walking over to her and sitting down on the candle's far side. "Wax play?" he guessed, with a smile.

"No...well...maybe? But not right now." She shifted and pulled a piece of paper out of her back pocket, before he could pull anything out of his. "You know what this is, right?" she asked, showing it to him.

He recognized it, of course. Her mother's letter from that troubling night. "I do."

"You haven't mentioned it again," she said, holding it in her lap.

"Because it's not mine to mention."

She unfolded the paper, without looking down. "You know I told Danny I'd burned it."

He nodded. "And I had a feeling that was a lie, but again, I wasn't going to press."

Her gaze caught his and he saw the worry in her eyes. "What does your dragon think of this?"

"That's easy to answer. He wants you to be safe, and has told me so repeatedly."

"You're safe now," she said, like that was an answer.

"For now," he corrected her. "But we both know that can change. Which is one of the reasons we play so roughly, I think," he said, looking around the room Grim had created for her, remembering all the other ones they'd shared. "How do you feel about that, princess?" he asked, gesturing to what she held.

"I think I like who I am, just the way I am now," she told him. "I just hope that that's not disappointing."

Knowing what he'd picked tonight here to do, to propose to her, wholeheartedly.... "No, princess. There is no possible way you could ever disappoint me." He gave her a mystified look. "Has this been worrying you this whole time?" He offered her his arms and lap, and she crawled around the candle to take them, nestling against him like a cat, wrapping her arms around his body.

"On and off," she said and squeezed. "I just don't want you to be hoping I'll turn into something more."

"I don't think I could handle any more of you, honestly," he said, rubbing his face in her hair. Getting to scent her all the time was maybe the best part of her living with him now, apart from all the sex.

"So, you're okay if I burn it?"

"Of course."

She looked up at him. "And your dragon won't be mad?"

"Princess," he began softly. "He will be understandably disappointed. But he knows the world we live in, as well as I. And he can always show you how much he loves you, through me."

She swallowed and nodded, and reached over with her hand. The paper she held caught fire in an instant and poofed into acrid smoke as the flame ate it and it disappeared.

"There," he told her, regathering her arm to hold all of her near. "Do you feel better now?"

"No. I feel the same. But that's what I wanted, Damian." She looked up and gave him an ever-so-earnest smile. "I love you, and I love being here, and I even kind of sort of love work now, mostly because then I get to come home to you afterward," she said and laughed.

"Good, although you going to work is the least favorite part of my week, but I suppose we all have to make accommodations." He leaned down to kiss her shoulder, and then looked up at her out of the corner of his eye. "Let me show you how I feel, princess," he murmured, lips hovering just above her skin, and felt her shiver in response.

"Okay," she whispered.

He sat up straight and held her closer, thinking on everything they'd put one another through and all that they had done. "Put your hand out for me?"

She stretched her right hand out first, and he quickly thought of earthly etiquette. "No, please, the other one."

Andi laughed warmly at his game, whatever it was. He felt the pleasant tremble of it in his arms, and it only made him want to hold onto her more tightly.

"Andi Ngo," he said, reaching behind himself to pull the velvet box out. "Who has decided to not be a dragon, and yet remains the most mysterious and alluring and intelligent woman in the world and all the Realms to me...can we get married?"

Damian opened the box, revealing the oval diamond ring, and he heard her gasp. "Damian, oh my God, you shouldn't have."

He tensed. "Why not?"

She took the ring and held it in both her hands, eyes wide. "Because there's no way this will ever fit underneath my gloves at work!"

"Does that mean we can't get married?" he asked her, genuinely.

"No," she protested. "I mean...yes. Of course...yes!" she said, twirling in his arms to face him.

"Put it on," he urged because he wanted to see her wear it. The necklace that she wore was one thing, a part of him, a private secret. But the ring on her finger was an announcement to the world that Andi Ngo was taken.

And she was. *She so was.* By decree of both him and his dragon. Neither one of them would ever let anything separate them from her, not ever again. He watched her slide it onto her finger and hold her hand out to the candle, where the facets on the stone reflected and refracted the light into a hundred different beams, just like the brightness from her soul. His fierce and courageous princess, the woman who'd warmed his ice and tamed his dragon, who'd fought her destiny and won his heart.

Andi, his inevitable and irrevocable, mate.

"Yes," she repeated, beaming at him.

He kissed her, and then took her to the ground.

WE HOPE you enjoyed this journey to Andi and Damian's happy ending!

Want to find out how Sammie ends up finding her very own dragon? DRAGON'S CAPTIVE is the first in our new Wardens of the

Otherworld series. Each book will feature a couple with a complete stand-alone story.

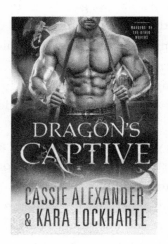

Sammy O'Connor didn't mean to steal a dragon's necklace...she just kind of did.

Little did she know that the viciously hot and muscled Rax Janvier who would come to claim it—and her—would be willing to do anything to get it back. It's a fragment of a key that opens up a lock to his past—and hers.

Can she survive being kidnapped by a sea dragon who's obsessed with her? And what happens if she starts to want him back?

Click here to grab DRAGON'S CAPTIVE at your favorite ebook retailer!

Or turn the page for the first chapter!

DRAGON'S CAPTIVE - CHAPTER 1 SAMPLE

"So, Damian doesn't know any eligible guys, like at all?" Sammy was sitting across from her best friend and old roommate, Andi, at Jones and Shah Coffee. They were hanging out before their separate evening plans: Sammy, hostessing at a high-end restaurant downtown, and Andi, going in early to the hospital to work into a nightshift.

The small café was lightly crowded, full of the scent of strong coffee and the iced lemon scone Sammy'd bought to wolf down before work tonight. Other people's conversations wrapped around them, as spinning spoons clanked against glasses and the espresso machine hissed. One woman laughed loudly in a corner as she flirted too hard on a first date—Sammy recognized both the woman's tone and her date's slight expression of horror.

First dates always suck, Sammy thought.

"Sammy," Andi said flatly, giving her a maternal headshake, calling her attention back to the table. "No. You do not want this kind of hassle, trust me." Her best friend waved a hand over herself. Andi was dressed in purple scrubs and wearing Dansko shoes with a cute checkered print on them, and the blue streak in her black hair was barely visible in her 'I'm going to work' bun. Tearing off a bite of the scone to push into her mouth, Sammy had absolutely no idea what Andi was even talking about.

"The *hassle* of someone giving me a three-carat diamond ring?" Sammy licked icing off her finger and then mimed difficulty raising her coffee with her left hand, even though Andi wasn't wearing jewelry right now. "Oh yeah, I can see how that must be a really heavy arm workout," Sammy teased.

Andi laughed. "A ring that I can't wear to work because, while gorgeous, it's ridiculous. But no, really Sammy, you know what I mean." And Andi gave her that look that was all: *We've talked about this before. You know I'm engaged to a dragon-shifter, right?*

Which meant it was Sammy's turn to give her a meaningful, *But why can't I ever see him as a dragon?* stink-eye, back, until both of them grinned.

"Honestly, Sammy," Andi said, getting real, looking around the room they were in and leaning forward. "There are at least three security cameras in this coffee shop, ever since that attempted robbery. And I guarantee you that right now all of them are pointed at me."

Sammy pushed a wave of red hair out of her face as she glanced up to see the little plastic bulbs set in the coffee shop's ceiling, which were new. Andi was right. "Why?"

"Because I don't want to have a bodyguard. This is our compromise."

Sammy pretended to think. "So...you're kind of like Beyoncé, is what you're saying?"

Andi laughed again. "No. Although I do sing better than you do." She stuck out her tongue at Sammy. "Damian's people have better things to do than to watch over me personally—but there's a trade-off. If I get to pretend to have a normal life, then someone's going to be low level watching over me all the time. Or listening in," she said, tapping at her phone on the table between them. "So don't say anything lewd."

"Who? Me? I would fucking never." Sammy put an affronted hand to her chest, laughing as Andi laughed too, before taking a sober inhale. "It's...just hard to believe that your life's changed so much, Andi. Don't get me wrong, I *do* believe you." Sammy knew the long term consequences of not being believed—she had known her best friend for too many years and they'd gone through too much stuff together for her not to. If Andi said her man was a dragon, well then, he really was. *Somehow.* "It's just different is all," she said with a half-shrug. "I mean, who would've guessed a few months ago that Andi Ngo would become a dragon's most valuable possession?"

"Yeah," Andi said, giving Sammy one of those dreamy 'hope-lessly-in-love' smiles that she'd been prone to, ever since she and Damian had become serious—the kind that made Sammy really happy for Andi, but a little sad for herself. Sammy knew it wasn't fair, but she was also only human, so she tried not to beat herself up about it. She shoved another tart bite of scone into her mouth.

"Although he doesn't treat me like a possession," Andi went on, in her man's defense. "He's not an asshole.... Well, actually, he is, just not to me."

Sammy laughed, then picked up Andi's phone to talk into it like it was a microphone. "Did you hear that? Damian's *not*, I repeat, *not* an asshole," she said loudly before setting it back down and grinning at her friend. "There. You're covered."

Andi snickered and pocketed her phone. "All right, girlie, so, enough about my relationship. Why are you asking about eligible men? What happened with the smart guy, Mr. Working-on-his-PhD?"

"Yeah," Sammy began slowly, sinking toward the table to massage her temples with the first two fingers of each hand, bringing her closer to the comforting scent of her coffee. "Remember the research project he was working on so hard? I guess you could say it was a 'group project.'"

"No!" Andi gasped, already knowing which way this story was

going to go. "Don't tell me that! By which I mean, do tell me, so I can go and murder him!"

"I bet your phone caught that too," Sammy said with a head-shake, although she and Andi had probably watched enough true crime shows on TV together in their time as roommates to get away with actual murders if they put their mind to it.

"How'd you find out?" Andi pressed.

"I drove over to pick him up from campus and because I miraculously found good parking I decided to surprise him—and caught him boning some other grad student on his desk."

"Ugh!" Andi said, furious on her behalf. "I mean, you're so much better off without him, obviously, but the gall!"

"Down girl, I know."

Andi's eyes narrowed and she frowned. "Sammy, why didn't you tell me?"

Sammy looked across the table at her best friend and couldn't really say what she was thinking: *Because. You look so happy—you make things look easy—why can't they be easy for me?* Andi reached across the table to grab her hand, reading a little of it on her anyhow, and Sammy squeezed her hand back.

"It just happened two days ago," Sammy said, blowing things off. "And I knew I was seeing you today—now that you're not living with me it's a lot harder for me to keep track of whether you're sleeping or not.. Plus, I'm not wrecked or anything. More just disgusted with the gender."

Andi let go of her hand but kept staring at her, and Sammy knew she was being *nursified*.

"I feel bad leaving you all alone, Sammy. What if...you get another roommate? Or—a cat? Or a puppy? I mean now that Damian's bought the building—"

"Don't think I don't appreciate that, Andi, because I do." Not having to pay rent, thanks to Andi's *bajillionaire* fiancé's largess was pretty damn amazing. "But a cat is not the same as a person— though it can't just be any person, you know?"

"No, it can't, can it," Andi said, agreeing with her—then getting a wicked gleam in her eye. "I mean, I probably am pretty irreplaceable as a roommate."

"Yeah, I'm not sure how that Craigslist ad would go: 'Roommate wanted, 20-something woman, must be into serial killer documentaries and cars.'"

"Hey now, I wasn't into cars."

"Well, if I'm going to bother replacing you, I might as well aim for perfection."

Andi laughed. "Actually? Yeah. You should. Hold out for the good stuff, always." She pulled out her phone to check the time and grumbled. "I'm sorry, Sammy, I've got to get going." Andi got up and navigated to the condiment bar to grab a to-go lid, while Sammy not so subtly tried to see if the security cameras really did watch as she returned. "Dress shopping? This weekend?" Andi asked.

"Wouldn't miss it for the world," Sammy said. "And you'd better wear your ring then."

"Why?" Andi questioned, picking up her bag.

"So if we get into trouble, without any bodyguards, you can punch somebody out with it," Sammy told her, pretending to give someone a left hook.

"I don't need bodyguards, Sammy, when I have you." Andi beamed and gave her a careful not-spilling-her-coffee hug. "Talk tomorrow?"

"For sure," Sammy said, and air-kissed her cheek.

SAMMY WAITED until Andi was off to the bus stop knowing that Andi wouldn't accept a ride into work unless she was going to be seriously late. Although maybe being on a bus was safer for her than being on the open road, because Sammy was going to have to break a few traffic laws to make it to her apartment in time to change and drive back downtown.

She parked outside her building, jogged up the stairs to the blue door of her apartment, let herself inside, and ran for her closet.

Andi was right—it was a little lonely here. Especially because Eumie wasn't downstairs in their bakery anymore—they were off doing God knew what. Sammy'd lost both her nearby best friends in the space of a few months.

Andi wasn't really *lost*-lost, but she was busy. Hanging out with Damian or letting him dote on her. Sammy had been over for a few awkward dinners at their place, and it wasn't the same as it had been —and it wasn't even Damian's fault. He was an excellent sport, and he played the host nicely. It was just that things were different now, what with Andi living there, was all. The last time she'd gone over and they'd tried to make a girls' night of it, watching the latest Netflix murder-show, some horrible sounding alarm had gone off in the middle of things. Sammy about peed her pants it was so loud, and Andi wouldn't tell her what was going on, "For your own safety, I mean it," and then had been tense until a few hours later when Damian had come back.

From...where? Doing...what?

Dragon-stuff?

Sammy supposed Andi knew, and she knew she didn't have a right to know. But now that they were keeping secrets from each other, things just weren't the same.

Then again, she'd been keeping a pretty big one from Andi—and everyone else she'd ever met, for the most part—her whole life.

Sammy sighed and tugged down the tight cream-colored dress she'd be wearing tonight, then de-sexed it with a loose pink silk scarf around her neck and a fitted navy blazer. She pushed her feet into matching navy flats—she was verging on stewardess, but that was okay, as long as she looked like she worked for a high-class airline.

It would just take time for their friendship to find a new normal, was all. Sammy knew that, and she could be patient. It wasn't like she had a ton of other friends besides. Acquaintances, maybe, and a string of disappointing men, for sure. But none of them were as solid as Andi, and Sammy just had to believe that if she waited out this phase in Andi's life—even if she wasn't sure of what it *was* or *how long it would last*—that they'd be strong again.

In a new way.

Eventually.

Right?

She looked at herself in her bathroom mirror, pulling her long curly red hair into a loose bun, swiped some lipstick on, poofed herself with blush, used the same blush for her eyeshadow, grabbed her purse, and ran for the door.

She swung it open to find a small box on her stoop—clearly labeled for their address, but not to anyone in particular.

Seeing as she hadn't ordered anything lately, it had to be for Andi.

She swiped her phone open and found Andi's contact in it as 'Lefty' because once upon a time when they'd still lived together, pre-Damian, Andi had expressed a desire to date Vin Diesel and Lefty from the *Fast and the Furious* movies was as close as she could get. (Plus, it was kind of funny, since Andi didn't know how to drive.)

There's a mysterious box here for you, she texted using voice-to-text as she brought it inside. *Don't worry, it's too small to be a body part.*

Andi texted back an eye roll emoji, faster than Sammy would've thought—she must've still been on the bus. *D warned me this might happen. That people would send us stuff just because, to try to get in his good graces.*

Sammy snorted softly. *Well, it's not a toaster or a shoe rack, so I know they didn't get it off your registry—oh wait, you don't have a registry,* she said. Sammy had maintained that people would still want to buy them gifts, whereas Andi said that was silly because they already had everything.

Andi sent her back an emoji with its tongue sticking out. *If it's not ticking, and there's no loose powder, want to open it?*

Sammy hesitated—yes, she might be late, but.... What the hell would anyone send someone like Damian Blackwood's fiancée to try to get on his good side? As Andi's old roommate, she already knew that Andi's most useful possessions were an infinite number of pens and sharpies—there must've been some nurse version of the sock-eating dryer monster that lived in the hospital basement, subsisting entirely on black ink. Or maybe it was a small box of Vietnamese instant coffee packets....

She set it down on her kitchen counter and opened the packaging. Inside the shipping box was another box—fancy and old, made of very structurally sound black cardboard that was embossed with tiny ripples—and inside of that, she found a dark purple velvet jewelry box.

Sammy knew she probably should've slowed her roll, but she also felt the need to just confirm that it really wasn't any body part at this point, and her get-to-work-on-time clock was ticking. She flipped the lid and inside, cradled in more purple velvet, was a lovely teardrop-shaped red cabochon the size of her thumb, strung on a delicate gold chain.

She pulled it out of the box so it could swing freely. It looked old —and old-timey—because girls her age hardly ever wore jewelry like this.

Then again, could someone her age afford something like this? She honestly didn't think so.

She snapped a photo and sent it to Andi.

Oh God—gorgeous, but so not me. Who is it from?

Sammy investigated the rest of the box thoroughly. *No clue. No card.*

Well, I'll ask around, I guess? Although I don't think anyone in my contacts list sent that....

Me either. They both knew their friend group was more of the gift-card or booze set.

Your brother? Sammy guessed although she felt it extremely doubtful. The only jewelry Andi's brother had ever gotten Sammy when they'd dated was a little peridot solitaire ring for her birthday.

She still wore it sometimes at work on her left ring finger to detour creepers.

No way, Andi agreed, and then went on: *Hey, so, don't hate me, but...I think I'm going to have to pass on dress shopping.*

Sammy stared at her phone, mysterious jewelry and upcoming job forgotten. *If you picked a dress out without me, I will not be your best friend anymore, so help me God,* she typed, followed quickly by: *joking-NOT-JOKING.*

It's not that! Andi protested. *We're taking a last-minute trip to Italy.*

But what about your job? Sammy asked, knowing full well that Andi only worked because she wanted to.

We just bought my hospital a new wing. They'll manage without me for a month just fine. And I've been thinking of going part-time, anyways.

Sammy huffed at her phone. That was the first she'd heard of it. But just like she hadn't run straight to Andi to tell her about Mr. PhDickhead, maybe Andi was pulling back a little, too.

We'll dress shop the day I get back, I promise, okay? Andi sent her.

Sure. Love you, Sammy sent, with an emoji smooch.

Sammy put her phone in her blazer's pocket and stared at the necklace for a little bit longer. If no one knew who it was from...and Andi didn't like it...and if they'd shared clothes *all the time* back when Andi used to live with her—Sammy's hands rose, and she clasped the necklace around her neck quickly. The flat back of the cold stone warmed up quickly against her skin as she hid the gemstone with her scarf, and voila, no one would be the wiser.

Click here to grab DRAGON'S CAPTIVE at your favorite ebook retailer!

ALSO BY CASSIE ALEXANDER

PRINCE OF THE OTHER WORLDS (co-written with Kara Lockharte)

(Andi & Damian's story)

Dragon Called

Dragon Destined

Dragon Fated

Dragon Mated

WARDENS OF THE OTHER WORLDS (co-written with Kara Lockharte)

(each book is a standalone)

Dragon's Captive (Sammy & Rax)

Wolf's Princess (Austin & Ryana)

Wolf's Rogue (Zach & Stella)

Dragon's Flame (Tarian & Seris)

...and don't forget to join Cassie's newsletter for access to an exclusive Andi and Damian prequel story, *Dragons Don't Date*, plus *Bewitched*, a Jamison and Mills novella!

THE DARK INK TATTOO SERIES

Blood of the Pack

Blood at Dusk

Blood by Moonlight

Blood by Midnight

Blood at Dawn

Cassie's Stand Alone Books

The House: Come Find Your Fantasy -- a choose your own adventure erotica

Rough Ghost Lover

Her Future Vampire Lover

Her Ex-boyfriend's Werewolf Lover

The Edie Spence Urban Fantasy Series

Nightshifted

Moonshifted

Shapeshifted

Deadshifted

Bloodshifted

Sign up for more news from Cassie here!

ALSO BY KARA LOCKHARTE

Dragon Lovers

Betrothed to the Dragon

Belonging to the Dragon

Bonded to the Dragon

Dragon Lovers Complete Vol. 1

The Space Shifter Chronicles

(Science Fiction Romances)

NOVELS

Wanted by the Werewolf Prince

Taken by the Tigerlord

Desired by the Dragon King (coming soon)

SHORT STORIES

The Boy Who Came Back a Wolf (free to newsletter subscribers)

The Lady and the Tigershifter

In Search of Skye

About the Author

On her own, Cassie's a nurse by day and writer by night, living in the Bay Area with her husband, two cats, inside a massive succulent garden.

Whereas Kara's a California transplant by way of NYC and is still, to this day, searching for the perfect bagel (although the no-snow and strawberries out here help to make up for it.)

Follow Cassie's newsletter for a free book and bonus content! https://www.cassiealexander.com/newsletter

Follow Kara on Facebook, www.facebook.com/karalockharte or get a free book at her website, www.karalockharte.com/signup